INAPPOSITENESS
OF
THE INDIVIDUAL
CULTURAL SYSTEM

On the Origin of the Tragedies
of the Protagonists in Thomas Hardy's Novels

个体性文化体系的失度

哈代小说主人公
悲剧根源研究

刘 磊——著

中国民航大学外语学科发展专项经费资助

天津市高等学校人文社会科学研究一般项目
"伦理的社会属性——哈代小说伦理内涵研究"（20142232）资助

南京大学出版社

Acknowledgements

First of all, I wish to express my sincere gratitude to my Ph. D. supervisor, Professor Shi Zhikang. His passion for the English language and his profound insights into British and American literature motivate me to conduct my research with all my efforts. The patient guidance by Professor Shi provides me with a source of inspiration and his enlightening suggestions facilitate the successful completion of my dissertation upon which this book is based. I also wish to thank Professor Yang Renjing from Xiamen University, Professor Zhou Zhong'an from Donghua University, Professor Chen Bing from Nanjing University, Professor Wang Xin, Professor Wu Gang, Professor Wang Yixuan and Professor Gu Yue from Shanghai International Studies University. Their illuminating suggestions help me to improve my dissertation. I also would like to thank all other professors at Shanghai International Studies University whose lectures help me lay a solid foundation in literature research. Last, I shall also express my sincere gratitude to Professor Edward Mendelson at Columbia University, USA, where I once stayed as a visiting scholar. Professor Mendelson's lectures and instruction broaden my horizons and assist me a lot in my academic growth.

目　录

Contents

前　言

　　悲剧维度是托马斯·哈代小说最重要的维度之一。对于主人公悲剧根源的探索有助于研究哈代小说的思想内涵及其历史意义。哈代小说主人公的悲剧根源(即他们的灾难性结局的根源)可以从文化角度来阐释。在雷蒙·威廉斯文化唯物主义理论的基础上,个体性文化体系的合度与失度之阐释框架可以发展出来,用以托马斯·哈代小说主人公悲剧根源的研究。在一定意义上,个体性文化体系的失度(简称为文化失度)导致了小说主人公的灾难性结局。道德、性格、身份和价值观是个体性文化体系的四个主要维度。个体性文化体系在这四个维度的合度状况能够根本地影响人们的生活,托马斯·哈代小说主人公的生活也与此四维度密切相关。

　　在道德维度,《还乡》的主人公克林、《德伯家的苔丝》的主人公苔丝和《无名的裘德》的主人公裘德都遭受了个体性文化体系的失度。利他性充分与利他性适中之间的冲突以及积极道德与消极道德机制之间的冲突构成了克林的文化失度并导致了他的灾难性结局。精神化道德与物质化道德机制的冲突构成了苔丝的文化失度并导致了她的灾难性结局。内容导向的道德与形式导向的道德机制之间的冲突构成了裘德的文化失度并导致了他的灾难性结局。通过展现造成主人公灾难性结局的道德维度文化失度,哈代小说演绎出其道德观念,这些观念呼应与阐释着功利主义的特定方面。

　　在性格维度,苔丝和《卡斯特桥市长》的主人公亨查德都遭受了个体性文化体系的失度。负面倾向和基于情绪的攻击性构成了亨查德的文化失度并导致他的灾难性结局。心理节奏的失衡构成了苔丝的文化失度并导致她的灾难性结局。通过展现造成主人公灾难性结局的性格维度文化失度，哈代小说演绎出其性格观念，这些观念呼应与阐释着进化论的特定方面。

在身份维度，苔丝和亨查德遭受了个体性文化体系的失度。显性平等身份与显性身份不平等之间的冲突以及隐性平等身份与隐性身份不平等之间的冲突构成了苔丝的文化失度并导致了她的灾难性结局。宗法制家长的身份与现代身份机制之间的冲突构成了亨查德的文化失度并导致了他的灾难性结局。通过展现导致主人公灾难性结局的身份维度文化失度，哈代小说演绎出其身份观念，这些观念呼应与阐释着马修·阿诺德文化观念的特定方面。

在价值观维度，裘德、克林和苔丝都遭受了个体性文化体系的失度。知识价值观与共时性价值霸权的冲突以及爱情价值观与历时性价值霸权的冲突构成了裘德的文化失度并导致了他的灾难性结局。外部导向的价值观与内部导向的价值机制之间的冲突构成了克林的文化失度并导致了他的灾难性结局。精神化价值观与物质化价值机制之间的冲突构成了苔丝的文化失度并导致了她的灾难性结局。通过展示导致主人公灾难性结局的价值观维度文化失度，哈代小说演绎出其价值观念。这些观念也呼应与阐释着马修·阿诺德文化观念的特定方面。

在本书所论述的四部哈代小说中共有十种文化失度，其中只有两种源于个体性文化体系内部存在的失度，而有八种源于内外关系失度（即内部存在与外部存在之间的冲突）。可见，相对于个人特性中的问题，哈代小说更加重视个人——社会关系中的问题所能给人的生活带来的危害。对于八种源于内外关系失度的文化失度中的三种，哈代小说没有对冲突双方中的任何一方表现出倾向性。在另外五种中，哈代小说倾向于内部存在并形成对于内部存在的肯定。借此，哈代小说演绎出一种观点：在一些情况下，内部存在与外部存在的和谐关系的重建应该通过双方的调整，以及双方之间更加有效的交流与互动得以实现。但是，在更多的情况下，内外关系和谐的重建应当依靠对于内部存在的保护和对于外部存在的改造。如此，个人和社会能够得到更好的发展机会。可以看出，哈代小说将人类救赎的希望更多地寄托于社会的改进而非个人的改进。从另一个角度来看，十种文化失度中没有源于外部存在失度的情况，这说明哈代小说中的社会批判相对温和，没有蕴含社会机制激烈变革的主张。哈代小说中文化失度导致悲剧的总体格局在文学的领域内实现了对亚瑟·叔本华宿命论和悲观主义的阐释。这种总体格局显示出一种尤其强调社会机制改造的改良主义思想，从文学视角实现了对约翰·罗斯金和奥古斯特·孔德改良主义思想的阐释。

Foreword

The tragic dimension is one of the most prominent dimensions of Thomas Hardy's novels. The investigations into the origin of the protagonists' tragedies are instrumental for the research of the connotations of Hardy's novels and the research of their historical significance. The origin of the protagonists' tragedies (namely the origin of their disastrous conclusions) in Thomas Hardy's novels can be interpreted from the perspective of culture. On the basis of the theory of cultural materialism of Raymond Walliams, the interpretative framework of the appositeness and inappositeness of the individual cultural system can be developed for the research of the origin of the protagonists' tragedies in Thomas Hardy's novels. In a certain sense, it is the inappositeness of the individual cultural system (shortened as cultural inappositeness) that causes the disastrous conclusions of the protagonists in the novels. Morality, disposition, identity and value concept are the four major dimensions of the individual cultural system. The appositeness condition of the individual cultural system in these four dimensions can fundamentally influence people's lives and the lives of the protagonists in Thomas Hardy's novels are also closely related to these four dimensions.

In the dimension of morality, Clym, the protagonist of *The Return of the Native*, Tess, the protagonist of *Tess of the d'Urbervilles*, and Jude, the protagonist of *Jude the Obscure*, suffer from the inappositeness of the individual cultural system. The conflict between the sufficiency of altruism and the moderation of altruism，and the conflict between the affirmative morality and the negative morality mechanism constitute the cultural inappositeness of Clym and lead to his disastrous conclusion. The conflict between the spiritualized morality and the materialized morality mechanism constitutes the cultural inappositeness of Tess and results in her disastrous conclusion. The conflict between the content-directed morality and the form-directed morality mechanism constitutes the cultural inappositeness of Jude，and brings about his disastrous conclusion. By demonstrating the cases of cultural inappositeness in the dimension of morality which cause the disastrous conclusions of the protagonists, the novels of Thomas Hardy develop certain ideas about morality. These ideas correspond to and interpret certain aspects of utilitarianism.

In the dimension of disposition, Henchard, the protagonist of *The Mayor of Casterbridge* and Tess both suffer from the inappositeness of the individual cultural system. The negative tendency and the mood-based aggressiveness constitute the cultural inappositeness of Henchard and give rise to his disastrous conclusion. The imbalance of psychological rhythm constitutes the cultural inappositeness of Tess and results in her disastrous conclusion. By demonstrating the cases of cultural inappositeness in the dimension of disposition which cause the disastrous conclusions of the protagonists, the novels of Thomas Hardy develop certain ideas about disposition. These ideas correspond to and interpret certain aspects of evolutionism.

In the dimension of identity, Tess and Henchard are subjected to the inappositeness of the individual cultural system. The conflict between the identity of explicit equality and the explicit identity inequality，and the conflict between the identity of implicit equality and the implicit identity inequality constitute the cultural inappositeness of Tess and result in her disastrous conclusion. The conflict between the identity as a patriarch and the modernized identity mechanism constitutes the cultural inappositeness of Henchard, and gives rise to his disastrous conclusion. By demonstrating the cases of cultural inappositeness in the dimension of identity which cause the disastrous conclusions of the protagonists, the novels of Thomas Hardy develop certain ideas about identity. These ideas correspond to and interpret certain facets of the cultural notions of Matthew Arnold.

In the dimension of value concept, Jude, Clym and Tess are subjected to the inappositeness of the individual cultural system. The conflict between the value concept of knowledge and the synchronic value hegemony, and the conflict between the value concept of love and the diachronic value hegemony constitute the cultural inappositeness of Jude and bring about his disastrous conclusion. The conflict between the exterior-oriented value concept and the interior-oriented value mechanism constitutes the cultural inappositeness of Clym, and leads to his disastrous conclusion. The conflict between the spiritualized value concept and the materialized value mechanism constitutes the cultural inappositeness of Tess and results in her disastrous conclusion. By demonstrating the cases of cultural inappositeness in the dimension of value concept which cause the disastrous conclusions of the protagonists, the novels of Thomas Hardy develop certain ideas about value concept. These ideas also correspond to and interpret certain facets of the cultural notions of Matthew Arnold.

In the four novels of Hardy under discussion in this book, there are altogether ten cases of cultural inappositeness. Among them, there are only two cases that derive from the inappositeness of the internal existence of the individual cultural system. In contrast to that, there are eight cases that derive from the inappositeness of the relationship between the internal existence and the external existence (namely the conflict between the internal existence and the external existence). It can be seen that the novels of Thomas Hardy place more importance upon the problems in individual-society relationship rather than upon the problems in the individual characteristics as the factor that can harm people's lives. For three of the eight cases of cultural inappositeness that derive from the inappositeness of the internal-external relationship, the novels of Hardy do not take sides with either of the two parties in conflict. For the other five, the novels of Hardy take sides with and approve of the internal existence. Thereby the novels develop the view that in some cases the reestablishment of the harmony between the internal existence and the external existence should be realized through modifications on both sides, together with more efficient communication and interactions between them. However, in more cases, the reestablishment of the harmony of internal-external relationship should be achieved through the protection of the internal existence and the transformation of the external existence. In that way, individuals and the society can get better chances of development. It can be seen that the novels of Hardy place the hope of the redemption of humanity more upon the improvement of the society than upon the improvement of individuals. From another perspective, none of the ten cases of cultural inappositeness derive from the inappositeness of the external existence. That shows that the social criticism in Hardy's novels is relatively moderate, not harboring the claim for radical changes of social mechanisms. The overall format of cultural inappositeness leading to tragedies in the novels of Thomas Hardy accomplishes the literary interpretation of the fatalism and pessimism of Arthur Schopenhauer. The overall format shows reformist ideas which especially emphasize transformation of social institutions, achieving the interpretation of the ideas of reformism of John Ruskin and Auguste Comte from the literary perspective.

Introduction

Thomas Hardy (1840 – 1928) is one of the greatest men of letters in the later Victorian era of Britain. Hardy was born in the village of Higher Bockhampton in Dorset. In his youth, Hardy once pursued his career as an architect in London. Several years later, he returned to Dorset and remained there for most of his life. Hardy's hometown Dorset exerts a permanent influence upon his artistic creation. Dorset leads a kind of literary existence in the Wessex created in Hardy's literary works. Hardy excels both in the creation of fiction and in the creation of poetry and he is especially well known across the world for his novels. During his lifetime, Hardy altogether created fifteen novels (His first novel *The Poor Man and the Lady* is not published). Most of Hardy's representative novels show the sufferings and downfalls of the main characters, and the writer is thus widely recognized as an artist of tragedy.

In the celebrated *A Glossary of Literary Terms*, M. H. Abrams and Geoffrey Galt Harpham give a definition of tragedy. According to Abrams and Harpham, the term tragedy "is broadly applied to literary, and especially to dramatic, representations of serious actions which eventuate in a disastrous conclusion for the protagonist (the chief character)". (Abrams, Harpham, 2009: 370 – 371) Most of Thomas Hardy's representative novels involve "serious actions" and "a disastrous conclusion for the protagonist", and therefore could be classified as tragedies. Two kinds of tragedies shall be differentiated from each other here. First, the tragedy is a literary genre or a specific literary work that belongs to that genre as described in the quoted definition. Second, the tragedy can denote the life experience of the protagonist which leads to a disastrous conclusion in the tragedy in the first sense. The tragic dimension is one of the most significant dimensions of Hardy's novels. The design of the origin of the protagonists' tragedies is of vital importance for the composition of the novels. This book will investigate into the origin of the tragedies of the protagonists in Hardy's novels and thereby carry out research upon the connotations of the novels and their historical significance. The disastrous conclusion is the decisive stage in the protagonist's tragedy. It is the disastrous conclusion that makes the protagonist's tragedy a tragedy. Therefore, the factors that cause the protagonist's disastrous conclusion are just the factors that cause the protagonist's tragedy. In other words, the origin of the protagonist's tragedy consists in the origin of his or her disastrous conclusion. In the investigation into the origin of the protagonists' tragedies in this book, for the convenience of discussion, analysis will be focused upon the origin of their disastrous conclusions.

0.1　Literature Review

Since the years during which Thomas Hardy's novels were published (from the 1870s to the 1890s), abundant researches have been conducted on those fictional masterpieces both in Britain and across the world. There are a large number of journal articles, monographs and Ph. D. dissertations which are dedicated to Hardy research. Among the large body of scholarship in the domain of Thomas Hardy study, the researches since the 1970s are especially enlightening for the conception and composition of this book; therefore, the literature review will be focused upon those recent researches. There are researches upon the origin of the protagonists' tragedies in Thomas Hardy's novels. They directly lay a foundation for the research in this book. There are also researches which, although not focused on the origin of the protagonists' tragedies in Thomas Hardy's novels, provide insights into the matter of morality, disposition, identity and value concept in those novels. Morality, disposition, identity and value concept are the four major dimensions of the individual cultural system, and the investigation into the inappositeness of the individual cultural system in this book will be carried out from these four perspectives. Therefore, the aforementioned researches concerning the four spheres also lay a foundation for the research in this book in their own ways. Moreover, there are researches which bear relation to the reformist tendency of Hardy's novels. These researches are helpful in the further analysis of the ideas of reformism in the novels, and thus instrumental in the interpretation of the historical significance of the overall format of cultural inappositeness leading to tragedies in the novels. As a consequence, the review of the researches upon Thomas Hardy's novels will be conducted first from the perspective of the origin of the protagonists' tragedies, then from the four perspectives which are significant for the individual cultural system, namely the sphere of morality, the sphere of disposition, the sphere of identity and the sphere of value concept, and last from the perspective of the reformist tendency of the novels. For all the six perspectives from which review of the researches will be conducted, the researches in foreign countries, especially those in Britain and the United States, will be reviewed first, and then the researches in China will be reviewed.

The tragic aspect is one of the most prominent aspects of Thomas Hardy's novels. However, there is only a relatively limited number of researches devoted to the origin of the protagonists' tragedies in Hardy's novels in a concentrated way. In *Fatalism in the Works of Thomas Hardy* (1932), Albert Elliott explains the tragedies of the protagonists of Hardy's novels from a supernatural perspective. According to Elliott, the tragedies in the novels result from the workings of the Immanent Will. The monograph treats the Immanent Will, embodied in the unescapable fate, as reflected in five concrete spheres, "chance and coincidence", "time", "nature", "woman", and "convention and law". Thus, natural and social elements attain their meanings in a supernatural framework. In *Thomas Hardy: The Forms of Tragedy* (1975), Dale Kramer investigates into the formal features of Thomas Hardy's tragic novels. Kramer traces the diachronic development of Hardy's tragic forms and links the explorations of the formal aspect of the novels with the explorations of the thematic aspect. In the research of the forms employed in Hardy's tragic novels, the monograph also achieves an interpretation of the origin of the tragedies of the protagonists. Kramer writes, "Foolishness and failure to act cause tragedy in *Tess of the d'Urbervilles* and *Jude the Obscure*, a refusal to look at the truth causes disaster in *The Return of the Native*, [...] and *The Mayor of Casterbridge* traces the career of a man impelled by his very character to take actions the least advantageous to himself. Thus Hardy's protagonists merit their fates and justify to man the ways of the universe." (Kramer, 1975: 16) It can be said that the monograph generally attributes the tragedies of the protagonists to the defects of their own characters.

The Ph. D. dissertation "Thomas Hardy's Tragic Forms" (1977) by Carol Louise Beran investigates into the similarities and differences among Hardy's tragic novels from the perspective of five common elements in those novels, namely "Hardy's characteristic setting, his similar rustic characters, his typical major characters, his abundant coincidences, and his characteristic 'twilight view of life'" (Beran, 1977: 11). In the process of discussion, the dissertation reveals both elements in the protagonists' characters and elements in the environment that are responsible for the protagonists' tragedies. However, the internal elements and external elements are explained and summarized by the functioning of a fate brought about by the Providence. In the final analysis, the dissertation accomplishes the interpretation of the origin of the protagonists' tragedies in Thomas Hardy's novels from a supernatural perspective. In *Tragedy in the Victorian Novel: Theory and Practice in the Novels of George Eliot, Thomas Hardy and Henry James* (1978), Jeannette King claims that "His [Hardy's] [novels] are tragedies of situation, rather than of character." (King, 1978: 99) According to King, the tragedies in Hardy's novels are effected by the circumstances in which individuals exist rather than by the characteristics of the individuals themselves. In line with King's view, this quality of the tragedies in Thomas Hardy's novels derives from the Aristotelian tragic theory. The influence of the Aristotelian tragic theory upon Hardy, King asserts, is most evidently shown in the novels' arrangement of the relationship between event and character. "For him [Hardy], as for Aristotle, the plot was the most important element." (King, 1978: 99) Therefore, the circumstances (or the situation), which are interrelated with the plot, cause the tragedies.

New Studies in Thomas Hardy (2009) by Wu Di conducts a panoramic study of the thematic and formal aspects of Hardy's fictional and poetical productions. The monograph achieves an in-depth interpretation of Hardy's pessimistic ideas. According to this monograph, evolutionary meliorism lies at the core of the pessimistic ideas of Hardy and constitutes a defining feature of those ideas. The monograph puts forward the view that Hardy believes in the existence of an Immanent Will in the universe and the functioning of the Immanent Will constitutes an important theme of Hardy's novels. From the perspective of this monograph, it can be seen that "Hardy places emphasis upon the conflict between human beings and the fate", while "neglecting the role of the social factors" in the formation of tragedies. As a result, "the novels are limited in terms of critical strength and social significance". (吴笛, 2009: 105 – 108) In effect, the monograph achieves the interpretation of the protagonists' tragedies from the supernatural perspective.

The previous researches upon the origin of the protagonists' tragedies are instrumental for the interpretation of the connotations of the novels of Hardy. As has been discussed, in previous researches, the supernatural perspective is the most prominent perspective from which the tragedies of the protagonists are explained. The Providence or the Immanent Will is treated as the primary force which causes the protagonists' tragedies. The research from the supernatural perspective is fairly fruitful. However, to interpret the origin of those tragedies from the supernatural angle can only reveal one aspect of Hardy's fictional art. Besides, the tragedies of the protagonists in Hardy's novels have also been interpreted from the mundane perspective. The tragedies are explained either as the results of the characteristics of the protagonists themselves or as the consequences of the elements in the social environment. However, the relationships between the characteristics of the protagonists themselves and the elements in the social environment have not received adequate critical attention. Therefore, this book will develop the interpretive framework of the appositeness and inappositeness of the individual cultural system for the more systematic research of the origin of the protagonists' tragedies in Hardy's novels. This book, availing itself of the perspective of the appositeness condition of the individual cultural system, will combine the individual angle and the social angle, deepening the understanding of the roles of individual characteristics and social elements in the formation of the tragedies through the establishment of their correlations and mutual references in a panoramic view. The research in this book is conducted on the basis of previous researches, and it also goes beyond the sphere of previous researches and throws new light upon the connotations of the novels.

In addition to the interpretation of the origin of the protagonists' tragedies in Hardy's novels that is carried out in a concentrated manner, there are researches concerning the four major dimensions of the individual cultural system. These researches are also illuminating for the composition of this book.

Firstly, the review could be conducted from the perspective of morality.

In the Ph. D. dissertation "A Study of the Role of the Woman in Thomas Hardy's Novels" (1976), Ruth Essex focuses on the characteristics and functions of the female characters in Hardy's fictional art. She discusses the lack of proper parental guidance in life and the problems in their characters which are formed thereby. She discusses the negative force that female characters exercise upon other characters and also pays attention to their positive features. In the discussion of the female characters, the dissertation reveals the moral aspects of the women in the novels and facilitates the understanding of the moral aspects in the concrete historical and literary context. The Ph. D. dissertation "Wandering Women: Sexual and Social Stigma in the Mid-Victorian Novel" (2000) by Lisa Hartsell Jackson discusses the wandering women as a literary paradigm in the novels of Charlotte Brontë, Charles Dickens, Thomas Hardy and George Eliot, emphasizing the difficult circumstances and the unfair treatments these women face in the Victorian society. Jackson writes, "Wandering is the symbolic equivalent of the difficult life path women in the nineteenth century often faced if they failed to stay within the limiting bounds of propriety." (Jackson, 2000: 145) Focusing upon the dimension of morality, the dissertation provides insights both into the social morality of Victorian Britain and into the individual moralities of the female figures in the works of the aforesaid novelists including Thomas Hardy. In *Thomas Hardy, Sensationalism, and the Melodramatic Mode* (2011), Richard Nemesvari discusses the elements of melodrama in Hardy's novels. He writes, "In attempting to represent the conflicts of his age he [Hardy] utilized melodramatic tropes not because of artistic inability or imaginative failure, and not even simply because they were part of a dominant and popular contemporary form, but rather because they provided a way of exploring a late-Victorian culture" (Nemesvari, 2011: 5 - 6). He claims that, "Hardy's fiction attempts to portray, and constitute, an ethical engagement between the individual and society in a world without deity or divinity." (Nemesvari, 2011: 5) In the monograph, melodramatic elements are not treated as artistic defects but as a necessary literary device for the handling of the culture of that transitional era, especially the ethical perspective of that culture. The monograph, by investigations into the melodramatic aspect of Hardy's fiction, sheds light on the moral tendencies in the fiction both on the individual level and on the social level. In *Thomas Hardy and Victorian Communication: Letters, Telegrams and Postal Systems* (2016), Karin Koehler probes into the subjectivity of Hardy's characters from the perspective of the various modes of communication in the Victorian era. According to the point of view of Koehler, "nineteenth-century [Nineteenth-century] developments in communication technology [...] impacted upon the literary imagination and upon representational possibilities." (Karin, 2016: 3) The understanding of the subjectivity of characters as reflected in methods of communication is especially helpful for the investigations into the moral tendencies in the novels.

The Research on the Ethical Ideas in Hardy's Fiction (2008) by Ding Shizhong presents a panoramic view of the ethical ideas reflected in Hardy's novels. The monograph treats the development of ethical ideas in Hardy's novels as a continuation of the emphasis upon ethical ideas in the British literary tradition. The monograph carries out the investigation into the ethical ideas in Hardy's novels under the background of the British literary history which runs from the days of *Beowulf* to Hardy's contemporary times. In the monograph, detailed analysis is made about different kinds of ethics in Hardy's novels, including ethics of love and marriage, ethics of the family, ethics of religion, ethics of the patriarchal native place, and ethics of ecology, etc. The journal article "On Chastity from *Tess of the d'Urbervilles* by Hardy" (2011) by Ji Shenglei, Feng Mei and Qiao Jianzhen probes into the idea about chastity of Thomas Hardy as reflected in the novel *Tess of the d'Urbervilles*. As regards Hardy's idea about chastity, the article puts forward the view that Hardy deems the purity of the spirits as more important than the immaculateness of the body. (姬生雷, 冯梅, 乔建珍, 2011: 102 - 103) In the discussion of Hardy's idea about chastity, the article reveals the novel's moral stance, together with the characters' moral attitudes. The Ph. D. dissertation "Loving-Kindness and Purity: The Two Dimensions of a New Religion in Thomas Hardy's Fiction" (2012) by Hao Tugen inquires into the ideas of the new religion of Thomas Hardy as reflected in his novels. According to the dissertation, the new religion of Hardy concentrates upon the ideas of loving-kindness and purity which originate from the teachings of Jesus Christ, while giving up the mystical and supernatural elements of Christianity. By probing the religion of loving-kindness and the religion of purity manifested in Hardy's novels, the dissertation presents views about the moral dimension of these novels.

As discussed above, in the previous works of research concerning the dimension of morality, there are both panoramic analyses of the ethical ideas in Hardy's novels and concentrated discussion of the moral features of female characters, which are widely acknowledged as an important focus in the characterization of the novels. In the previous works of research concerning morality, there are both investigations into the moral characteristics of individuals and those into the moral characteristics of the society. Attention has also been paid to the interpretation of individual moralities in the historical and social context. The previous works of research have also covered the roles that special textual components, such as the melodramatic mode and the methods of communication, play in the revelation of features of morality. Besides, the previous works of research have also probed into the dimension of morality of Hardy's novels through the discussion of the related categories such as the idea about chastity and the ideas of the new religion, etc.

Secondly, the review could be conducted from the perspective of disposition.

Thomas Hardy: Distance and Desire (1970) by J. Hillis Miller utilizes the concepts of distance and desire to build a framework of interpretation for Hardy's fiction and poetry. The monograph treats "distance as the source of desire and desire as the energy behind attempts to turn distance into closeness" (Miller, 1970: Xii). In the discussion of distance and desire, dispositional factors of the characters which are intertwined with the functioning of distance and desire also come into view. The Ph. D. dissertation "Psychology of Character in Thomas Hardy and D. H. Lawrence" (1976) by Romey Thomas Keys explores the "psychological theories of personality" formed by Hardy and Lawrence. In the exploration, both non-fictional works and novels are utilized for intertextual references. In the process of exploration, the psychological ideas of the authors and the psychological characteristics of the fictional characters form a relationship of interaction and mutual interpretation. In *Thomas Hardy: Psychological Novelist* (1981), Rosemary Sumner concentrates upon the psychological explorations conducted by Thomas Hardy in the creation of novels. Sumner emphasizes the necessity of "A [a] realisation of both the range and the immense depth of Hardy's psychological insights" (Sumner, 1981: 11), and devotes her monograph to the detailed study of the psychological traits, especially the psychological problems of Hardy's characters. *Thomas Hardy: The "Dream-country" of His Fiction* (1987) by Anne Alexander probes into the dream-country in Hardy's novels which is alienated from the reality in the physical sense, but more closely related to the reality in the spiritual sense. The dream-country depends upon symbols and myths and emphasizes the irrational, the unconscious and the supernatural. The dream-country is the tool with which Hardy investigates into the human condition. The monograph, by the analysis of the dream-country, facilitates the understanding of the dispositions of the characters in Hardy's novels.

In the Ph. D. dissertation "Sex in Mind: The Gendered Brain in Nineteenth-century Literature and Mental Sciences"(2003), Rachel Ann Malane discusses the psychological dimension of the novels of the Victorian writers Charlotte Brontë, Wilkie Collins and Thomas Hardy in the intellectual context of nineteenth-century mental sciences. According to Malane, the three writers have integrated the new findings in contemporary mental sciences into their vision of mental functions, upholding "the notion that mental functions are inherently, biologically gendered" (Malane, 2003: 247). According to Malane, Hardy investigates into the dangers that the efforts to share mental spaces can bring about. As slightly differentiated from the other two authors, Hardy emphasizes the harms of "excessive male reason" and "overwhelming female emotion" (Malane, 2003: 248). By revealing the different psychological tendencies of different genders, the dissertation provides a glimpse into the dimension of disposition in Hardy's novels. In *Thomas Hardy's Brains: Psychology, Neurology, and Hardy's Imagination* (2014), Suzanne Keen writes, "Thomas Hardy's representations of brains were conceived in light of Victorian brain science, his imagery of nerves depicted in keeping with Victorian medical neurology." (Suzanne, 2014: 4 - 5) Keen carries out researches upon the psychological aspect of Thomas Hardy's artistic creation within the intellectual context of brain science, neurology and psychology. In *The Madder Stain: A Psychoanalytic Reading of Thomas Hardy* (2015), Annie Ramel uses the madder stain imprinted on Tess's arm as the beginning point of discussion and draws upon the Lacanian concepts "the Real", "object-gaze" and "object-voice" etc. to conduct explorations into the psychological and dispositional aspects of Thomas Hardy's novels.

The journal article "The Relationship Between 'Character' and 'Environment' in Hardy's Novels of Character and Environment" (2004) by Li Zeng and Wang Ding elucidates the character, the environment and the relationship between the two parties in Hardy's novels. The article differentiates the natural environment from the social environment, and distinguishes the natural character from the social character. Correlations between the natural environment and the natural character, together with the correlations between the social environment and the social character are established in the article. Thereby the article uncovers certain aspects of the dispositions of the characters in the novels.

As discussed above, the previous works of research concerning the dimension of disposition have paid attention both to the psychological traits of fictional characters and to Thomas Hardy's ideas about psychology. The two aspects in research promote each other and form a relationship of mutual interpretation. In previous works of research, adequate attention has been rendered to the function of certain textual designs, such as the distance and desire and the dream-country, in the development and demonstration of dispositional traits of characters. In previous works of research, analysis has been made of the role of Victorian psychological sciences in Hardy'sconception of fictional characters and the development of the characters' dispositional traits. Besides, 20th century psycho-analytic theories like that of Lacan's have also been utilized in the explanation of the fictional characters' dispositional tendencies. Moreover, binary oppositions have been established to facilitate the interpretation of dispositional traits of characters, such as the opposition between male and female figures and the opposition between characters and different types of environment.

Thirdly, the review could be carried out from the perspective of identity. *The Decline of the Goddess: Nature, Culture and Women in Thomas Hardy's Fiction* (1995) by Shirley A. Stave discusses the variety of qualities possessed by the female characters in Hardy's novels and the difficulties that the female characters meet in the Victorian society. Thereby, the monograph attains insights into the issue of female identity in the Victorian patriarchal society. In *The Novels of Thomas Hardy: A Study in Existential Perspectives* (2001), Amrit Lal Pandey explores Hardy's novels from the angle of existentialist philosophy. According to the analysis in this monograph, search for the self is one of the major concerns of Hardy's novels. "The human psyche, unfortunately, owing to its radical fragmentation, fails to disclose the basis of individual identity." (Pandey, 2001: 173) The analysis in this monograph reveals that because of the limitations of the human psyche and because of unfavorable forces in the society, characters in Hardy's novels suffer from problems of identity.

In *Thomas Hardy's Vision of Wessex* (2003), Simon Gatrell presents a panoramic view of the Wessex visualized in the artistic works of Hardy, including both his fiction and his poetry. The Wessex depicted by Hardy is interpreted under the background of the social conditions of the transitional era in Britain. Therefore, Gatrell successfully investigates into the historical significance of Hardy's Wessex. The study of Wessex by Gatrell is especially illuminating for this book's analysis of the dimension of identity in the individual cultural system which is closely related to the social conditions of the transitional era as reflected in the picture of Wessex. In the journal article "Reconstructing Tess" (2003), Oliver Lovesey analyzes Tess's virginity and its symbolic reconstruction, together with the cultural and religious significance of the reconstruction for Angel. He says, "The symbolic reconstruction of Tess's virginity, figured in the recuperative allegory of Tess's mouth and in the person of her sister Liza-Lu, [...] allows Angel to retain his deified, homogenized view of women and to accept the benevolence of a natural order without God."

(Lovesey, 2003: 914) This analysis conducted under the ideological background of the Victorian obsession with female virginity sheds new light upon the matter of identity in terms of gender relationships and social relationships. In *Social Transformations in Hardy's Tragic Novels: Megamachines and Phantasms* (2003), David Musselwhite employs "the territorial formation", "the despotic formation" and "the capitalist formation"—concepts of Deleuze and Guattari's typology of social formations as the basis for the interpretation of Hardy's novels. Besides, the psychoanalytical concept of phantasm, closely linked to the postmodern discourses of Deleuze and Guattari, is also employed in the interpretation of Hardy. On the theoretical basis made up of these concepts, social transformations in the novels come into analytical view and the identities of the characters also get a new mode of interpretation.

Dysfunctional Families in the Wessex Novels of Thomas Hardy (2005) by Lois Bethe Schoenfeld "concentrates on Hardy's use of dysfunctional families as a frame of reference" (Schoenfeld, 2005: 1) and thereby studies a variety of thematic elements in Hardy's novels. The dysfunctional families precipitate and witness the problematization of the dimension of identity, and shed light on the matter of identity in Hardy's novels. In *Critical Issues: Thomas Hardy* (2009), Julian Wolfreys discusses the confessions of the other in *The Woodlanders*, *Tess of the d'Urbervilles* and *Jude the Obscure*. Wolfreys writes, "For Hardy true or authentic dwelling in an existential sense in the second half of the nineteenth century is inaccessible, so removed have his characters become from their worlds, as a result of their modernity." (Wolfreys, 2009: 184) Wolfreys in effect handles the matter of identity of Hardy's characters in terms of the relationship between the individual and the environment. The characters somewhat become outsiders and the other, with their identity alienated from the surroundings.

In *Landscape and Gender in the Novels of Charlotte Bronte, George Eliot, and Thomas Hardy: The Body of Nature* (2011), Eithne Henson examines the treatment and representations of landscapes in Charlotte Brontë, George Eliot, and Thomas Hardy's works. It is found out that landscapes, elements of the nature and ideas about the nature are utilized as tools to express gender attitudes and gender identities in the works of the three writers. *Thomas Hardy's Legal Fictions* (2013) by Trish Ferguson dedicates itself to the revelation of "Hardy's deep concern not only with specific legal issues under debate, but with the ideological basis of the law and the principles on which legal reform was undertaken" (Ferguson, 2013: 163). The institutions of law, as an integral part of social institutions, provide a panoramic view of the social institutions as a whole. The monograph is especially illuminating for the understanding of the identity relationships in the context of the institutions of law and the social institutions at large.

The monograph *Thomas Hardy: A Study of his Novels* (1992) by Nie Zhenzhao classifies Hardy's novels into three groups in accordance with the chronological order. The first group of novels, namely those created in the early phase of Hardy's career as a novelist, express an idyllic ideal. The second group of novels, namely those written in the middle phase of Hardy's career, reveal the decline and destruction of the patriarchal society, as well as the tragedies of the peasants in Wessex. The third group of novels, namely those written in the later phase of Hardy's career, show the replacement of patriarchy by capitalism in Wessex and the life of the people in this new era. The monograph is especially illuminating for the understanding of the changing identities of the Wessex people in the successive historical periods. The journal article "The Evolution of the Native Land Complex of Hardy" (2006) by Lu Chunfang deals with the native land complex of Hardy and the diachronic development of the complex in the sequence of the writer's novels. The article discusses the decline of the traditional patriarchal society in Wessex, and sheds light on the features of the identities of the novels' characters in the era of transition. *Love and Marriage, Woman's Rights, Fiction: Thematic Research of the Fiction of Hardy and Lawrence* (2009) by Gao Wanlong probes into the theme of love and marriage and the theme of female rights in the fiction of Thomas Hardy and D. H. Lawrence, incorporating the discussions of the two thematic aspects into an integrated whole. The monograph covers several related fields, including the Oedipus complex, opposition and harmonization in love and marriage, marriage and the abolition of marriage, etc. Besides, the monograph both analyzes fiction focused upon female characters and fiction focused upon male characters. By the research of the theme of love and marriage and the theme of female rights, the monograph throws light on the characteristics of the identities of both female characters and male characters in Hardy's novels.

As discussed above, in the previous works of research, the dimension of identity in Hardy's novels has been explored sufficiently. Gender has been chosen as a significant angle from which one can get a glimpse of the dimension of identity in the novels. The characteristics of the identity of female figures have been analyzed. Besides, the identities of female characters and the identities of male characters have been put in juxtaposition for comparison and mutual interpretation. The previous works of research also attach importance to the analysis of the changing social environment in the interpretation of the identities of the characters in the novels. The previous research makes analysis of the relationship between the Wessex depicted in Hardy's novels and the social conditions in the late Victorian era, achieving the interpretation of the significance of the Wessex under the specific historical background. The previous research traces the stages in the change and development of the society in the novels, unravelling the process of the destruction of patriarchy and its replacement by capitalism. By discussing the evolution of the native land complex, the previous research also provides a more sentimental perspective to understand the social changes as reflected in the novels. All these ways to explore the changing social environment shown in the novels are quite instrumental in the interpretation of the identities of the characters.

Moreover, in the previous works of research, some special textual arrangements are explored in a way which is enlightening for the understanding of the dimension of identity in the novels. For instance, the symbolic reconstruction of virginity, the dysfunctional families, the specially represented landscapes, specific and general legalissues, etc. Besides, philosophical perspectives are employed in the research of the novels in a manner that is illuminating for the interpretation of the fictional figures' identities. Existentialism and the typology of social formations by Deleuze and Guattari are utilized in the explorations of Hardy's novels. Furthermore, the matter of the existential dwelling of the characters comes into the critical view, with the alienation of the characters from the surroundings interpreted. To summarize, in the previous works of research, the special textual arrangements as internal resources instrumental in the cognition of the matter of identity, have been sufficiently utilized. Different philosophical perspectives, as external resources for the interpretation of the matter of identity, have also been put into employment.

Last, the review could be carried out from the perspective of value concept, or in other words the perspective of values. (In the book, the term value concept is used synonymously with the term values.)

In *Thomas Hardy: Towards a Materialist Criticism* (1985), George Wotton employs a materialist method in the research of Hardy's novels. According to Wotton, "the aim of a materialist criticism is [...] an understanding of the historical conditions of the production of writing and the ways in which literature operates in the process of reproducing the relations of production of class society." (Wotton, 1985: 2) Wotton asserts that "it is important and necessary to understand literature not only in terms of the production of meaning but also the production of value, of ideology and ideological discourses, aesthetic and otherwise, and crucially the production and reproduction of the relations of production in class society." (Wotton, 1985: 211) In literature the production of value is achieved in the context of the reproduction of the relations of production in class society. Through explorations into the reproduction of production relations in Hardy's novels, the monograph provides an insight into the material basis of the production of value and greatly facilitates the investigations into the values in those novels. The Ph. D.

dissertation "Different Countries: A Study of Unrequited Love in the Novels of Charles Dickens, Anthony Trollope, and Thomas Hardy" (1992) by Karen Ann Luten discusses the treatment of the matters of gender, love and marriage in the novels of the Victorian writers as mentioned in the title. The dissertation probes into the continuation and the defiance of the mainstream views about marriage in literary productions of these authors. The dissertation provides an analysis of the problems in the pursuit of romantic love and the difficulties that pursuit can meet with in the novels of Thomas Hardy. The dissertation sheds light upon the matters about the value concept of love in Hardy's novels.

The Ph. D. dissertation "Men Writing Women: Male Authorship, Narrative Strategies, and Woman's Agency in The Late-Victorian Novel" (2002) by Molly C. Youngkin discusses the novels of George Gissing, Thomas Hardy, George Meredith, and George Moore from the perspective of feminist influence upon these male writers. This dissertation develops the view that the novels of these writers incorporate the literary principles of liberal-feminist realism to different degrees, representing the difficult conditions of women and the triumphs they can sometimes achieve against those difficult conditions. The dissertation analyzes how *Tess of the d'Urbervilles* and *Jude the Obscure* show that female characters assert agency in face of unfavorable or even hostile conditions. The insight into the manner in which females assert agency sheds light upon the process in which they engage in their pursuit and aspire after their fulfillments, thus providing enlightenment about the connotations of their values. The Ph. D. dissertation "Darwinism in the Art of Thomas Hardy" (2005) by Michiko Seimiya discusses the profound impacts that Darwinism exerts upon Hardy's fiction and poetry. In this dissertation, around the analysis of the influence of Darwinism upon Hardy's art, the influence of other ideological discourse systems, including Christianity and Comte's positivism etc., also gets interpretation. On the background of the variety of ideological systems, the ambitions and pursuits of the characters in Hardy's novels come into a clearer view. Thereby, the dissertation provides enlightenment for the study of the values of the characters in the novels. In the Ph. D. dissertation "Thomas Hardy: Timely Exits" (2008), Tracy A. Ford discusses the employment of the literary technique of timely exits in Thomas Hardy's fiction. The characters in Hardy's fiction engage in a battle between themselves and the environment and work for a kind of fulfillment which is not allowed by the social surroundings. Therefore, they conduct timely exits to free themselves. Realized by suicide and other methods, timely exits, identical with the "voluntary isolation" proposed by Sigmund Freud in a certain sense, provide an escape for the characters and fulfill the empowerment of them. From another perspective, timely exits also present a demonstration of Hardy's fatalistic view of the world. (Ford, 2008: 5) In the discussion of the timely exits, the dissertation reveals aspects of the characters' pursuits in their particular social contexts. Thereby, the dissertation accomplishes the probing into the dimension of value concept in the novels.

　　In *Thomas Hardy and Desire: Conceptions of the Self* (2013), Jane Thomas deals with the forms and manifestations of desire in Hardy's works. Thomas writes, "This book is an exploration of desire in relation to that 'discovery' which, for Hardy's characters, may be equated with falling in love and, for Hardy the writer, with the struggle of the creative subject to achieve 'its little modicum of purpose'." (Thomas, 2013: 2) The desire discussed in the book is closely related to an individual's pursuit in life, which is conducted under the guidance of the individual's value concept. Therefore, the monograph is instrumental for the discussion of value concepts in this book. In *The Novels of Thomas Hardy: Illusion and Reality* (2013), Penelope Vigar utilizes the relationship between illusion and reality as an angle for the interpretation of Hardy's novels, together with their characters and events. She writes, "His [Hardy's] view of life often seems as if channelled to us through a sort of dream-consciousness, tinged with a nightmare reality." (Vigar, 2013: 52) In the monograph, the illusion-reality relationship functions as a tool for the investigation into the pursuits and values of the characters and effectively deepens the understanding of those pursuits and values.

The journal article "On the Religious Thoughts of Thomas Hardy" (2003) by Ma Xian discusses the religious ideas of the writer which are reflected in his literary works. According to this article, Hardy's attitudes towards Christianity incorporate belief, doubt, rebelliousness, and reflections. Quite complicated, Hardy's religious thoughts are full of contradictions and they are always in a process of change. (马弦, 2003: 115) In the exposition of Hardy's religious thoughts, the article sheds light upon the manners in which Hardy's works treat the characters' pursuits and values. These manners are influenced by Christianity and on the same time they constitute a revolt against certain propositions of Christianity. The journal article "On the New-Woman Image in Hardy's Novels" (2004) by Ma Xian presents a discussion of the depiction of new women in Thomas Hardy's novels. Moreover, the article achieves a revelation of the contradictions in the artistic images of these new women. The new women in Hardy's novels "aspire after freedom and democracy, and they are in pursuit of the integrity and independence of the personality" (马弦, 2004: 79). The defining feature of the new women is what they aspire for and what they pursue. The discussion of the new women in this article is especially illuminating for the comprehension of the values of the female characters.

As discussed above, in the previous works of research concerning the dimension of value concept, certain critical tendencies can be detected. There are interpretations of the outward forces that determine or influence Hardy's explorations of value and his representations of the characters' values. The novels of Hardy are understood as "the production of value, of ideology and ideological discourses", and as "the production and reproduction of the relations of production" (Wotton, 1985: 211). The spiritual production in the novels, including the production of values, is elucidated with reference to its material basis. Thus, the production of values in the novels is interpreted under the background of the material conditions of the late Victorian society. The outward forces not only exist in the material sphere but also exist in the spiritual sphere. The previous research also shows the influence of ideological systems upon Hardy's exploration and representation of value and value concepts. These ideological systems include feminism, Darwinism, and Christianity, etc. The previous research also covers some special textual arrangements in Hardy's novels which are endowed both with thematic significance and with formal significance. These arrangements include requited and unrequited love, timely exits, the forms and manifestations of desire, illusion and reality, the focused characterization of new women, etc. The analysis of these arrangements facilitates the elucidation of the dimension of value concept in Hardy's novels from a variety of specific perspectives.

To sum up, the previous works of research about the origin of the protagonists' tragedies in Thomas Hardy's novels lay a solid foundation for the research in this book. They directly facilitate the research here. The previous works of research concerning the dimensions of morality, disposition, identity and value concept assist in the explorations of the individual cultural systems of the protagonists, thus also facilitating the research here from their specific perspectives.

Besides the previous works of research about the origin of the protagonists' tragedies and the previous works of research concerning the four dimensions, there are also some works of research which shed light on the reformist tendency of the novels of Thomas Hardy; they assist in this book's investigation into the reformist ideas of Hardy's novels, and in turn facilitate the book's research of the historical significance of the overall format of cultural inappositeness leading to tragedies in the novels.

The Ph. D. dissertation "Metropolitan Dissent in Thomas Hardy's Fiction: Class, Gender, Empire" （2017） by Rena Jackson dissects the tripartite social structure of the fictional Wessex and analyzes the imperial manifestations in Hardy's novels. Moreover, the dissertation draws parallels between class and gender inequality and oppression in Wessex and colonial pursuits that go beyond the boundaries of metropolitan Britain then. According to the dissertation, the novels of Thomas Hardy launch a protest against the exploitation of empire for the purpose of achieving class and gender oppression. (Jackson, 2017) The dissertation combines the criticism of colonialism and the criticism of domestic social inequality, thereby shedding light on the progressive and reformist dimension of Hardy's novels. The book *Thomas Hardy and History* (2017) by Fred Reid interprets Hardy's novels under a historical view and elucidates the historical significance of Hardy's novels in relation to contemporary thinkers such as John Stuart Mill and Auguste Comte who have developed their own philosophies of history. The work locates specific connections between Hardy's novels and contemporary historical conditions and incidents, and also gives consideration for tendencies of meliorism in the novels. (Reid, 2017)

The book *Food in the Novels of Thomas Hardy: Production and Consumption* (2017) by Kim Salmons probes into Hardy's novels under concrete economic and social backgrounds, using the production and consumption of food as a material link that bridges the gap between historical existence and literary existence, and confirming the realist aspect of Hardy's fictional art. The work provides a specific material perspective from which further considerations on the reformist tendency in the novels could be possibly made. (Salmons, 2017) The Ph. D. dissertation "Gender, Form, and Interiority in the Novels of Thomas Hardy" (2017) by Bailey Justine Shaw accomplishes the investigation of gender representations in Hardy's novels under the light of Hardy's formal experiments and his treatment of the matter of interiority and subjectivity. Analysis of Hardy's explorations of fictional form provides a perspective from which one could unravel the mysteries in the novelist's complicated and paradoxical gender treatments, while the manners of handling interiority and subjectivity equip the novels with a vantage point from which they could evoke in readers reconsiderations of the matters of form arrangement and gender representations. The dissertation sheds light on Hardy's progressive and reformist views concerning matters of gender in association with complicated historical context and in combination with nuanced social and ideological implications. (Shaw, 2017)

The journal article "Hardy's Community Building in *Tess of the d'Urbervilles*" (2018) by Wang Zhimin and Wu Tingjing discusses the cultural community imagination in *Tess of the d'Urbervilles*. According to this article, different from the idea which is prominent in Matthew Arnold's educational notions that Hebraism in the British spirit and culture should be balanced with Hellenism, the novel refuses to acknowledge the possibility of reconciling the two cultural stances, proposes the negation and overcoming of Hebraism in the British spirit and culture, and places the hope for a harmonious cultural community totally on the development and flourishing of Hellenism. Along this line of argumentation, it can be seen that the novel ardently advocates the value of the spontaneousness, sensuousness and enterprise of Hellenism. In addition, the novel advocates the necessity of broader physical and intellectual sphere for the development of individuals and economy, which also shows the influence of Darwin's evolutionism and the tendency of progressivism. (王智敏, 吴亭静, 2018) From the discussion in the article, it can be inferred that Hellenism functions as a pivot for the scheme of social reform and progress in *Tess of the d'Urbervilles*, and the development and flourishing of Hellenism shall be proposed as a central belief in the reformist ideas in the novel. The journal article "The Narrative of Educational Theme and Characteristics of the Era in Hardy's *The Return of the Native* and *Far from the Madding Crowd*" (2020) by Luo Ying discusses the two novels by Hardy under the background of the educational reform campaign in Britain that is contemporary with their creation. The article investigates the relationship between social class interaction and educational environment, paying attention to the role that education can play for the upward mobility of lower classes. (罗影, 2020) In that way, the article sheds light on the reformist tendency in Hardy's novels from the perspective of education.

0.2   The Methodology and Organization of the Book

The tragic novels of Thomas Hardy involve the problems of the protagonists' individualities and the inharmoniousness between individuals and the social environment, both of which should be held responsible for the tragedies of the protagonists. In order to get a systematic perception of that, an interpretative framework need to be developed.

On the theoretical basis of cultural materialism put forward by Raymond Williams, a famous British cultural research scholar, the interpretative framework of the appositeness and inappositeness of the individual cultural system could be developed to analyze the origin of the protagonists' tragedies in Thomas Hardy's novels, and thereby to investigate into the social ideas manifested in those novels.

In the development of cultural materialism, Raymond Williams conducts the interpretation of culture on the basis of the materialist conception of history. Concerning the materialist conception of history, Williams writes:

> The original notion of "man making his own history" was given a new radical content by this emphasis on "man making himself" through producing his own means of life. [...] It offered the possibility of overcoming the dichotomy between "society" and "nature", and of discovering new constitutive relationships between "society" and "economy". As a specification of the basic element of the social process of culture it was a recovery of the wholeness of history. (Williams, 1977: 19)

The materialist conception of history lays a foundation for cultural materialism and its interpretation of culture. In the theoretical vision of cultural materialism, culture is the whole way of the life of people. Williams comments:

> [...] the [The] recognition of a separate body of moral and intellectual activities, and the offering of a court of human appeal, which comprise the early meanings of the word, are joined, and in themselves changed, by the growing assertion of a whole way of life, not only as a scale of integrity, but as a mode of interpreting all our common experience, and, in this new interpretation, changing it. (Williams, 1983: Xⅷ)

Culture, as a whole way of life, can constitute a constructive agent and source of vitality. Culture is endowed with the force to put new perspectives upon and provide new forms to human existence and experience. Culture, as a whole way of life, is embedded in a web of interrelationships with particular material contexts. Culture depends on the material context as the basis for its existence and development. On the other hand, the material context finds in culture a chance for innovation and reconstruction. "Williams insists that culture be understood through the representations and practices of daily life in the context of the material conditions of their production. This Williams calls cultural materialism [...]" (Barker, Jane, 2016: 51). The representations and practices of daily life and the context of the material conditions are mutually complementary and mutually dependent aspects of human existence. The former one, concentratedly expressed as culture, takes roots in and extends its influence to the latter one. The context of material conditions for the production of culture mainly consists in economic relations. The role that culture assumes in its relationship with economic relations is either passive or active, according to the perspective adopted in the assessment of that role. Culture is determined by the economic factors, in a certain sense, but it is not a completely passive existence. Culture could generate physical forces and influence people's existence and development. Culture derives from the material realm and transmits its influence to the material realm. Therefore, culture has a kind of materiality.

Since culture is in some sense determined by economic relations, the analysis of culture shall begin with the assessment of the manner in which culture is determined by economic relations. About the relationships of determination between the economic sphere and the cultural sphere, scholars point out:

> He [Raymond Williams] discusses the relations between the economic and the cultural in terms of "setting limits". By this he means that the economic sets limits to what can be done or expressed in culture. However, it does not determine the meaning of cultural practices in a direct one-to-one relationship. Rather, Williams speaks of "the variable distances of practices". By this he means that the social relationships embedded in the wage labour process are the critical and dominant set of social

relations. Other relations and practices are set at "variable distances" from this central set of practices, thereby allowing for degrees of determination, autonomy and specificity. (Barker, Jane, 2016: 66 - 67)

Different cultural relations and practices, set at variable distances from the economic relations at the center, accordingly attain different degrees of freedom in development and the expression of meanings. As a consequence, cultural elements in basically the same economic context, set at different distances from the central economic relations, demonstrate different degrees of diversity. Therefore, there is the possibility that the cultural elements in basically the same economic context form sharp contrasts to each other in the same dimension.

Culture can be studied both on the macroscopic level and on the microscopic level, both on the collective level and on the individual level. Cultural analysis on the individual level is particularly effective for the investigation into the causes of particular patterns of individual existence and development. Raymond Williams says:

> We are seeking to define and consider one central principle: that of the essential relation, the true interaction, between patterns learned and created in the mind and patterns communicated and made active in relationships, conventions and institutions. Culture is our name for this process and its results, and then within this process we discover problems that have been the subject of traditional debate and that we may look at again in this new way. Among such problems, that of the relationship between an individual and his society is evident and crucial. (Williams, 2011A: 95)

On the individual level, a certain person's cultural individuality and cultural setting (the cultural part of the person's social environment) constitute the person's way of life, namely his individual cultural system. The relationship between the cultural individuality and the cultural setting forms the cultural aspect of the relationship between an individual and his society. The cultural individuality comprises the "patterns learned and created in the mind", and the cultural setting consists in " patterns communicated and made active in relationships, conventions and institutions ". The relationship between the former and the latter, of central importance, exerts profound influence upon an individual's existence and development. By the analysis of the individual cultural system, made up of the cultural individuality and the cultural setting, new light can be shed on the relationship between an individual and the society. Besides this relationship which receives a new light, other problems in traditional debate, such as morality, disposition, identity and value concept, could also be interpreted from a new perspective. These four aforementioned problems make up four major dimensions of the individual cultural system which are of vital significance for the system and will be explained later. The cultural individuality of a person is the internal existence of the individual cultural system; the cultural setting of the person is the external existence of the individual cultural system. Besides, the individual cultural system covers different dimensions, among which the major ones include morality, disposition, identity and value concept. If the internal existence or the external existence of the individual cultural system in one dimension is generally harmless for individual existence, it shall be regarded as in appositeness. Accordingly, if the internal existence or the external existence of the individual cultural system in one dimension is generally harmful for individual existence, it shall be regarded as in inappositeness. If the relationship between the internal existence and the external existence of an individual cultural system in one dimension is predominated by harmony and therefore generally harmless for individual existence, the relationship shall be considered as in appositeness. Accordingly, if the relationship between the internal existence and the external existence in one dimension is predominated by conflict and therefore generally harmful for individual existence, the relationship shall be considered as in inappositeness.

The appositeness condition (namely whether a cultural construct is in appositeness or in inappositeness) of the individual cultural system depends upon the appositeness conditions of the internal existence, the external existence and the internal-external relationship of the system. In one dimension, if the internal existence, the external existence and the relationship between the internal existence and the external existence are all in appositeness, the individual cultural system will stay in appositeness in that dimension. Nevertheless, in one dimension, if the internal existence, the external existence or the internal-external relationship is in inappositeness, the individual cultural system will be plunged into inappositeness in that particular dimension. The appositeness of an individual cultural system in a major dimension will generate a conspicuous stabilizing force that can establish a cultural foundation for the existence of an individual. The conspicuous stabilizing force generated by the appositeness of an individual cultural system in a major dimension consists in the appositeness of the internal existence, the external existence and the internal-external relationship. The inappositeness of the internal existence, external existence or internal-external relationship, or in other words the inappositeness of the individual cultural system in a major dimension, will generate a conspicuous destructive force that can culturally threaten an individual's existence and fundamentally do harm to the individual's life. Both the aforementioned stabilizing and destructive forces are the embodiment of the materiality of culture.

The appositeness condition of an individual cultural system is determined by the appositeness conditions of the internal existence, the external existence and the relationship between the internal existence and the external existence of the system. Besides, the appositeness condition of an individual cultural system involves a variety of dimensions. Morality, disposition, identity and value concept are essential to an individual's life as well as the individual cultural system and they constitute the major dimensions of the system. Among them, morality is the basis, disposition is the keynote, identity is the core and value concept is the orientation. The individual morality, the individual disposition, the individual identity and the individual value concept are major constituents of the cultural individuality of a person, whereas the social mechanism of morality, the social mechanism of disposition, the social mechanism of identity and the social mechanism of value concept are major constituents of the cultural setting in which the person lives. (The social mechanism of value concept, in the context of this book, can also be called the social mechanism of value, for brevity.) The aforementioned social mechanisms are constituted by certain social institutions, which incorporate both organizational social institutions and ideological social institutions.

"The humanistic idea appears at the very beginning of the human civilization, and gets its first systematic and comprehensive interpretation from the humanists during Renaissance in Europe." (刘磊, 胡婷婷, 2012A: 1) The humanistic idea "combines the feature of emphasizing reason of Hebrew-Christianity Civilization and the feature of emphasizing humanity of Ancient Greek Civilization" (刘磊, 胡婷婷, 2012B: 129), and is of vital importance for the Western Civilization. The novels of Thomas Hardy receive influence from the Renaissance; they highlight the value of humans and constitute an embodiment of the humanistic idea. During the Renaissance period, the God-centered concept and the human-centered concept coexist and intermingle with each other in their development. (刘磊, 2016: 100) Created in a new era characterized by industrialization, Hardy's novels present a more obvious human focus. By virtue of the distinct focus on humans and the detailed and vivid depictions of various aspects of individuals and their settings of life in the novels, the appositeness of the individual cultural system can serve as a valid and feasible perspective for the interpretation of the origin of the protagonists' tragedies.

In the investigation into the origin of the protagonists' tragedies in Thomas Hardy's novels, this book chooses four representative ones *The Return of the Native* (1878, shortened as *The Native* afterwards in this book), *The Mayor of Casterbridge* (1886, shortened as *The Mayor* afterwards in this book), *Tess of the d'Urbervilles* (1891, shortened as *Tess* afterwards in this book) and *Jude the Obscure* (1896, shortened as *Jude* afterwards in this book). In *The Native*, along with the unfolding of the plot, the protagonist Clym's mother and wife gradually get estranged from him and successively die in bitterness. Moreover,

Clym's fellow villagers at Egdon Heath, despite all the efforts and sufferings of Clym, still misunderstand him at the ending of the novel. Clym is rejected both by his mother and his wife. He is also rejected by his fellow villagers in a certain sense. Clym's ending in rejection constitutes his disastrous conclusion. In *The Mayor*, the protagonist Henchard in the end goes to death in despair, which constitutes his disastrous conclusion. The despair of Henchard has two levels of meanings. First, his business meets with downright failure. He feels despair about business. Second, he loses the love of family members. He feels despair about the family. In *Tess*, the protagonist Tess is executed in the end. Her execution constitutes her disastrous conclusion. In *Jude*, the protagonist Jude can neither attain the higher education at Christminster University nor preserve the love of Sue. He eventually dies in disillusion, which constitutes his disastrous conclusion. Through analysis, it is found out that in a certain sense the inappositeness of the individual cultural system, shortened as cultural inappositeness, constitutes the origin of the disastrous conclusions of the protagonists in these novels. By showing the cases of cultural inappositeness which cause the protagonists' disastrous conclusions, the novels of Thomas Hardy develop certain ideas about the four major dimensions of the individual cultural system, namely morality, disposition, identity and value concept. (In an essential sense, the ideas about the value concept are also ideas about value. In other words, they fall under the category of the ideas about value.) These ideas do not exist in isolation. Instead, they are caught in a web of intertextuality together with contemporary ideological discourses. Utilitarianism, evolutionism and Matthew Arnold's cultural notions are prominent constituents of the intellectual atmosphere of the Victorian era in Britain. It is natural for these systems of ideological discourses to exert some influence upon the creation of Thomas Hardy's novels. Besides, Thomas Hardy himself had read the works of utilitarianism, evolutionism and the works by Matthew Arnold. He had received much influence from these works. Therefore, it is highly reasonable and probable for Thomas Hardy's novels to bear some correspondence to certain aspects of utilitarianism, evolutionism and Matthew Arnold's cultural notions. Through the correspondence to the systems of ideological discourses, the novels can accomplish the interpretation of certain aspects of these systems in the literary way. Therefore, the novels facilitate the understanding of the systems of ideological discourses and the systems of ideological discourses facilitate the interpretation of the novels.

The main body of the book is divided into five chapters, each of the first four chapters dealing with one of the four major dimensions of the individual cultural system, while the fifth chapter dealing with the historical significance of the overall format of cultural inappositeness leading to tragedies in Hardy's novels. The first chapter deals with the dimension of morality. Cultural inappositeness in the dimension of morality fulfills a function in the formation of the disastrous conclusions of Clym, Tess and Jude, respectively the protagonists of *The Native*, *Tess* and *Jude*. Because cultural inappositeness in the dimension of morality is particularly important for the development of the disastrous conclusion of Clym, two sections are devoted to the discussion of *The Native* for detailed analysis. The conflict between the sufficiency of altruism and the moderation of altruism and the conflict between the affirmative morality and the negative morality mechanism constitute the inappositeness of Clym's individual cultural system and lead to his disastrous conclusion. The conflict between the spiritualized morality and the materialized morality mechanism makes up the inappositeness of Tess's individual cultural system and results in her disastrous conclusion. The conflict between the content-directed morality and the form-directed morality mechanism makes up the inappositeness of Jude's individual cultural system and brings about his disastrous conclusion. By demonstrating the cases of cultural inappositeness in the dimension of morality which cause the protagonists' disastrous conclusions, the novels of Hardy develop certain ideas about morality which correspond to and interpret certain aspects of utilitarianism.

The second chapter deals with the dimension of disposition. Cultural inappositeness in the dimension of disposition fulfills a function in the formation of the disastrous conclusions of Henchard, the protagonist of *The Mayor* and Tess, the protagonist of *Tess*. For cultural inappositeness in the dimension of disposition is particularly significant for the development of the disastrous conclusion of Henchard, two sections are devoted to the discussion of the case of cultural inappositeness in disposition in *The Mayor* for detailed analysis. The negative tendency and the mood-based aggressiveness constitute the inappositeness of Henchard's individual cultural system and give rise to his disastrous conclusion. The imbalance of psychological rhythm constitutes the inappositeness of Tess's individual cultural system and results in her disastrous conclusion. By demonstrating the cases of cultural inappositeness in the dimension of disposition which cause the protagonists' disastrous conclusions, the novels of Thomas Hardy develop certain ideas about disposition which correspond to and interpret certain aspects of evolutionism.

The third chapter deals with the dimension of identity. Cultural inappositeness in the dimension of identity fulfills a function in the formation of the disastrous conclusions of Tess and Henchard. Because cultural inappositeness in the dimension of identity is particularly significant for the development of the disastrous conclusion of Tess, two sections are dedicated to the case of cultural inappositeness in *Tess* for detailed analysis. The conflict between the identity of explicit equality and the identity of explicit inequality and the conflict between the identity of implicit equality and the implicit identity inequality constitute the inappositeness of Tess's individual cultural system and result in her disastrous conclusion. The conflict between the identity as a patriarch and the modernized identity mechanism constitutes the inappositeness of Henchard's individual cultural system and gives rise to his disastrous conclusion. By demonstrating the cases of cultural inappositeness which cause the protagonists' disastrous conclusions, the novels of Hardy develop certain ideas about identity which correspond to and interpret certain aspects of Matthew Arnold's cultural notions.

The fourth chapter deals with the dimension of value concept. Cultural inappositeness in the dimension of value concept fulfills a role in the formation of the disastrous conclusions of Jude, Clym and Tess. Since the cultural inappositeness in the dimension of value concept is particularly significant for the development of the disastrous conclusion of Jude, two sections are dedicated to the discussion of the case of cultural inappositeness in *Jude*. The conflict between the value concept of knowledge and the synchronic value hegemony and the conflict between the value concept of love and the diachronic value hegemony constitute the inappositeness of Jude's individual cultural system and bring about his disastrous conclusion. The conflict between the exterior-oriented value concept and the interior-oriented value mechanism constitutes the inappositeness of Clym's individual cultural system and leads to his disastrous conclusion. The conflict between the spiritualized value concept and the materialized value mechanism constitutes the inappositeness of Tess's individual cultural system and results in her disastrous conclusion. By demonstrating the cases of cultural inappositeness which cause the protagonists' disastrous conclusions, the novels develop certain ideas about value concept which also correspond to and interpret certain aspects of Matthew Arnold's cultural notions.

The fifth chapter deals with the historical significance of the overall format of cultural inappositeness leading to tragedies. The overall format of cultural inappositeness leading to tragedies in the novels of Thomas Hardy accomplishes the literary interpretation of the fatalism and pessimism of Arthur Schopenhauer. The overall format shows reformist ideas which especially emphasize transformation of social institutions, achieving the interpretation of the ideas of reformism of John Ruskin and Auguste Comte from the literary perspective.

The conclusion gives a summary of the cases of cultural inappositeness in all four major dimensions which cause the protagonists' disastrous conclusions. The conclusion also accomplishes the revelation of the ideas about the redemption and development of humanity in Hardy's novels which are related to the origin of the protagonists' tragedies in these novels. In the novels, only two out of the ten cases of cultural inappositeness are caused by the inappositeness of the internal existence of the individual cultural system. The other eight cases are caused by the inappositeness of the relationship between the internal existence and the external existence. It can be seen that the novels attach more importance to the unfavorable conditions in the relationship between individuals and the society than to the unfavorable characteristics of individuals themselves as the factors which can threaten the existence of individuals. In three cases out of the eight cases of cultural inappositeness which are caused by the inappositeness of internal-external relationship, the novels do not take sides either with the internal existence or with the external existence. In all other five cases, the novels achieve the approval of the internal existence and foster the anxiety that unfavorable conditions in the society may pose threats to individuals and the society itself. It can be seen that the novels place the hope of the redemption of humanity more upon the transformation of the society than upon the improvement of individuals. The overall format of cultural inappositeness leading to tragedies in the novels is arranged in concrete historical conditions, demonstrating considerable historical significance.

Chapter One
Cultural Inappositeness in
the Dimension of Morality

In an academic work about ethics, Wang Zeying provides a definition of morality:

> In essence, morality is a social ideological structure peculiar to human beings which is determined by certain social material relations. It is the spiritual actions in human practice with ethical values which reflect and regulate various social relations through non-compulsory forms like norms of good and evil, criteria, obligation and conscience, etc. (王泽应, 2012: 64)

Morality is the basis of the individual cultural system and it constitutes a major dimension of the system. The inappositeness of the individual morality, the social mechanism of morality or the relationship between the individual morality and the social mechanism of morality will plunge the individual cultural system into inappositeness in the dimension of morality. The inappositeness of the individual morality, the social mechanism of morality or the relationship between the individual morality and the social mechanism of morality, or in other words the inappositeness of the individual cultural system in the dimension of morality will generate a destructive force which can culturally threaten an individual's existence.

1.1 *The Native:* The Conflict Between the Sufficiency and the Moderation of Altruism

"All moral systems should be established on the basis of the recognition of the fundamental status of good." (刘磊, 2011: 79) Nevertheless, different moral systems or different moral stances foster different conceptions of good. Correspondingly, different moral systems or different moral stances also develop different modes of treating altruism, a category closely correlated with good. In *The Native*, in the individual morality of the protagonist Clym, the principle of the sufficiency of altruism is in a dominant position, whereas the social mechanism of morality in which Clym lives is dominated by the principle of the moderation of altruism. Conflict exists between the sufficiency of altruism as a kind of moral principle and the moderation of altruism as another kind of moral principle. The individual morality of Clym is a type of affirmative morality while the social mechanism of morality that Clym faces shall be classified as a type of negative morality mechanism. There is also the conflict between the affirmative morality and the negative morality mechanism in Clym's individual cultural system in the dimension of morality. The conflict between the sufficiency of altruism and the moderation of altruism and the conflict between the affirmative morality and the negative morality mechanism, from their respective angles, drive the individual cultural system of Clym into inappositeness in the dimension of morality. Terry Eagleton says, "[...] the notion of cultural materialism is in my view of considerable value. For it is as though it extends and completes Marx's own struggle against idealism, carrying it forcefully into that realm ('culture') always most ideologically resistant to a materialist redefinition." (Eagleton, 1989: 169) In the theoretical vision of cultural materialism, culture gets the material quality and can conspicuously influence people's lives. The inappositeness of Clym's individual cultural system in the dimension of morality, as a major cultural feature of the young man, engenders a negative force which fundamentally does harm to his life and leads to his ending in rejection, his disastrous conclusion. From another perspective, it can also be said that the conflict between the sufficiency of altruism and the moderation of altruism and the conflict between the affirmative morality and the negative morality mechanism lead to Clym's disastrous conclusion.

Clym Yeobright returns from the prosperous metropolis Paris to his native place, the bleak Egdon Heath, supposedly for the celebration of Christmas. In Paris, Clym is the manager of a diamond business and leads a well-off and prosperous life. However, Clym does not intend to go back to Paris. Instead, with much determination, he plans to start a school at his hometown. In Clym's mind, this would probably be his final choice for life and has great significance for him.

Clym's plan to start a school in his hometown is made for the purpose of promoting the welfare of the villagers there. In this plan and the persistent efforts to carry it out, the principle of the sufficiency of altruism in Clym's individual morality is demonstrated. Clym thinks that the folks at Egdon live in isolation and could not get access to enough knowledge and proper enlightenment. Therefore, they could not prosper in life both intellectually and physically. Clym hopes that he, by starting a school at Egdon, can provide knowledge and guidance to the local people, thereby rendering better life to them. "He wished to raise the class at the expense of individuals rather than individuals at the expense of the class. What was more, he was ready at once to be the first unit sacrificed." (Hardy, 1995: 145) In order to promote the welfare of his fellow villagers at Egdon, Clym is ready and willing to sacrifice his well-off life in Paris. He voluntarily retreats into the crude and difficult surroundings at Egdon Heath and makes up his mind to serve his fellow villagers wholeheartedly in his own way. "his [His] love of humanity and courage in self-sacrifice is sincere and sublime" (Zhang, 2010: 89). Clym's choice and behavior which are focused upon the interests of others instead of those of himself present a manifestation of the principle of the sufficiency of altruism in his individual morality. George Wotton says, "Clym loves Egdon and he loves its people; it is just that he no longer sees them, but gazes past them, beyond them to that utopian vison of a conflict-free altruistic world of universal consciousness." (Wotton, 1985: 118) The realization of the education scheme of Clym may be quite difficult and the feasibility of his plan is something which can easily evoke controversy. However, the principle of the sufficiency of altruism shown by him is evidently adorable. Though adorable in a certain way, the principle of the sufficiency of altruism in Clym's morality is not understood by others and it is in conflict with the principle of the moderation of altruism of the social morality mechanism which is embodied by various characters around the protagonist. The conflict between the sufficiency of altruism and the moderation of altruism leads to Clym's ending in rejection, his disastrous conclusion.

First, the conflict between the sufficiency of altruism and the moderation of altruism leads to Mrs. Yeobright's estrangement from Clym and her unnatural death which constitute one aspect of Clym's ending in rejection. Clym's plan to open a school at Egdon is resolutely opposed by his mother Mrs. Yeobright. At her son's assertion that he will not return to Paris to continue his career as the diamond business manager and he intends to start a school to benefit his fellow residents at Egdon, Mrs. Yeobright says, "I hadn't the least idea that you meant to go backward in the world by your own free choice." (Hardy, 1995: 147) Unlike Clym, Mrs. Yeobright sets one's own interests before the interests of others. From her perspective, Clym shall fully utilize the foundation of the career which has already been laid with many efforts. He shall continue steadily onwards on his way towards greater affluence and prosperity instead of going backwards. There is no reason for Clym to sacrifice his personal interests for the interests of others and his personal prosperity for the enlightenment of the local people. In Mrs. Yeobright's morality, there is not the sufficiency of altruism which can be found in Clym. The morality of Mrs. Yeobright is a reflection of the social morality mechanism, and the view of Mrs. Yeobright is a demonstration of the principle of the moderation of altruism in the social morality mechanism then and there. Concerning the issue of whether Clym should stay at Egdon or return to Paris, a fissure grows in the relationship between the son and the mother and the mother is gradually estranged from the son. That fissure in essence is brought about by the conflict between the sufficiency of altruism in Clym's individual morality and the moderation of altruism in the social morality mechanism.

The conflict between the sufficiency of altruism and the moderation of altruism also harms Clym's relationship with his mother indirectly through his relationship with his wife. Clym's wife Eustacia Vye is another major character in the novel who manifests the moderation of altruism in the social morality mechanism. Eustacia's primary wish is to escape from Egdon Heath. She despises and hates the bleakness of the heath. She longs for a glittering, affluent and prosperous life which can by no means be realized on the heath. She hopes that Clym can bring her to the glittering Paris, the place where he prospers as a diamond business manager, so that she can begin the life as a wealthy lady. Eustacia regards her own welfare as the criterion for making judgments, without paying much attention to the welfare of others. She reflects the principle of the moderation of altruism in the social morality mechanism then and there. Governed by the social morality mechanism which is controlled by the moderation of altruism, Eustacia could not understand and accept Clym's decision to remain at the bleak heath and pursue a much less prosperous career of a schoolmaster. When the decision of Clym seems irreversible and the desire of Eustacia appears unquenchable, the fragile happiness of their marriage collapses and discord begins to dominate their marital life. The discord in Clym and Eustacia's marriage is in essence effected by the conflict between the sufficiency of altruism and the moderation of altruism. Eustacia grows estranged from Clym and begins to spend time with her old lover Damon Wildeve, which suggests the gloomy prospects of her marriage with Clym.

After some frictions between Mrs. Yeobright and the couple, the mother goes to visit her son and her daughter-in-law, in an attempt to repair her relations with them. At that time, Clym is asleep. Eustacia is having a meet with her lover Damon. Afraid of being caught together with Damon at home, Eustacia does not open the door for Mrs. Yeobright, assuming that her husband will be awakened by the knock at the door and open it. Contrary to her expectation, Clym is not wakened and Mrs. Yeobright, thinking that her son and daughter-in-law refuse to meet her, goes away in extreme disappointment. The conflict between the sufficiency of altruism and the moderation of altruism brings about the discord between Clym and Eustacia which in turn leads Eustacia to turn to her old lover. In Eustacia's secret meet with Damon, Mrs. Yeobright fails to attain admission into her son's residence, which plunges her into extreme disappointment. That extreme disappointment and the fissure in Mrs. Yeobright and Clym's relationship which also arises out of the conflict between the sufficiency of altruism and the moderation of altruism together plunge Mrs. Yeobright into great mental agonies. Having been refused admission, Mrs. Yeobright goes towards her own home through the heath. The weather is extremely hot and the old woman is exhausted both by the trudge and by the heat. More importantly, she feels heart-broken and suffers from great mental agonies. On the way, she meets a boy named Johnny Nunsuch. To him, Mrs. Yeobright describes herself as "a broken-hearted woman cast off by her son." (Hardy, 1995: 238) This description clearly shows the state of Mrs. Yeobright. She is in utter helplessness both physically and mentally. In this utter helplessness, Mrs. Yeobright is unable to fight against the threats from the outside world. At last, she is bitten by an adder and dies.

Mrs. Yeobright's abortive visit and unexpected death constitute one of the central episodes of the novel. The episode and its preparatory actions are narrated in Book Fourth of the novel and the episode proper is committed to the narration of the final four chapters of Book Fourth. From the perspective of narrative tempo, a sharp contrast is established between Book Third and Book Fourth. Book Third covers six months, while in Book Fourth the temporal coverage is only two months. Moreover, in the interior of Book Fourth, the narrative tempo is also on the decrease—the last four chapters of Book Fourth are concentrated upon the narration of a single day. Accumulating drama is achieved by the decreasing tempo, by the intensifying ratio between the quantity of textual materials assigned to narration and the length of time narrated. (Ireland, 2014: 77) The episode of the abortive visit and unexpected death of Mrs. Yeobright, by the decrease of narrative tempo and the obtainment of relatively more textual space in comparison to episodes in its narrative context, gets the status of one major narrative focus of the novel. The abortive visit and unexpected death of Mrs. Yeobright are brought under the spotlight, with their moral implications greatly magnified. The conflict between the sufficiency of altruism and the moderation of altruism, to a large extent negatively influences Mrs. Yeobright's psyche and drives her into an exceedingly difficult condition which takes shape both in the physical sense and in the psychological sense. The unnatural death of the old lady is just the direct result of this difficult condition. The moral conflict estranges Mrs. Yeobright from her son and finally leads to her death on the heath. Facing the estrangement of his mother from him and the death of his mother for which he himself is also responsible, Clym sinks into great agonies. The estrangement of Mrs. Yeobright from Clym and her unnatural death haunt Clym's heart forever and constitute one aspect of Clym's ending in rejection, his disastrous conclusion. To summarize, the conflict between the sufficiency of altruism and the moderation of altruism leads to the estrangement between Clym and his mother and his mother's unnatural death, which constitute one aspect of Clym's ending in rejection, his disastrous conclusion.

Second, the conflict between the sufficiency of altruism and the moderation of altruism also leads to the estrangement of Eustacia from Clym and her unnatural death, which constitute another aspect of Clym's ending in rejection, his disastrous conclusion. Under the influence of the principle of the moderation of altruism of the social morality mechanism, Eustacia considers her own affluence as the principle for making decisions. "Lacking in loving-kindness for heath-dwellers, Eustacia burns with an ambition to leave Egdon Heath". (郝涂根, 2012: 21 - 22) The ambition of leaving Egdon Heath together with the people there and the lack of loving-kindness for the heath people show the influence exerted by the principle of the moderation of altruism of the social morality mechanism upon Eustacia. As discussed before, there is the principle of the sufficiency of altruism in Clym's individual morality. According to the principle of the sufficiency of altruism, Clym regards the welfare of the residents at Egdon Heath as the principle for making decisions. The conflict between the sufficiency of altruism and the moderation of altruism plunges the marriage of Clym and Eustacia into crisis. In the novel, Hardy writes:

> She was hoping for the time when, as the mistress of some pretty establishment, however small, near a Parisian Boulevard, she would be passing her days on the skirts at least of the gay world, and catching stray wafts from those town pleasures she was so well fitted to enjoy. Yet, Yeobright was as firm in the contrary intention as if the tendency of marriage were rather to develop the fantasies of young philanthropy than to sweep them away. (Hardy, 1995: 200)

Influenced by the principle of the moderation of altruism in the social morality mechanism, Eustacia's mind is focused upon her own "pleasures". Eustacia is not a person without any sense of altruism. Although she and Clym are not happy in their marriage, "She [she] is not only physically protective of Clym, but she also forbids any adverse criticism of him no matter how much she secretly desires to hear it." (Essex, 1976: 170) Eustacia's care and protection of Clym show a certain amount of altruism in her. However, that altruism, under the influence of the moderation of altruism in the social mechanism of morality, is weak. Quite different from Eustacia's morality, Clym's morality is characterized by the sufficiency of altruism and his mind is focused upon "philanthropy". Holding her own affluence as the principle for making decisions, Eustacia is in great eagerness to escape from Egdon Heath where people could only lead a poor and obscure life. Her wish is directed toward the metropolis Paris where all prosperity seems ready for her to occupy. Totally different from her, Clym, holding the welfare of the residents at the heath as the principle for making decisions, is in all eagerness to start a school in his hometown. In that way, he hopes he could provide enlightenment to the folks at Egdon and stimulate their wisdom. He dreams of substantially enriching their intellectual life, thereby promoting their welfare. The conflict between the sufficiency of altruism and the moderation of altruism casts a chill upon Clym and Eustacia's love and sets a block on their route towards happiness through marriage. As a consequence, the two newlyweds are increasingly estranged from each other. Frustrated in her pursuit, Eustacia "see[s] herself as a tragic heroine trapped in the toils of a sadistic super-power" (Dutta, 2000: 38). Lacking altruistic spirits, Eustacia concentrates on her own interests. The failure in promoting her own interests as she wishes will inevitably plunge her into agonies. Feeling disappointed with her life, Eustacia begins to search for new consolation and new hope. Gradually she is attracted to and eventually regained by her old lover Damon. Eustacia can no longer tolerate the life at Egdon. She and Damon make a plan about the escape from the heath. In a stormy night, Eustacia and Damon secretly flee from their homes and head for Paris. Unfortunately, Eustacia falls into a weir on the heath. She and Damon who dives into the weir to save her both get drowned. Were it not for the help from Diggory Venn, another major figure in the novel, Clym who comes to rescue Eustacia would also lose his life. The conflict between the sufficiency of altruism and the moderation of altruism creates the crisis of Clym and Eustacia's marriage and the estrangement between them. Driven into this unhappy condition, Eustacia again turns to Damon and together with him attempts the dangerous flee from the heath which precipitates their death. After the death of his mother, the unnatural death of his wife deals a further blow to Clym. A further layer of gloom gathers around him. His wife turns away from him and looks for love from another man; therefore, Clym is rejected by his wife spiritually. Eustacia elopes with Damon and unluckily loses her life. Clym can never meet his wife again; in this sense, he is rejected by his wife physically. The estrangement of Eustacia from Clym and her unnatural death haunt Clym forever and constitute another aspect of his ending in rejection. Therefore, by bringing about the estrangement of Eustacia from Clym and her unnatural death, the conflict between the sufficiency of altruism and the moderation of altruism leads to Clym's ending in rejection, his disastrous conclusion.

1.2 *The Native:* The Conflict Between the Affirmative Morality and the Negative Morality Mechanism

The conflict between the internal existence and the external existence of Clym's individual cultural system in the dimension of morality is not only projected upon the magnitude of altruism but also upon the dynamics of morality. The dynamics of morality is the principle according to which the morality shall be constructed. It involves whether morality should be constructed as a kind of affirmative existence—affirmative morality or should be constructed as a kind of negative existence—negative morality. The affirmative morality requires people to actively pursue virtues, whereas the negative morality only requires people to passively obey moral disciplines. The individual morality of Clym is an affirmative morality, whereas the social mechanism of morality in which Clym lives is a negative morality mechanism. The conflict between the affirmative morality and the negative morality mechanism, as another one of the factors that constitute the inappositeness of Clym's individual cultural system in the dimension of morality, also leads to the protagonist's ending in rejection, his disastrous conclusion. Clym once says:

> I get up every morning and see the whole creation groaning and travailing in pain, as St Paul says, and yet there am I, trafficking in glittering splendours with wealthy women and titled libertines, and pandering to the meanest vanities—I, who have health and strength enough for anything. I have been troubled in my mind about it all the year, and the end is that I cannot do it any more. (Hardy, 1995: 148)

Clym dedicates himself to the active pursuit of moral attainments rather than stay satisfied with the passive compliance with moral commandments. In other words, Clym engages in the active construction of virtues instead of the passive observance of disciplines. As a result, when Clym faces people in pains, he could not refrain from trying all what he can to render assistance to them. The sharp contrast between his affluence and others' pains drives him to hasten his steps towards the self-sacrifice for the welfare of others. It can be seen that Clym upholds an affirmative morality. Under the guidance of the affirmative morality, Clym cannot get satisfied with merely keeping away from what moral commandments prohibit him to do. To stay passively submissive to moral principles without actively fostering virtues can create a sense of guilt in Clym's psyche and that highly unpleasant sense is suffocating and virtually intolerable for him. The central element in Clym's affirmative morality is free will. Only when he carries out practices of virtue actively by his free will instead of passively through external pressure, can Clym get moral satisfaction.

Contrary to Clym, under the control of the negative morality mechanism of the society then, Mrs. Yeobright demonstrates passive moral tendencies. To Clym, Mrs. Yeobright says, "Manager to that large diamond establishment— what better can a man wish for? What a post of trust and respect!" (Hardy, 1995: 148) Under the negative morality mechanism, Mrs. Yeobright's moral satisfaction comes from passively complying with moral disciplines. With the compulsory moral requirements met, she is unwilling to further sacrifice personal interests to actively develop virtues. The failure in moral advancements beyond compulsory moral requirements is considered by Mrs. Yeobright as something natural, and it will by no means create a sense of guilt in her psyche. Therefore, she holds the view that Clym shall naturally and happily pursue the career of the diamond business manager. Not required by any moral discipline, from her perspective, it is unnecessary and unnatural for Clym to sacrifice himself for the welfare of others. Mrs. Yeobright holds Clym's position of the manager as "a post of trust and respect", because in her view the choice for the position is definitely beyond reproach in the moral sense. As a consequence,

Mrs. Yeobright considers Clym's plan to give up his glittering profession and start a school for the local folks unreasonable and unacceptable. She is firmly opposed to Clym's plan and thus frictions develop between the mother and the son.

Similar to Mrs. Yeobright, Eustacia also demonstrates passive moral tendencies under the control of the negative morality mechanism. In eagerness, Eustacia once says, "Yes, take me to Paris, and go on with your old occupation, Clym! I don't mind how humbly we live there at first, if it can only be Paris, and not Egdon Heath." (Hardy, 1995: 205) Unlike Clym who places much emphasis upon the active construction of virtues, Eustacia does not feel the moral necessity to do that. Clym intends to sacrifice his own prosperity to bring enlightenment and welfare to the residents of Egdon Heath. Nevertheless, Eustacia does not regard the endeavors of her husband as understandable or acceptable. In her view, just not to break the moral rules is enough to establish one's moral justification and enable one to live without any moral burden. To actively construct virtues at a level much higher than what moral commandments require, just like what her husband resolves to do, is not a wise choice from her perspective. As a result, Eustacia insists upon going to Paris. She does not care the possible humbleness and difficulty at the beginning. But in the long run, she should live a wealthy and glittering life, which is her aim. Making judgments from the angle of the negative morality mechanism, Eustacia does not feel her purpose of life and choice for life are morally improper. The conflict between the affirmative morality and the negative morality mechanism is harmful for the marriage between Clym and Eustacia. It erodes their love and frictions develop between them.

As discussed before, the conflict between the affirmative morality and the negative morality mechanism generates frictions between Clym and his family members. Disharmony increases in the relationship between Clym and his mother and in the relationship between him and his wife. This disharmony causes Mrs. Yeobright to trudge on the heath lonely and helplessly and she finally dies by an accident which is not so accidental. This disharmony drives Eustacia to flee away audaciously on a stormy night and finally she dies unfortunately with implications far beyond the sphere of fortune. The deaths of Mrs. Yeobright his mother and Eustacia his wife deal heavy blows to Clym. He sinks into a helpless gloom step by step. Clym is permanently rejected by his mother and his wife, the dearest people in his life; the disharmony between Clym and his family members and the unnatural deaths of his family members haunt his heart forever. The disharmony and the unnatural deaths constitute aspects of Clym's ending in rejection, his disastrous conclusion. Therefore, the conflict between the affirmative morality and the negative morality mechanism is one factor that leads to Clym's disastrous conclusion.

1.3 *Tess*: The Conflict Between the Spiritualized Morality and the Materialized Morality Mechanism

In *Tess*, the individual morality of the protagonist Tess is a spiritualized morality. However, the social mechanism of morality in which she lives is a materialized morality mechanism. Conflict predominates the relationship between the spiritualized morality and the materialized morality mechanism, plunging Tess's individual cultural system into inappositeness in the dimension of morality. The conflict between the spiritualized morality and the materialized morality mechanism, or in other words, the inappositeness of the individual cultural system in the dimension of morality produces a destructive force which is partly responsible for the disastrous conclusion of Tess.

Alec, the main villain in the novel, takes advantage of Tess sexually during their night ride in a wood called the Chase. When that incident takes place, Tess is still an unexperienced girl, and more importantly she is asleep and therefore in an unconscious state. As a consequence, she is spiritually unstained, although physically humiliated by Alec. The individual morality of Tess is a spiritualized morality. This kind of morality is strengthened and made more prominent after her humiliated experience. Tess "instituting [institutes] a split between self and body [...], and essentially disavowing [disavows] her materiality [...]. Her body becomes the object to which random events happen, and upon which random acts of violence and domination are inscribed—her real self remains beyond." (Law, 1997: 251) By differentiating the self from the body, Tess is asserting her spiritualized morality, which is independent of material interference. According to Tess's own understanding, she is morally immaculate. However, in line with the materialized social mechanism of morality, Tess is morally defective because of the sexual relationship between her and Alec out of matrimony. This judgement on the basis of the materialized social mechanism of morality is made without reference to whether or not the girl goes through the experience of her own free will.

After the humiliation by Alec, Tess returns to her own native village Marlott. Basically, she is tortured during the ensuing days. "A wet day was the expression of irremediable grief at her weakness in the mind of some vague ethical being whom she could not class definitely as the God of her childhood, and could not comprehend as any other." (Hardy, 1993A: 75) The materialized social mechanism of morality establishes itself as an outward authority over individuals, explicit or implicit, and creates ethical pressure upon the psyche of Tess, depriving her of the easiness of the blooming days of youth. Gossip about Tess and Alec spreads among the village folk, posing a threat to her name and a hurt to her heart. In the local church, whispers with hues of discrimination go about and reach the perception of Tess. "She knew what their whispers were about, grew sick at heart, and felt that she could come to church no more." (Hardy, 1993A: 75) The fellow villagers, with the materialized social mechanism of morality prevailing in their cognition of Tess's affair, regarding Tess as a bad example in the moral sense. Their whispers and gossips, though not necessarily ill-intentioned, present an insulting negative assessment of Tess's morality which makes the girl painful. In Victorian society, a female who gives birth to an illegitimate child is sure to become the target of condemnation. (丁世忠, 2008: 109) In front of Tess, there appears "an intolerant society that could condemn a woman of Tess's integrity and courage and humility" (Weber, 1940: 129). The society shows intolerance and condemns Tess because the materialized morality mechanism in the society holds those virtues of hers meaningless when she has already lost virginity in the material sense. "The Victorians' rigid social code made few allowances for alternate lifestyles, and their intense fear of diversion from duty and morality demanded either conformity or censure." (Jackson, 2000: 71) The morality upheld by the Victorians is rather rigid and that rigidity derives from the materiality of the morality. Preoccupied with the material aspects of affairs, the materialized morality of Victorians overlooks the moral value of people's spirituality, leaving little space for the development of variant modes of life.

Facing the prejudice and gossip and being placed under various forms of pressure, Tess lives on with a sturdy attitude. (丁世忠, 2008: 110) The spiritualized morality of Tess renders moral confidence and moral courage to the girl and helps foster a sturdy attitude toward life. The sturdy attitude in turn constitutes an expression of the spiritualized morality of Tess. Nevertheless, public opinions about Tess, generated under the dominion of the materialized social mechanism of morality and spread through gossips, make the protagonist's days at her native village Marlott miserable. She considers herself as an innocent victim of her experience at the Chase; nevertheless, she is fixed in the position of a sinner by the villagers. Sharp contrast between the moral judgements made by Tess herself and those made by the community places Tess at the status of a sheer outcast, "a stranger and an alien." (Hardy, 1993A: 78) The conflict between the spiritualized morality and the materialized morality mechanism engenders tremendous social pressure upon Tess and creates a sense of being alienated and persecuted in her psyche, constituting a source of great mental suffering to her.

The conflict between the spiritualized morality and the materialized morality mechanism is also dramatically revealed in the confrontations between Tess and a native man of Trantridge. While doing shopping with Angel, Tess's true love whom she finds after much suffering, in a nearby town before their wedding, Tess confronts that man for the first time. The Trantridge man insults Tess about her past, which is overheard by Angel. Angel strikes a heavy blow to the man. Later, after being deserted by Angel, Tess trudges to Flintcomb-Ash farm to join her friend Marian and look for work there. On the way, Tess again meets that malicious man. Upon his allusion to her painful past, Tess flees away, anguish stimulated from the depths of her heart. Once at the farm, Tess devotes herself to work together with her friends. Out of all expectations, she eventually finds that the Trantridge man that haunts her like a ghost is just the owner of the farm. The harsh words of the malicious man again pour into Tess's delicate ears, "You thought I was in love with 'ee I suppose? Some women are such fools, to take every look as serious earnest. But there's nothing like a winter afield for taking that nonsense out o' young wenches' heads." (Hardy, 1993A: 255) The Trantridge man regards Tess as profligate and especially interested in romantic affairs. He uses the word "wench" for Tess. The word can either denote a maid in the common sense or denote a woman of loose moral, or even a prostitute, in an archaic sense. The word with twofold meanings, in this context, carries the moral judgement by the Trantridge man, transmitting his derogatory signals to Tess, as well as to the readers.

Tess's persecutor Alec "has not only physical strength but knowledge of the world and the power derived from wealth and social status on his side" (Page, 2001: 152). As a result, although Tess wants to resist Alec's advances, it is exceedingly difficult for her to successfully fend him off. According to the spiritualized morality, being taken advantage of in that helpless situation, "Tess has been less a sinner than one sinned against" (Page, 2001: 152). In sharp contrast to that, the Trantridge man's moral judgement of Tess relentlessly defines her as a sinner. The Trantridge man is a representative of the materialized morality mechanism which permeates the society then. Through the Trantridge man, the materialized morality mechanism accentuates its negative moral judgement of Tess. In that way, Tess's sexual experience with

Alec, although passive and rather unconscious, means the permanent loss of moral virginity, something to be condemned severely for an unmarried female. Nonetheless, in the spiritualized moral framework of Tess, one can come to a completely different conclusion. The Trantridge man pours bitter words upon Tess and grows hypercritical about Tess's work. The bad attitudes are the result of the man's anger at Angel's treatment of him, and more importantly they are the result of his moral depreciation of Tess. Under his despotic power, Tess fearlessly retorts. The retorts by Tess are the rebellion against the unfairly fastidious criticism about her work and more importantly, they are the rebellion against the materialized morality mechanism. The fearless retorts by Tess constitute an expression of her spiritualized morality. From Tess's fearless and self-dependent struggles after being deserted by Angel, the moral confidence and moral courage of the protagonist could be felt. "Patience, that blending of moral courage with physical timidity, was now no longer a minor feature in Mrs Angel Clare; and it sustained her." （Hardy, 1993A: 249 - 250）Although lacking enough physical strength and rather insufficient in face of strenuous agricultural labor, Tess works hard to support herself and render financial aid to her impoverished family. In her frame of spiritualized morality, Tess is the victim of sin rather than a sinner, a bearer of moral positivity rather than moral negativity. The spiritualized morality fuels the self-justification of Tess and provides a source of self-confidence for her, accomplishing her "moral courage" and encouraging her forward. The moral confidence and moral courage of Tess which originate from the spiritualized morality enable the girl to retort upon the Trantridge man and call for justice. In the confrontations between Tess and the haunting Trantridge man and in the relationship between the girl and the villagers at Marlott, the conflict between the spiritualized morality and the materialized morality mechanism is shown. In the moral conflict, Tess suffers from much social pressure and great mental agony. In the stifling psychological condition that results therefrom, Tess more easily loses control of herself and stabs Alec to death when certain circumstances arise. Therefore, it can be said that the conflict between the spiritualized morality and the materialized morality mechanism results in the execution of Tess, her disastrous conclusion.

1.4 *Jude*: The Conflict Between the Content-Directed Morality and the Form-Directed Morality Mechanism

In *Jude*, the protagonist Jude's morality is a content-directed morality, while the social mechanism of morality he lives in is a form-directed morality mechanism. The conflict between the content-directed morality and the form-directed morality mechanism plunges the individual cultural system of Jude into inappositeness in the dimension of morality. The inappositeness of Jude's individual cultural system in the dimension of morality engenders a negative force that brings about the protagonist Jude's disastrous conclusion. In other words, the conflict between the content-directed morality and the form-directed morality mechanism leads Jude towards his disastrous conclusion.

An entity or a phenomenon can be divided into two parts—the content and the form. Both the content and the form can be regarded as virtuous or not virtuous. The matter of marriage can serve as an example. The shared life of the married people constitutes the content of the marriage, while the matrimonial procedures constitute the form of the marriage. If the married people lead a happy life, then the content of the marriage shall be considered virtuous. If the married couple have observed the matrimonial procedures that are acceptable according to social customs, the form of the marriage shall be considered virtuous. The morality of Jude is a content-directed morality. This kind of morality leads him to pay more attention to the virtue of content rather than to the virtue of form. In the novel, readers can detect "Jude's movement toward the awareness that moral worth must be searched for behind or beyond conventional platitudes" (Nemesvari, 2011: 203). The conventional platitudes are constituted by solidified moral stipulations. They emphasize the virtue of form and tend to sacrifice the virtue of content for the preservation of the virtue of form. Jude's search for moral worth "behind or beyond conventional platitudes" demonstrates his content-directed morality. In line with the content-directed morality, if the virtue of content and the virtue of form are put in juxtaposition, Jude will render priority to the virtue of content. When the virtue of content and the virtue of form are in harmony, the content-directed morality of Jude cannot be easily detected; however, when the virtue of content and the virtue of form are in discord, the content-directed morality of Jude will be shown clearly.

After getting divorced from their respective former spouses and freed from their unhappy marriages, Jude and Sue are in possession of freedom again. Jude requests to marry Sue formally. Nonetheless, Sue still appears to have antipathy against the procedures of marriage. Sue's moral tendencies are reflective of those of Jude's. At the request of Jude, Sue protests, "I think I should begin to be afraid of you, Jude, the moment you had contracted to cherish me under a Government stamp, and I was licensed to be loved on the premises by you—Ugh, how horrible and sordid! Although, as you are, free, I trust you more than any other man in the world." (Hardy, 1993B: 227) With the endorsement of a Government stamp and the accompanying public recognition, the Victorian procedures of matrimony guarantee the virtue of form of a marriage in the social conditions then. However, in the eyes of Sue, that virtue of form, together with its consequences, is in fact "horrible and sordid". From her perspective, "the civil institution of marriage is ill-suited to human needs and emotions" (Karin, 2016: 121), and the virtue of form of the marriage is by no means valuable. In the view of Sue, matrimonial procedures, with the binding force, could only suffocate their nature and twist their souls and the "'iron contract' would extinguish tenderness" (Pinion, 1968: 329). Contrary to that, being free from the fetters of marital procedures, Sue and her lover could retain the wholesomeness of their individualities and use their unstained inner purity as a more natural guarantee for their love and mutual trust. For Sue, to save the souls of herself and her lover from suppression and to save their love from adulteration can accomplish the virtue of content. That endeavor and the state of life coming thereby do not present the virtue of form, which is perceptible to the people around. Instead, they constitute a fountain of happiness for the people concerned. As a result, Sue prefers not to go through the procedures of marriage with Jude. Jude says in his response, "People go on marrying because they can't resist natural forces, although many of them may know perfectly well that they are possibly buying a month's pleasure with a life's discomfort." (Hardy, 1993B: 227) Jude, with the content-directed morality, holds a hierarchy with the virtue of content as the superior virtue and the virtue of form as the inferior virtue. He does not go to extremities as Sue does. Jude sees some necessity in the maintenance of the virtue of form. Thus, he intends to marry Sue formally. However, from his perspective, the virtue of form is of comparatively minor significance. So, when Sue puts forward the standpoint about the harmfulness of marriage procedures for their happiness and the unjustifiability of their going through the procedures, Jude hesitates and becomes ready to compromise. He does not want to preserve the virtue of form at the cost of hurting Sue and thus harming the happiness and the virtue of content. The happiness of the parties concerned, Jude and Sue in this case, is the criterion of the virtue of content. Jude is willing to first guarantee their happiness in practical terms and give priority to the virtue of content. The content-directed morality of Jude is also indirectly shown by his strong sense of sympathy. Jude's strong sympathy extends from humans to animals like birds and pigs. As "an advanced moral type", Jude "experience[s] acute sympathy in a society in which it is not universal" (Sumpter, 2011: 676). Sympathy, largely depending upon instincts, is not confined to any definite moral form and is not required by social customs and conventions. It revolves around the content of morality. Jude's strong sense of sympathy reflects and confirms his content-directed morality from a certain perspective.

In the continuous exchange of views with Jude, Sue proceeds to say, "Fewer women like marriage than you suppose, only they enter into it for the dignity it is assumed to confer, and the social advantages it gains them

sometimes—a dignity and an advantage that I am quite willing to do without."
(Hardy, 1993B: 228) Sue holds the view that only "a dignity and an advantage"
which are not necessary could be attained through marriage, and she
understands matrimonial procedures as a social requirement which could be
dispensed with. In fact, Sue is questioning the virtue of form in the matter of
marriage. Through airing her view about marriage in this way, she is in effect
claiming the righteousness of the marriage justified solely by the virtue of
content. In contrast to the view of Sue, the social mechanism of morality which
permeates the social surroundings of Jude and Sue is a form-directed morality
mechanism, emphasizing the virtue of form in the matter of marriage. According
to that mechanism, the virtue of form gains advantages over the virtue of
content. With the virtue of form and the virtue of content in discord, priority
will be rendered to the former one when moral judgments are made. Under the
control of the form-directed morality mechanism, people around Jude and Sue
tend to neglect whether or not the pair concerned could attain happiness
through the procedures of marriage; what interests them is the indispensability
of the matrimonial procedures as a virtue of form. Although having realized the
moral pressure from the social mechanism, Sue is oblivious to its magnitude and
what it really means for the life of her and her lover. Afterwards, Jude
complains about the lack of an expression of love from Sue. However, at last
Jude totally compromises. "Sue, my own comrade and sweetheart, I don't want
to force you either to marry or to do the other thing—of course I don't!"
(Hardy, 1993B: 228) In the view of Jude, the happiness of Sue and himself,
especially that of his beloved Sue, without any infringement of others' rights to
happiness, is the first consideration in his moral judgment in this case. If Jude
follows Sue's opinion and does not seek to marry her formally, maybe they
could be happier as she believes. More importantly, to satisfy Sue's requirement
could make her joyous, which in Jude's moral judgment, is especially virtuous.
Jude follows Sue's requirement in the intention of enhancing the joys and
happiness first of his beloved and then of himself. That advancement of joys and

happiness realizes the virtue of content, which is attained at the cost of the virtue of form. The procedures of matrimony, a requirement of the virtue of form, are sacrificed in this case. The choice made by Jude in the matter of marriage shows his content-directed morality.

The form-directed morality mechanism exerts an influence upon the life of Jude and Sue and they could not get rid of that influence. The conflict between the content-directed morality and the form-directed morality mechanism makes it difficult for Jude and his lover to lead a life. People in the neighborhood become unfriendly to them, regarding them as outsiders or even sinners who have inflicted shame upon the community. "The baker's lad and the grocer's boy, who at first had used to lift their hats gallantly to Sue, when they came to execute their errands, in these days no longer took the trouble to render her that homage, and the neighbouring artisans' wives looked straight along the pavement when they encountered her." (Hardy, 1993B: 262) Those people in the neighborhood think that probably Jude and Sue have failed to fulfill the requirement of the society and go through proper marital procedures and they hold that failure as an offense to self-evident moral principles. In their view, Jude and Sue are thus immoral figures, unworthy of their respect. They are not interested in whether or not the pair could by their choice better promote their happiness without any harm to the happiness of others. In other words, under the control of the form-directed morality mechanism, they are indifferent to the virtue of content while preoccupied with the virtue of form. The unfavorable attitudes of these people in the community deal a blow to Jude and Sue and to a large extent mould their psychological experience of life. Jude, together with his lover Sue, becomes the target of public criticism, due to the conflict between their individual moralities and the social mechanism of morality. Perceiving that "an oppressive atmosphere began [begins] to encircle their souls" (Hardy, 1993B: 263), Jude feels suffocated in life. The conflict between the content-directed morality and the form-directed morality mechanism inflicts a wound upon the psyche of Jude and spiritual agonies thus come into being. The moral conflict finally engenders the emotional and physical breakdown of Jude, bringing about his death in disillusion, his disastrous conclusion.

1.5   The Ideas about Morality in *The Native* and Their Historical Significance

As discussed before, *The Native* demonstrates that the conflict between the principle of the sufficiency of altruism and the principle of the moderation of altruism leads to the protagonist's disastrous conclusion. In this process of demonstration, the novel simultaneously justifies the principle of the sufficiency of altruism and the principle of the moderation of altruism. Thereby the novel develops the inquietude that the entangled relationships between the sufficiency of altruism and the moderation of altruism may endanger individuals and the society. (The entangled relationships between the sufficiency of altruism and the moderation of altruism have two layers of meanings. First, the principle of the sufficiency of altruism and the principle of the moderation of altruism are in disagreement with each other, and therefore the conflict between the two sides is possible. Second, the principle of the sufficiency of altruism and the principle of the moderation of altruism have their respective justifiability and there is no sign of definite supremacy of one over the other. Therefore, both principles can easily appeal to people and exert continuous influence upon their respective followers. As a consequence, the probability of the formation of the conflict will be greater. Moreover, once the conflict is formed, the difficulty of its resolution will also be greater.)

In the process of demonstrating the conflict between the principle of the sufficiency of altruism and the principle of the moderation of altruism, *The Native* shows the justifiability of both sides. The protagonist Clym manifests the principle of the sufficiency of altruism. Surprising everyone around him, Clym gives up his promising position as a diamond establishment manager in the world-renowned metropolis Paris where a luxurious life is just at his hand. Even more surprising for people around him, Clym makes all this sacrifice not for himself but for the interests of the residents at the heath. For Clym, the interests of others carry more weight than the interests of himself. In the making of his judgments and decisions, priority goes to the welfare of others instead of that of himself. By his unusual and unexpected choice of life, Clym shows his strong altruistic tendencies. Through his own choice and his persistent efforts to put his choice into practice, Clym demonstrates the admirable quality of the principle of the sufficiency of altruism. An appeal to the readers about the justifiability of the sufficiency of altruism builds up in the text thereby. Meeting with Clym's highly altruistic choice of life, his family members and fellow villagers, under the control of the principle of the moderation of altruism, demonstrate different degrees of resistance, of course in different ways. The mother Mrs. Yeobright stands against the plan of his son, lamenting the wasted efforts made in the preparation for Clym's career which could otherwise bring about a future of prosperity. The wife Eustacia not only stands opposed to her husband's plan but also makes persistent efforts to change his mind and set him in a course that would lead to the prosperity both of him and of herself. The fellow villagers, at the revelation of Clym's plan, either think that he would not actually carry out the plan or hold the view that he has in effect made a wrong choice. They basically demonstrate a negative evaluation of Clym's choice. With the unfolding of the plot, the opinions of Mrs. Yeobright, Eustacia and the villagers are made clearer and clearer and they gain justifiability gradually. The novel transmits the feeling that their view that Clym need not sacrifice his own interests to such a high degree for the welfare of others is reasonable. It seems that his moral considerations are out of balance and his choice is not only detrimental to himself but also unfeasible in the promotion of the welfare of the folks at Egdon Heath. It seems that, maybe in line with the view of Mrs. Yeobright, Eustacia and the villagers, "the confrontation between the self and the other can be resolved" and "individuals can establish more harmonious relationships" (刘磊, 2013:35) which are more stable. In that way, the principle of the moderation of altruism accumulates its justifiability and its appeal to readers. To summarize, *The Native* as an integrated field of meanings, shows the justifiability both of the principle of the sufficiency of altruism and of the principle of the moderation of altruism. First, it advocates the sufficiency of altruism; second, it also advocates the moderation of altruism. According to the principle of the sufficiency of altruism, one shall put the interests of others and of the collective before the interests of his own. When the individual interests and the collective interests are in conflict, one shall give up individual interests in order to preserve and promote collective interests. In accordance with the principle of the moderation of altruism, one has a right not to put the interests of others and of the collective before his own individual interests if he has sound reasons. When there are conflicts between individual interests and collective interests, one has the right not to give up individual interests for the preservation and promotion of collective interests on the condition that he has sufficient reasons.

The principle of the sufficiency of altruism and the principle of the moderation of altruism are in disagreement with each other, and therefore, the conflict between the two sides is possible. Because the two principles have their respective justifiability, they can both easily appeal to people and continuously affect their followers. Therefore, the conflict between the two principles will be more likely to take shape. Furthermore, once the conflict takes shape, it will be more difficult to resolve it. In *The Native*, the conflict between the principle of the sufficiency of altruism and the principle of the moderation of altruism is just precipitated and made more difficult to resolve by their respective justifiability. In Thomas Hardy's novels, "his critique of cruelty and his promotion of altruism" (Cohn, 2010: 499) can be perceived. However, the problem of the extent to which altruism shall be pursued is left unresolved in the fictional world of Thomas Hardy. The simultaneous justifications of the principle of the sufficiency of altruism and the principle of the moderation of altruism in *The Native* bring that unresolved problem to the foreground. By demonstrating that the conflict between the principle of the sufficiency of altruism and the principle of the moderation of altruism leads to the protagonist Clym's disastrous conclusion, *The Native* develops the inquietude that the entangled relationships between the sufficiency of altruism and the moderation of altruism may endanger individuals and the society. This inquietude corresponds to the twofold ideas about the relationship between the principle of the sufficiency of altruism and the principle of the moderation of altruism which are implied in utilitarianism.

Utilitarianism, with the British thinkers Jeremy Bentham (1748 - 1832) and John Mill (1806 - 1873) as its main representatives, is one of the main schools of ethical ideas in the West of the modern period and it was especially influential in the 19th century which witnessed the production of the novels of Thomas Hardy. From one angle, it can be seen that utilitarianism is not immune to historical limitations and it shows certain tendencies of hypocrisy. From another angle, it can be seen that utilitarianism is a milestone in the development of ethics in Britain and it had exerted profound influence upon the production of contemporary literary discourses including the novels of Hardy. The core of utilitarianism is the greatest happiness principle which sets the highest degree of happiness for the largest number of people as the goal of morality. In *An Introduction to the Principles of Morals and Legislation*, Bentham writes:

> By the principle of utility [namely the greatest happiness principle] is meant that principle which approves or disapproves of every action whatsoever. according to the tendency it appears to have to augment or diminish the happiness of the party whose interest is in question: or, what is the same thing in other words to promote or to oppose that happiness. (Bentham, 2000: 14)

According to the principle of greatest happiness, the best deed is the deed which can realize the highest degree of happiness for the largest number of people. If a deed can realize the possibly highest degree of happiness for the possibly largest number of people in its concrete context, it can be accepted as the best possible deed in a certain condition. Then the degree of the deviation from the highest degree of happiness for the largest number of people constitutes a criterion for the judgement of the relative moral acceptability and justifiability of a deed. From another perspective, utilitarianism also recognizes the individual's inner drive to pursue his own happiness as natural and justifiable. Because any individual constitutes a component of the humankind, the pursuits by individuals of their own happiness increase the total happiness of the humanity in a certain way. Therefore, the acts by individuals for their own welfare also comply with the principle of greatest happiness. Then comes the problem of the relationship between the interests of the subject and the interests of others, and the relationship between the individual interests and the collective interests. On one hand, utilitarianism advocates the promotion of the interests of others and the collective interests, for the promotion of the interests of others and the collective interests is directly in line with the principle of greatest happiness. Thereby utilitarianism in effect justifies the principle of the sufficiency of altruism. On the other hand, utilitarianism also advocates the promotion of the interests of the subject and the individual interests, for the promotion of the interests of the subject and the individual interests provides a lasting internal drive for the implementation of the principle of greatest happiness. Thereby utilitarianism in effect justifies the principle of the moderation of altruism. In utilitarianism, one can perceive the coexistence of the justifications of the sufficiency of altruism and the moderation of altruism as two moral principles which are in disagreement with each other. Utilitarianism basically tries to resolve the problem by unifying interests of the subject and interests of others, and unifying individual interests and collective interests. Theorists of utilitarianism generally believe that, by certain methods, interests of the subject and interests of others could be unified, and individual interests and collective interests could also be unified, with potential conflicts avoided. However, the conflicts of interests under discussion cannot be effectively avoided in practice and the utilitarian belief of unification cannot render an ultimate solution to the moral difficulties in this case. Utilitarianism in reality leaves the problem of subject-object and individual-collective interest relationships unsettled. Justifying the principle of the sufficiency of altruism and the principle of the moderation of altruism at the same time, utilitarianism implicitly develops twofold ideas about the relationship between the principle of the sufficiency of altruism and the principle of the moderation of altruism.

As discussed above, the inquietude about the possible dangers of the entangled relationships between the principle of the sufficiency of altruism and the principle of the moderation of altruism is developed in *The Native*. That inquietude corresponds to the twofold ideas about the relationship between the sufficiency of altruism and the moderation of altruism in utilitarianism and constitutes a literary interpretation of those twofold ideas. In the development of the inquietude about the entangled relationships between the sufficiency of altruism and the moderation of altruism, the respective justifiability of the two principles is demonstrated along with the harmful conflict between them. In the literary interpretation of the twofold ideas, the conflict between the sufficiency of altruism and the moderation of altruism takes shape and leads to the disastrous conclusion of Clym. It can be seen that the novel pays more attention to the practical application of ethical principles and places more emphasis upon the actual dangers that problems in ethical principles and their relationships can bring about.

Besides the conflict between the sufficiency of altruism and the moderation of altruism, *The Native* also demonstrates the conflict between the affirmative morality of Clym and the negative morality mechanism in his cultural setting, which also leads to the disastrous conclusion of the protagonist. In this process of demonstration, the novel justifies the affirmative morality and the negative morality at the same time. Thereby the novel develops the inquietude that the entangled relationships between the affirmative morality and the negative morality may endanger individuals and the society. (The entangled relationships between the affirmative morality and the negative morality have two layers of meanings. First, the affirmative morality and the negative morality are contradictory to each other, and therefore, the conflict between the two sides is possible. Second, the affirmative morality and the negative morality have their respective justifiability, and there is no sign of definite supremacy of one over the other. Therefore, both sides can easily appeal to people and exercise continuous influence upon their respective followers. As a result, the probability of the formation of the conflict between the two sides will be greater. Moreover, once the conflict is formed, the difficulty of its resolution will also be greater.)

In the process of demonstrating the conflict between the affirmative morality and the negative morality mechanism, *The Native* develops the justifications of the affirmative morality and the negative morality simultaneously. By the protagonist Clym, the novel shows morality as an affirmative existence. Clym could not get satisfied with just obeying moral commandments without taking the initiative in the construction of virtues. His moral focus is set upon the active fostering of virtues when outward moral pressure is absent. No moral commandment requires Clym to sacrifice his own prosperous career to serve the residents at Egdon Heath. However, he still insists upon giving up his position as the manager of a diamond establishment and starting a school for Egdon Heath. Clym wants to establish himself as a man of morality and his morality is an affirmative existence which is based upon the active construction of virtues rather than the passive compliance with disciplines. Through the figure Clym, *The Native* justifies the morality as affirmative existence—the affirmative morality. In contrast to the affirmative morality of Clym, a negative morality mechanism prevails in the cultural setting. In accordance with the negative morality mechanism, people should devote themselves to the passive observance of moral disciplines and additional sacrifices beyond the requirement of disciplines are not necessary in the moral sense. Mrs. Yeobright, Eustacia and other residents at the heath are all supporters of the negative morality mechanism. From the perspective of these people, Clym's choice of self-sacrifice is not reasonable. It is unwise of Clym to sacrifice his own interests to such an extent for the welfare of others. For them, it is morally advisable for Clym to confine his virtues inside the sphere of moral disciplines and do no more additional self-sacrifices. The novel shows the justifiability of the view of these people, namely the justifiability of the negative morality. The novel transmits the feeling that it is too cruel for Clym as an individual to bear such a heavy moral burden for the whole community. It seems unfair for Clym to sacrifice his individual happiness to such an extent in the promotion of communal happiness. Therefore, there exist two contrary lines of argumentation in *The Native*, one line in the justification of the affirmative morality and the justification of the view of morality as affirmative existence, the other line in the justification of the negative morality and the justification of the view of morality as negative existence.

Because the affirmative morality and the negative morality are contradictory to each other, the conflict between the two sides is possible. Moreover, because the affirmative morality and the negative morality have their respective justifiability, both of them can easily appeal to people and exert continuous influence upon their respective followers. Therefore, the conflict between the two sides will be more likely to take shape. Moreover, once the conflict takes shape, it will be more difficult to resolve it. By demonstrating that the conflict between the affirmative morality and the negative morality mechanism leads to the disastrous conclusion of Clym, the novel *The Native* develops the inquietude that the entangled relationships between the affirmative morality and the negative morality may endanger individuals and the society. As discussed before, *The Native* has also developed the inquietude that the entangled relationships between the sufficiency of altruism and the moderation of altruism may endanger individuals and the society. The two kinds of inquietude constitute significant facets of the ethical connotations of the novel. Hardy's philosophy contains the standpoint that one cannot justifiably hold absolute standards and consistent views in the field of ethics. (Wilkie, 1972: 132) The two kinds of inquietude just reflect this dimension of ambiguity and open-endedness in Hardy's ethical philosophy. In *The Native*, Egdon Heath is the central constituent part of the natural environment, and it has manifold formal and thematic significance. Egdon Heath metaphorically suggests Hardy's theme of ambiguity and complexity. The suggestion is achieved from certain perspectives, the ambiguity of the relationship between Egdon and human beings, the variety of the tones that the descriptions of the heath show, and the lack of stability in the relationship between the heath and cosmic laws, etc. (Wilkie, 1972: 132 – 133). Egdon Heath functions as a metaphorical expression of the different forms of inquietude in *The Native* and the ambiguity and open-endedness in Hardy's ethical philosophy. The environmental image assists in the development of the novel's ethical significance. Like the inquietude about the entangled relationships between the sufficiency of altruism and the moderation of altruism, the inquietude about the entangled relationships between the affirmative morality and the negative morality does not exist in isolation. It corresponds to the twofold ideas about the dynamics of morality which are implied in utilitarianism.

  Utilitarianism demonstrates certain ideas about the dynamics of morality. First, utilitarianism demonstrates the tendency to justify the affirmative morality. Utilitarianism advocates the principle of greatest happiness as the central moral doctrine. From the perspective of utilitarianism, one should try the best to attain the highest degree of happiness for the largest number of people. The highest degree of happiness for the largest number of people constitutes the paramount virtue. The degree of happiness and the number of people who could enjoy the happiness determine to what an extent a deed or a subject of deeds is virtuous. Following this string of logic, morality shall be constituted by active and dynamic construction of virtues rather than passive and static observance of moral commandments. From this perspective, it can be said that utilitarianism justifies the affirmative morality and the view of morality as affirmative existence. Second, utilitarianism demonstrates the tendency to justify the negative morality. Utilitarianism encourages individuals to pursue their own happiness, because the promotion of one's own happiness also complies with the principle of greatest happiness in a certain sense. Then with life focused upon the pursuit of one's own happiness, an individual could not render sufficient attention to the promotion of the happiness of the whole humankind. In handling the relationship with others, an individual is only required to obey basic moral disciplines, which is already sufficient to justify the individual and his deeds. From this perspective, it can be said that utilitarianism also justifies the negative morality and the view of morality as negative existence.

In the discussion about the sanction of utilitarian morality, Mill says, "The ultimate sanction, therefore, of all morality (external motives apart) being a subjective feeling in our own minds, I see nothing embarrassing to those whose standard is utility, in the question, what is the sanction of that particular standard? We may answer, the same as of all other moral standards—the conscientious feelings of mankind." (Mill, 2009: 52) The cultivation and establishment of the ultimate sanction—conscientious feelings—is of crucial importance for the effective justification and implementation of utilitarian morality. However, there is an inherent difficulty in the cultivation and establishment of the ultimate sanction for utilitarianism. Should the conscientious feelings of mankind be based upon the view of morality as affirmative existence or the view of morality as negative existence? Should conscientious feelings get satisfied with the observance of compulsory moral disciplines and stop there, just staying insensitive and indifferent to further altruistic pursuit? Should conscientious feelings engage in the active construction of virtues within and especially beyond moral disciplines, craving for and promoting maximum altruistic endeavors? The conflict between the definitions of morality as a kind of affirmative existence and as a kind of negative existence takes root in the fundamental sphere of conscientious feelings and spreads its influence across the whole theoretical and practical structure of utilitarian morality. Caught between the view of morality as affirmative existence and the view of morality as negative existence, utilitarianism implicitly demonstrates twofold ideas about the dynamics of morality.

In *The Native*, the inquietude that the entangled relationships between the affirmative morality and the negative morality may endanger individuals and the society corresponds to the twofold ideas about the dynamics of morality in utilitarianism. Moreover, the inquietude achieves a literary interpretation of those twofold ideas. In the novel's development of the inquietude about the entangled relationships between the affirmative morality and the negative morality, the respective justifications of the affirmative morality and the negative morality are demonstrated along with the harmful conflict between the two sides. In the novel, the conflict between the affirmative morality and the negative morality mechanism leads to the disastrous conclusion of the protagonist Clym. It can be seen that the novel pays more attention to the practical application of ethical views and the dangers that the problems of ethical views and their relationships can bring about.

1.6   The Ideas about Morality in *Tess* and *Jude* Together with Their Historical Significance

The novel *Tess* demonstrates that the conflict between the spiritualized morality and the materialized social mechanism of morality results in the disastrous conclusion of the protagonist. In this process of demonstration, two layers of meanings could be detected. On the first layer, it is shown that the spiritualized morality of Tess contributes to her development as a human being. Thereby the novel achieves the approval of the spiritualized morality. On the second layer, it is shown that the spiritualized morality is beneficial for the realization of Tess's freedom and in a certain sense spiritualized morality is synonymous with freedom. It is shown that the materialized morality can jeopardize the spiritualized morality and the freedom. Moreover, it is emphasized that the oppression of the spiritualized morality by the materialized morality mechanism achieves a function in the creation of the protagonist's disastrous conclusion. Thereby the novel develops the anxiety that unfavorable social conditions may jeopardize the spiritualized morality and freedom, thus posing threats to individuals and the society.

In the novel, it is shown that the spiritualized morality contributes to Tess's development as a human being. By virtue of the spiritualized morality, Tess can hold the belief in her own innocence and immaculateness after the tribulations in her life. Therefore, under the affliction of misunderstandings and gossips, Tess can retain her confidence. Encouraged by this confidence, she can continue to pursue her love and happiness after the insult by Alec and other related humiliations. Encouraged by this confidence, Tess can stick to her belief in life after being deserted by Angel. Encouraged by this confidence, she can dauntlessly fight against Alec when he attempts to destroy her for a second time. This confidence gives strong backing to Tess in her development as a human being. In the novel, "Tess embodies a moral poise beyond the reach of most morality" (Mehta, 2014: 120). It is just the spiritualization of morality that enables Tess to accomplish the moral poise. Upholding the spiritualized morality, Tess conducts her moral endeavors in a variety of directions in a balanced way. She avoids being caught in one direction exclusively in the material sense and spreads her moral attention across various directions. The accomplishment of the moral poise is also a way in which the spiritualized morality contributes to Tess's development as a human being. By showing the contribution that the spiritualized morality does to Tess's development as a human being, *Tess* achieves the approval of the spiritualized morality. In the approval of the spiritualized morality, the novel transmits the view that Tess is forced to have a sexual relationship with Alec and she is sinned against rather than sinning voluntarily; it also transmits the view that she is innocent and does not really lose her virginity (姬生雷, 冯梅, 乔建珍, 2011: 103). This view about Tess's virginity constitutes the central connotations of the novel's approval of the spiritualized morality and accomplishes the fundamental moral assessment of the protagonist Tess.

Controlled by the materialized morality, an individual cannot be free. In order to remain morally justified or morally purified, the individual has to satisfy certain physical requirements which are often beyond the capabilities of the individual. Under the externally inflicted physical burden, the individual is often deprived of the right to determine his or her own moral status or moral definition, and in that way deprived of freedom. Although spiritually immaculate, Tess is still tortured by the materialized morality mechanism. In accordance with the materialized morality mechanism, since Tess has already had a sexual relationship with Alec out of marriage, she is inevitably morally stained, no matter whether she does so of her own accord or not. The materialized morality mechanism places an absolute emphasis upon facts in the physical sense while turning a blind eye to the actualities in the spiritual sense. Spiritual immaculateness is what Tess could choose freely, but it does not count in the reference system of the materialized morality mechanism. Physical immaculateness is what Tess could not manage by herself, but it counts a lot in the reference system of the materialized morality mechanism. In that way, the materialized morality mechanism deprives Tess of her freedom, the freedom to live decently and the freedom to decide her moral status and moral definition by herself. Under the despotic power of the materialized morality mechanism, Tess resorts to the spiritualized morality of herself. According to the spiritualized morality, Tess is pure since she has spiritual purity. Although she has had sexual experience out of marriage, she is still morally immaculate. The reason lies in the fact that Tess does not do that in exchange for interests and that incident even does not take place of her own free will. Relying upon her spiritualized morality, Tess gets a chance to enjoy freedom. It can be seen that the spiritualized morality is beneficial for the realization of Tess's freedom and in a certain sense spiritualized morality is synonymous with freedom. In the novel, the materialized morality impairs Tess's spiritualized morality and her freedom. Moreover, the oppression of the spiritualized morality by the materialized morality mechanism achieves a function in the creation of the disastrous conclusion of Tess. By that arrangement, the novel develops the anxiety that unfavorable conditions in the society may jeopardize the spiritualized morality and the freedom and thus pose threats to individuals and the society. The approval of the spiritualized morality and the anxiety about its social vulnerability correspond to the idea of liberty in utilitarianism and achieve a literary interpretation of that idea.

Liberty occupies a prominent place in the theoretical palace of utilitarianism. The emphasis upon liberty in utilitarianism is mainly achieved by John Stuart Mill. Mill's investigation into the concept of liberty is a concrete application of the principle of the greatest happiness. An 18th century rationalist might have interpreted liberty as a natural right of humanity. In contrast to that, Mill develops the view that liberty should be preserved because the greatest happiness of the largest number of people could be guaranteed by rendering various forms of freedom to people. (Jones, 1975: 166) Mill advocates the freedom of thought and discussion. (Kateb, Bromwich, Mill, 2003: 86 - 120) Moreover, Mill speaks highly of the free development of individuality. In *On Liberty*, he comments:

> As it is useful that while mankind are imperfect there should be different opinions, so is it that there should be different experiments of living; that free scope should be given to varieties of character, short of injury to others; and that the worth of different modes of life should be proved practically, when any one thinks fit to try them. It is desirable, in short, that in things which do not primarily concern others, individuality should assert itself. (Kateb, Bromwich, Mill, 2003: 122)

Individuality integrates one's specific thoughts, expressions and deeds. Individuality reflects a human being's liberty to design his or her life according to his or her own wishes without infringing upon others' reasonable rights. Individuality is an important dimension from which liberty could be effectively and thoroughly interpreted. By emphasizing individuality as an element of well-being, Mill pushes his discussion and advocacy of liberty to a further stage. In *Tess*, the freedom of the protagonist, which together with the spiritualized morality endures the suppression of the materialized morality mechanism, is closely related to individuality too. The process in which Tess demonstrates her spiritualized morality and thereby advocates the conviction in freedom is also a process of asserting her individuality. In her life experience and in her struggles against oppression, Tess builds up her spiritualized morality. She departs from and revolts against the materialized morality mechanism, refuting its definition of her as impure and defective. Tess develops a morality of her own, a lifestyle of her own and a reference system for her self-evaluation, whereby her individuality is solidly established. The individuality which differentiates Tess from other individuals and marks her out from her social environment constitutes a concentrated expression of the conviction in freedom.

In *Tess*, the approval of the spiritualized morality and the anxiety that unfavorable conditions in the society may jeopardize the spiritualized morality and freedom and thus pose threats to individuals and the society accomplish a literary interpretation of the idea of liberty in utilitarianism. In *Tess*, it is emphasized that the oppression of the spiritualized morality by the materialized morality mechanism achieves a function in the creation of the disastrous conclusion of the protagonist. In that process, Tess is also gradually deprived of her freedom by unfavorable social conditions. It can be seen that, like *The Native*, *Tess* pays adequate attention to the social context of the practical application of ethical views. By presenting the problems that ethical views may meet in application, *Tess* achieves the literary interpretation of the idea of liberty.

The novel *Jude* demonstrates that the conflict between the content-directed morality and the form-directed morality mechanism brings about the disastrous conclusion of the protagonist. In this process of demonstration, two layers of meanings can be detected. First, it is shown that the content-directed morality does contributions to the development of Jude as a human being. Thereby the novel accomplishes the approval of the content-directed morality. Second, it is shown that the form-directed morality can impair the content-directed morality and Jude's development as a human being. Furthermore, it is emphasized that the oppression of the content-directed morality by the form-directed morality mechanism eventually achieves a role in the formation of the disastrous conclusion of the protagonist Jude. Thereby the novel develops the anxiety that the unnecessary and overelaborate formalities may jeopardize people's practical interests, thus posing threats to individuals and the society.

The content-directed morality focuses the attention on the promotion and allocation of practical interests, while the form-directed morality mechanism places emphasis upon the observance of established formal requirements of society. Complying with the content-directed morality, Jude gives priority to the guarantee of happiness rather than to the observance of the formalities required by the society. Therefore, Jude chooses to live together with Sue without the procedures of marriage. By doing that, Jude avoids hurting the feelings of Sue and avoids undermining their relationship and their happiness. Driven by the content-directed morality, Jude enhances the sensibility to Sue's inner needs, enhances the sensibility to his own inner needs and broadens the channels of communication between himself and Sue. Jude learns to recognize, respect and preserve the natural humanity which is embodied both in individuals and in the relationship between individuals. The content-directed morality helps Jude to protect humanity against the alienation by nonhuman entities and forces. By that, the content-directed morality does contributions to Jude's development as a human being. Jude chooses a kind of life according to the content-directed morality. Because of that, Jude is afflicted by the pressure of the form-directed morality mechanism. Facing the prejudices of people around him, Jude cannot easily find employment and lodging. At last, his children die in difficulties and his love for Sue is plunged into destruction. The form-directed morality impairs Jude's content-directed morality and his development as a human being. By showing that the content-directed morality does contributions to Jude's development as a human being, *Jude* achieves the approval of the content-directed morality. By showing that the form-directed morality impairs Jude's content-directed morality and his development as a human being, and by emphasizing that the oppression of the content-directed morality by the form-directed morality mechanism achieves a role in the formation of Jude's disastrous conclusion, the novel develops the anxiety that unnecessary and overelaborate formalities may jeopardize people's practical interests, and may thus pose threats to individuals and the society. This approval and this anxiety correspond to the conviction in practical interests in utilitarianism.

Jeremy Bentham says, "Nature has placed mankind under the governance of two sovereign masters, *pain* and *pleasure*. It is for them alone to point out what we ought to do, as well as to determine what we shall do. On the one hand the standard of right and wrong, on the other the chain of causes and effects, are fastened to their throne." (Bentham, 2000: 14) From the utilitarian perspective, pain and pleasure constitute, justifiably, two primary driving forces for the thoughts and deeds of human beings. Humans should move, both in thoughts and deeds, in the direction of promoting pleasures and avoiding pains. Pleasure and pain fall under the category of practical interests. Moreover, they constitute a general summary of all spheres of practical interests. In fact, all forms of practical interests can be interpreted as specific kinds of the promotion of pleasure or the avoidance of pain. The important position that pleasure and pain occupy in the theoretical system of utilitarianism attests the conviction in practical interests of this ethical system. On another level, utilitarianism advocates the principle of greatest happiness, or in another term the principle of utility. It stipulates that the most morally superior deed is the one that realizes the highest degree of happiness for the largest number of people. Utilitarianism also holds the view that an individual is naturally and morally justifiable in the pursuit of the highest degree of happiness of his own, and in fact the pursuit of individual happiness also complies with the principle of greatest happiness in a certain way. Therefore, no matter on the macroscopic level or on the microscopic level, utilitarianism justifies, eulogizes and supports the pursuit of happiness, which is in a certain sense synonymous with practical interests.

The approval of the content-directed morality and the anxiety about the vulnerability of practical interests under the pressure of excessive requirements of formalities in *Jude* correspond to the conviction in practical interests in utilitarianism and achieve a literary interpretation of that conviction. In the novel, the content-directed morality is in conflict with the form-directed morality mechanism, and practical interests are not in harmony with the social requirements of formalities. Furthermore, it is emphasized that the oppression of the content-directed morality by the form-directed morality mechanism finally achieves its role in the formation of the protagonist's disastrous conclusion. It can be seen that, like *The Native* and *Tess*, *Jude* pays adequate attention to the practical application of ethical views. By manifesting the problems that may arise in the utilization of certain ethical views, the novel achieves the literary interpretation of the conviction in practical interests.

Chapter Two
Cultural Inappositeness in the
Dimension of Disposition

In *Introduction to Psychology*, scholars point out:

> Disposition is a person's stable attitudes towards reality and accustomed modes of behavior that fit in with those attitudes. Disposition is the most important and prominent psychological feature in a person's individuality and it is the primary symbol for a person's social quality and spiritual outlooks. Therefore, disposition plays a central role in the individuality.（张旭东, 刘益民, 欧何生, 2009: 161）

Disposition is the keynote in which an individual cultural system exists and operates and it constitutes one major dimension of the individual cultural system. Inappositeness of the individual disposition, the social mechanism of disposition or the relationship between the individual disposition and the social mechanism of disposition will plunge the individual cultural system into inappositeness in the dimension of disposition. The inappositeness of the individual disposition, the social mechanism of disposition, or the relationship between the individual disposition and the social mechanism of disposition, or in other words the inappositeness of the individual cultural system in the dimension of disposition, will generate a conspicuous destructive force which can culturally threaten an individual's existence.

2.1 *The Mayor:* The Negative Tendency

There are a variety of needs in people's psychology; needs generate energy and actuate individuals' deeds. Needs cannot always get satisfied and frustrated needs will produce negative energy. In the handling of the negative energy from frustrated needs, the human disposition could demonstrate two contrary tendencies, the positive tendency and the negative tendency, namely the tendencies to handle the energy positively and negatively respectively. Following the positive tendency, an individual would harbor and release the energy generated by frustrated needs in a constructive way. He or she would actively promote the solution of problems together with the amelioration of life and foster an optimistic view about life. The positive tendency creates a constructive pattern for the transformation from energy of frustrated needs into deeds. Following the negative tendency, an individual would hold and release the energy generated by frustrated needs in a destructive way. He or she would passively witness the exacerbation of problems as well as the deterioration of life and develop a pessimistic view about life. The negative tendency creates a destructive pattern for the transformation from energy of frustrated needs into deeds. A certain mode of psychology, namely a certain kind of disposition may generally be characterized by the positive tendency or by the negative tendency. In *The Mayor*, the individual disposition of the protagonist Michael Henchard is generally characterized by the negative tendency and that tendency constitutes a major constituent of Henchard's individual disposition. In Henchard's disposition, there is a rough and extremely egocentric need to struggle to success. (李增, 王丁, 2004: 64) The roughness and extreme egocentricity of Henchard's basic need make it difficult for him to deal with frustrations calmly and constructively. Henchard thus tends to handle the energy from frustrated needs destructively and demonstrates the negative tendency. Moreover, mood-based aggressiveness is another major constituent of the individual disposition of Henchard. The negative tendency and the mood-based aggressiveness mark the inappositeness of the internal existence of Henchard's individual cultural system in the dimension of disposition. In other words, the two features in the protagonist's individual disposition conspire to create the inappositeness of his individual cultural system. The negative tendency and the mood-based aggressiveness give rise to the disastrous conclusion of Henchard. It could also be said that the inappositeness of Henchard's individual cultural system in the dimension of disposition gives rise to his disastrous conclusion.

Following the negative tendency, Henchard often generates destructive impulses. "Hardy charts Henchard's tragedy as a psychological study of impulsive behavior and self-destruction." (Suzanne, 2014: 88) The character's self-destructive impulsiveness derives from his negative tendency and constitutes a manifestation of the negative tendency. In the novel, there is "the conflict of reason and impulse" (Chew, 1928: 46 – 47). Facing the frustration of needs, instead of actively designing methods and taking actions according to the reason for the solution of problems, Henchard usually passively follows his impulse only to plunge into his self-destruction. In brief, Henchard's negative tendency is closely correlated with his impulsiveness. There are a number of demonstrations of Henchard's negative tendency in the novel's plot. The negative tendency of Henchard is first demonstrated in his selling of his wife by auction at the beginning of his story. The protagonist Michael Henchard as a hay-trusser, and his wife with their little daughter in arms walk towards the village of Weydon-Priors. Near the village, Henchard gathers information from a turnip-hoer that neither work nor housing could be easily found in the village. Henchard is frustrated by his gloomy prospects here, and the dissatisfaction with life deposited bitterly in his heart is thus stimulated. The family enter a tent where porridge is sold. Henchard quickly finds out that, by the woman who runs the business there, liquor is surreptitiously added to the porridge at requests. The protagonist signals to the woman, enjoys his porridge mixed with rum one bowl after another and soon falls into drunkenness. Having got drunk, Henchard complains that his plighted situation is just caused by his untimely marriage and unwanted wife. He even offers to sell his wife by auction then and there. "She shall take the girl if she wants to, and go her ways. I'll take my tools, and go my ways. 'Tis simple as Scripture history." (Hardy, 1994: 7) Henchard meets with difficulties in supporting the family. His need to lead a well-off life meets with frustration and energy accumulates in his frustrated mind. Instead of positively handling the energy from the frustrated need and actively searching for solutions to current adversities, he attributes the straitened conditions of life to the trammels that his wife and family supposedly inflict upon him. Facing the troubled family life, Henchard chooses to destruct the family instead of constructing it into a better one and he regards that destruction as the right way of handling the energy from his frustrated need. In this process, the protagonist shows the negative tendency in his disposition. Pessimism is one of the facets of the negative tendency. The reason why Henchard chooses to disintegrate his family instead of consolidating and ameliorating it, from a significant perspective, is just constituted by his pessimism. In difficulties of life, Henchard cannot perceive the hope of improvement. Although devoting himself to singing his own praises, he is in fact extremely unconfident of his talents and abilities. In the disillusion about the future, what Henchard most wants to do in the handling of his negative energy is to find someone else to bear the responsibility of all the failure. Thus, he chooses to complain about and sell his wife. The wife is most conveniently chosen as a scapegoat in accounting for all the husband's weaknesses and failures. In complaining about and offering to sell his wife, Henchard pessimistically handles the energy arising out of his frustrated need. Of course, Henchard's complaint of his wife and his offer to sell her are made in drunkenness. The drunken state also plays a role in the formation of Henchard's destructive behavior. However, in final analysis, that is just an external catalyst in the stimulation of what is inherent in the protagonist. The negative tendency functions more decisively than the drunken state in this episode. Fed up with all the humiliation Henchard repeatedly inflict on her, the wife Susan goes away with a sailor who accepts Henchard's offer and pays the required amount of money. At this point, Henchard begins to taste the bitterness of his own deeds. After several months of fruitless search for his wife and daughter, Henchard gives up and sets out for Casterbridge. All of Henchard's later miseries and his disastrous conclusion originate from this initial error of the abandonment of his family which is precipitated by the negative tendency. In the handling of the negative energy arising out of the frustrated need of leading a well-off life, the negative tendency in Henchard's disposition comes to the foreground and shows how it triggers a process which at last leads to the protagonist's disastrous conclusion.

Many years have elapsed before Henchard's wife Susan, together with Elizabeth-Jane the grown-up daughter, tries to search for Henchard after the supposed loss at sea of the sailor who makes the purchase of the abandoned wife. With some efforts, Susan and Elizabeth-Jane finally trace the whereabouts of Henchard to the city of Casterbridge. Out of all expectations, Henchard has become the mayor of Casterbridge. At the time of Susan and Elizabeth-Jane's arrival at the city, a Scotchman named Donald Farfrae also gets there. With his outstanding abilities, Farfrae wins favor from Henchard and is appointed the manager of the mayor's corn business. At first Henchard and Farfrae cooperate smoothly and agreeably. However, Henchard gradually feels that Farfrae surpasses him in capabilities and is not willing to remain in total subordination. A fissure begins to grow between the boss and the manager. Then there comes a festive day in celebration of a national event and that proves to be an occasion for the final breakup of Henchard and Farfrae's cooperation in business. The celebration event organized by Henchard turns into an utter failure because of a heavy rain. That event organized by Farfrae, however, runs rather smoothly and successfully in the rainy weather, thanks to an ingeniously designed tent. With people's mockery that the mayor is beaten by his young manager, Henchard can no longer control his envy and fires Farfrae. " 'He'll be top-sawyer soon of you two, and carry all afore him,' added jocular Mr Tubber. 'No,' said Henchard gloomily. 'He won't be that, because he's shortly going to leave me.' He looked towards Donald, who had again come near. 'Mr Farfrae's time as my manager is drawing to a close—isn't it, Farfrae?'" (Hardy, 1994: 83) Henchard, as the boss of his corn business, wants to keep his employee Farfrae in an inferior position. He wants Farfrae to accept the absolute authority of his boss and place himself in total subordination. He wants Farfrae to be capable, so that he could manage the business successfully; however, he does not want Farfrae's capabilities to surpass those of himself and cast a shadow upon the superiority of a boss or even overthrow that superiority. In short, Henchard has the need for superiority in the relationship with Farfrae. Nevertheless, Farfrae's capabilities which are more brilliant than those of Henchard's and the manager's unwillingness to yield to the supposedly unconditioned authority of his boss, naturally reveal themselves in daily affairs. In the process, the need for superiority of Henchard is gradually frustrated. The celebration of the national event is an occasion for the culmination of the frustration of Henchard's need. The energy arising out of the frustrated need tortures Henchard and makes him feel miserable; and Henchard chooses the dismissal of Farfrae as the way to handle the energy from his frustrated need. Henchard finds that the relationship between him and Farfrae does not meet the need for absolute superiority and feels that he is dragged into unhappiness by the energy which is generated by the frustration of his need. Therefore, he just ends that relationship and hopes to release the energy of his frustrated need thereby. That is a destructive way of dealing with negative energy, and the negative tendency of Henchard reveals itself in the destructiveness. The relationship based upon the absolute superiority of Henchard the boss is one that deprives Farfrae of the dignity as an independent human being. That is repugnant to a person of strong self-esteem and the spirit of independent thinking like Farfrae. Henchard has not fostered the habit of introspection of his needs. He never considers the possibility of adjusting his need and developing his relationship with Farfrae in a more realistic way. Following his negative tendency and releasing his impulses, he chooses a destructive way of getting rid of his negative energy which is bound to bring about a sequence of unfavorable consequences. The destructiveness of the method of Henchard's handling of the negative energy gives the method the high efficiency in releasing the energy. In effect, the most destructive is usually the most efficient, of course in a negative manner. The negative tendency of Henchard decides that he will adopt the efficient yet destructive method to deal with the energy from the frustrated need. "However vehemently Henchard approaches another person, the shadow cast between them by his own soul will remain as an impenetrable obstacle, his consciousness forbidding union with any of the people he loves." (Miller, 1970: 150) The negative tendency is one of the means by which Henchard's soul casts the shadow between himself and the person he approaches. Because of the negative tendency, Henchard always deals with frustrated needs in interpersonal interactions in a destructive way, thus ruining his relationships with others and making unions with others impossible. After the dismissal, Farfrae buys a small corn and hay business of his own. For Henchard, an able helper disappears and a strong opponent appears, which in the end brings his business to the downfall. Besides, the estrangement between Henchard and Farfrae brings negative effects to the former's family relationships, especially to his relationship with his daughter Elizabeth-Jane whom Henchard cherishes as an emotional prop in his later phases of life. The bitterness on the part of Elizabeth-Jane in turn deals a fatal emotional blow to Henchard. The failure in business and the loss of the emotions of Elizabeth-Jane are both critical factors that affect Henchard's disastrous conclusion. In brief, both from the perspective of business and from the perspective of family, Henchard's dismissal of Farfrae, engendered by the negative tendency in his disposition, is responsible to a large extent for the protagonist's disastrous conclusion.

The negative tendency in Henchard's disposition is also shown in his deception when the sailor Newson comes to look for Elizabeth-Jane. Susan falls ill and dies soon after her remarriage to Henchard. In her dying days, Susan leaves a letter to Henchard telling him that his daughter dies shortly after their departure at Weydon-Priors and this grown-up Elizabeth-Jane is in fact the daughter of the seaman Newson. As the prosperity of the business gradually declines and eventually vanishes, Henchard's need for stable family ties intensifies and Elizabeth-Jane becomes an emotional anchorage for him. However, the fact that Elizabeth-Jane is not his daughter in the biological sense renders a sense of frustration to Henchard. The claim for Elizabeth-Jane by the authentic father Newson poses a threat to Henchard's current relationship with Elizabeth-Jane and constitutes a high tide in the frustration of his need for stable family ties. Faced with this situation, Henchard chooses to deceive Newson and assert that Elizabeth-Jane is dead. The sailor asks, "They told me in Falmouth that Susan was dead. But my Elizabeth-Jane—where is she?" (Hardy, 1994: 227) "Dead likewise" (Hardy, 1994: 227), Henchard answers. The frustration of the need for stable family ties generates negative energy in Henchard's psyche. The negative energy makes him feel insecure and painful, and at the same time makes him especially resentful towards the sailor who triggers a large proportion of his pains. In dealing with the negative energy together with the unpleasant feelings associated with it, Henchard chooses a method that is on the surface simplest and the most efficient while essentially the most destructive. In this process, the negative tendency in Henchard's disposition reveals itself. By deceiving Newson, Henchard releases the negative energy from his frustrated need instantaneously. He immediately drives the threat away and temporarily alleviates his anxiety. At the same time, he vents his spite upon Newson thereby. With the negative treatment of the energy from the frustrated need, Henchard temporarily gets freed from his psychological burden. However, Henchard's treatment of the negative energy carried out under the negative tendency is essentially destructive to his need for stable family ties and destructive for his life. Afterwards, he will be haunted and tortured by the fear of his lie being exposed to others. In the end, the deception is found out by Elizabeth-Jane and Newson, which radically undermines Elizabeth-Jane's trust for Henchard and deals a fatal blow to her love for him. Shortly after, deprived of the much-cherished love, Henchard dies in loneliness. The deception by Henchard, brought about by the negative tendency in his disposition, is a direct cause of the protagonist's disastrous conclusion. "self-destructiveness [Self-destructiveness] is the key to Henchard's character" (Langbaum, 1995: 131). Accordingly, the negative tendency marked by destructiveness constitutes a major component of Henchard's disposition and exerts profound influence upon his life route. In Henchard's treatment of his wife Susan, his cooperator Farfrae, and the sailor Newson, it can be seen that the negative tendency gives rise to his disastrous conclusion.

2.2 *The Mayor:* The Mood-Based Aggressiveness

In the psychology of Henchard, mood-based aggressiveness also shows itself. Henchard is often made aggressive by his bad mood and "The [the] possibly self-destructive aspect of his aggressiveness" (Sumner, 1981: 61) exerts a significant influence upon his life. The mood-based aggressiveness of Henchard has two layers of connotations. First, Henchard easily interprets others' words and deeds as offences. Confronted with offences, including minor ones, Henchard cannot make efficient use of his reason and work out constructive responses and ways of settlement. Instead, he sinks into bad moods and renders no timely check on those moods, leaving them running wild. Second, the rampant bad moods always engender and heighten Henchard's hostility towards others. The mood-based aggressiveness, like the negative tendency, gives rise to the protagonist's disastrous conclusion, his death in despair.

After Susan's death, Henchard gets the information that Elizabeth-Jane is in fact not his daughter. Following the mood-based aggressiveness, Henchard feels offended and bitterness grows in Henchard's heart out of this offence. The bad mood of Henchard produces excessive hostility towards the innocent girl. One time, Henchard bitterly criticizes the handwriting of Elizabeth-Jane, denouncing that as becoming for people from lower strata. The genial disposition of Elizabeth-Jane leads her to do some manual labor in person rather than leave everything to servants. Moreover, she inclines to express gratitude to a parlour-maid for every service. Regarding Elizabeth-Jane's deeds as the degrading of herself and a disgrace to the family and to himself, Henchard pours upon the girl hostile words which make her rather painful. Elizabeth-Jane sometimes serves provisions to Nance Mockridge, a female employee in Henchard's business. One day, Henchard sees the girl practice this charitable deed. Witnessing his daughter serve his inferior, Henchard is instantaneously enraged. "Haven't I told you o't fifty times? Hey? Making yourself a drudge for a common workwoman of such a character as hers! Why, ye'll disgrace me to the dust!" (Hardy, 1994: 102) Henchard does not have the willingness and ability to control his rampant bad mood and leaves it to trigger and heighten the hostility towards Elizabeth-Jane. These examples of Henchard's hostility towards Elizabeth-Jane directly arise out of some specific offences. However, the decisive offence is the fact that Elizabeth-Jane is not Henchard's daughter in the biological sense. The hostility from the father causes much pain to Elizabeth-Jane and can exert unfavorable effects upon their relationship.

As told in the preceding passage, Elizabeth-Jane is bitterly scolded by Henchard for serving provisions to Nance Mockridge. The scolding from Henchard is overheard by Mockridge. Incensed by her employer's insults upon her, the woman proclaims to Henchard in revenge that Elizabeth-Jane has once served at a local inn to earn money, which is much worse for Henchard's reputation. Henchard gets much agonized by this humiliation. Afterwards Henchard gets to know that it is Farfrae, the one who exceeds him almost in every aspect, who is served by Elizabeth-Jane at the inn. That fact exacerbates the sense of humiliation in Henchard's psyche. Henchard's feelings of being offended are heightened and the hostility from him is intensified. In effect, the hostility of Henchard is not only in the form of passionate scolding but also in the form of coldness. He tries to keep away from Elizabeth-Jane and even tries to get rid of her by showing Farfrae that he is no longer against his courting of Elizabeth-Jane. Elizabeth-Jane withstands the hostility in both forms from her father and in fact "his passion had [has] less terror for her than his coldness"

(Hardy, 1994: 101). Henchard's coldness furthers the devastating effects upon the fragile girl that passionate scolding initiates. Scolding, in fact, is not as destructive as coldness in this case. "The increasing frequency of the latter mood told her the sad news that he disliked her with a growing dislike." (Hardy, 1994: 101) The coldness on the part of Henchard deals ruthless blows to Elizabeth-Jane and plunders her into a gloomy state. Including both passionate scolding and coldness, the hostility from Henchard tortures Elizabeth-Jane and makes her rather thoughtful. On one occasion, "She [she] fell into painful thought on her position, which ended with her saying quite loud, 'Oh, I wish I was dead with dear mother!'" (Hardy, 1994: 105) The hostility from Henchard makes the girl quite disappointed with him and somewhat disillusioned about the possibility of building a harmonious family relationship. In this situation, Elizabeth-Jane's love for her father Henchard gradually fades and she grows more and more indifferent to Henchard. The mood-based aggressiveness of Henchard gives rise to the estrangement of Elizabeth-Jane from him and eventually to her rejection of him. In the end, the estrangement and rejection on the part of the daughter precipitates the breakdown of the tough man Henchard and he dies in despair.

The mood-based aggressiveness of Henchard is directed not only at Elizabeth-Jane but also at Farfrae. Donald Farfrae, a young gentleman from Scotland, helps Henchard make grown wheat wholesome again and is urged by the latter to serve as the manager of his corn business. At first, Henchard and Farfrae develop a sincere friendship. Nonetheless, as time passes by, Farfrae shows that he exceeds his boss in talents and accomplishments. Moreover, he is reluctant to stay in the total subordination which is desired by Henchard. A fissure appears between Henchard and Farfrae and it grows wider and wider. After parting company and each going his own way in business, they become competitors in commerce. Afterwards, Henchard fails in business because of ill management. After the failure of the former boss, the former employee purchases his business. Henchard feels much offended by Farfrae and deems that

Farfrae bears much responsibility for his misfortunes and failures. Hatred towards the young man accumulates in Henchard's psyche. Hatred, as a bad mood, creates and aggravates Henchard's hostility towards Farfrae. Henchard bitterly threatens to harm his rival. Later, it is said that a Royal Personage is going to pass through Casterbridge. Henchard, drunken, behaves improperly before the royal carriage and makes an indecent scene. Frarfrae, out of a sense of responsibility, stops Henchard and drags him away. This incident further intensifies Henchard's hostility towards Farfrae. Henchard forces Farfrae into a fierce wrestle. With his "more stable disposition" (Taylor, 2013: 122), Farfrae is unwilling to engage in the meaningless and dangerous wrestle, yet finds it difficult to avoid it. Considering that he is a much stronger man, Henchard ties an arm of his to make the fight a fair one. However, the sense of fairness does not bring the sense of mercy, and Henchard relentlessly grapples with his former cooperator. After much struggle, Henchard finally overpowers Farfrae. "'Now,' said Henchard between his gasps, 'this is the end of what you began this morning. Your life is in my hands.' 'Then take it, take it!' said Farfrae. 'Ye've wished to long enough!'" (Hardy, 1994: 213) At this point, the conflict between Henchard and Farfrae culminates and the hostility of Henchard towards Farfrae also comes to culmination. Although Henchard soon repents his aggressive treatment of the former friend and remorsefully withdraws his attack, this violent physical clash between the two men inevitably plunges the relationship between them into a more negative state. From a broader perspective, the hostility of Henchard towards Farfrae, which is brought about by the mood-based aggressiveness, erodes the emotions cherished in Farfrae's heart for his former friend. That hostility retards Farfrae's willingness to render assistance to Henchard, and in that situation Henchard's revival in business becomes more difficult. Furthermore, Elizabeth-Jane admires, supports and loves Farfrae. The hostility towards Farfrae worsens the attitude of Elizabeth-Jane towards Henchard. In both ways, the mood-based aggressiveness gives rise to Henchard's death in despair, his disastrous conclusion.

As discussed above, the mood-based aggressiveness of Henchard engenders the indifference and estrangement on the part of Elizabeth-Jane. Later, she even rejects him as her father. The mood-based aggressiveness also hampers the willingness to provide help on the part of Farfrae. Moreover, the aggressiveness directed upon Farfrae is also detrimental to Elizabeth-Jane's feelings for Henchard. The mood-based aggressiveness, no matter directed on Elizabeth-Jane or on Farfrae, always gives rise to Henchard's death in despair. In both ways, the mood-based aggressiveness draws Henchard nearer to his emotional and physical breakdown and death in despair, his disastrous conclusion. Besides, the hostility engendered and exacerbated by bad moods in turn causes the bad moods in Henchard's psychology to develop more destructively. The mood-based aggressiveness deprives Henchard's psychology of stability. In the unstable psychological state, Henchard cannot effectively control his emotions and feelings. Henchard becomes more and more pessimistic and unhappy, eventually dies in despair and goes to his disastrous conclusion.

2.3 *Tess:* The Imbalance of Psychological Rhythm

In *Tess*, the imbalance of the psychological rhythm dominates the internal existence of the protagonist Tess's individual cultural system in the dimension of disposition and makes that internal existence generally harmful for individual existence. As a consequence, Tess's individual cultural system is plunged into inappositeness in the dimension of disposition, generating a destructive force that finally results in the woman's execution, her disastrous conclusion. From another perspective, it can also be said that Tess's imbalance of psychological rhythm results in her disastrous conclusion.

In the novel, Tess strives for happiness. One's conception of happiness is related to what one wants—one's desire. Tess's "desire is a desire for the Other". (Ramel, 2015: 63) As a consequence, Tess's happiness, in her own conception, is inseparable from the other. She hopes to bring welfare to her family members and she hopes to find a worthy husband. These aims about "the other" achieve Tess's conception of happiness. In her struggle for happiness, Tess does not demonstrate an advantageous psychological condition. The internal existence of the individual cultural system of Tess in the dimension of disposition is predominated by excessive indecisiveness and excessive rashness, which could be summarized as the imbalance of psychological rhythm. The imbalance of psychological rhythm plunges Tess's individual cultural system into inappositeness in the dimension of disposition. *Tess* "suggest[s] sensitive nuances of an individual's feelings" and "suggest[s] the ultimate consequences of the destructive potential of human nature" (Alexander, 1987: 150). In Tess's nature, the destructive potential is just housed in her imbalance of psychological rhythm, her excessive indecisiveness and excessive rashness.

In some critical phases of her life, Tess manifests excessive indecisiveness which hinders her pursuit of happiness. At the beginning of her story, Tess is urged by her mother to go to Mrs. d'Urberville's estate to claim kin, in the hope of improving the financial condition of the family. Tess's own heart abhors the practice of lowering oneself to beg for charity. However, the excessive indecisiveness in Tess's disposition prevents her from making a final and absolute refusal to her mother's requirement. Under her mother's ceaseless exhortations, and in her unclear cognition of the essence of the affairs and the state of the circumstances, Tess agrees to go to Mrs. d'Urberville's estate to claim kin, and then eventually agrees to work at the rich lady's fowl-farm to win her favor. The excessive indecisiveness in the disposition deprives Tess of the opportunity to keep away from potential dangers, leaving her bogged down in the power field of the lustful Alec. At her mother's urges, Tess once says, "I don't altogether think I ought to go" (Hardy, 1993A: 37). However, shortly afterwards her attitudes are substantially softened, and she says, "It is for you to decide. I killed the old horse, and I suppose I ought to do something to get ye a new one. But—but—I don't quite like Mr. d'Urberville being there!" (Hardy, 1993A: 39) Although she does not want to sacrifice her dignity to claim kin and seek for charity, and although she finds Alec rather annoying, Tess still could not make a clear-cut decision to refuse her mother's request. The excessive indecisiveness in Tess's disposition places her in a state which is vulnerable to misguidance. The coaxing of her mother, coupled with her own sense of guilt for the death of their only horse, pushes Tess towards the acceptance of the job of tending fowls at the d'Urberville estate, a critical point in her life which leads to her disastrous conclusion.

After Tess agrees to go to Trantridge to work, Alec drives his fancy vehicle to fetch her. On the way to the d'Urberville estate, Alec tries to take liberties with Tess. He drives at a dangerously fast speed to scare Tess. He threatens to continue his reckless driving if Tess does not allow him to kiss her. Tess, scared, has to meet his demand. Exceedingly angry, Tess gets off the vehicle by some excuse and refuses to get on the vehicle again. She goes to the destination on foot. Due to the molestation from Alec, Tess's reluctance to go to the d'Urberville estate drastically increases. Nonetheless, impeded by the excessive indecisiveness in the disposition, Tess is not able to make a definite decision based upon her won wishes in time. Although refusing to take the vehicle, she still proceeds with the journey which is against her own will. At the d'Urberville estate, Alec continues to flirt with Tess and the latter still could not make a decision to go home and escape from this unpleasant and potentially dangerous place. Even after being taken advantage of sexually during the night ride in the Chase, Tess still could not immediately break away from Alec and the choice of life which he and his mother represent. It is "some few weeks subsequent to the night ride in The Chase" (Hardy, 1993A: 66) that Tess finally decides to return to her own home. She eventually comes to the conclusion that "the serpent hisses where the sweet birds sing" (Hardy, 1993A: 66). Alec, together with the lifestyle at the d'Urberville estate, is in conflict with Tess's view of life and happiness. Nevertheless, in the complication of interfering factors, the excessive indecisiveness in the disposition tremendously prolongs the time that Tess uses to make a redemptive decision. The much-delayed self-redemptive decision could not pull Tess away from the trajectory of life which leads to a disastrous conclusion through numerous sufferings.

In the early stages of her relationship with Angel Clare, Tess also shows excessive indecisiveness. More than two years after her bitter experience at Trantridge and the disgraceful return to her own home, Tess starts a new journey in life and begins her career as a milking maid at Talbothays Dairy. There Tess meets Angel Clare who is devoted to the study of agricultural techniques and the pursuit of a farming career. Mutually attracted, Tess and Angel naturally develop an intimate relationship. With the gradual revelation of love by Angel, Tess feels at a loss. On one hand, Tess resolves not to marry in her lifetime because of her "ignominious" past. One the other hand, she craves for love in the depths of heart and really finds hopes of true love in Angel. At Angel's repeated showing of love and proposals of marriage, Tess grows increasingly indecisive. "The struggle was so fearful; her own heart was so strongly on the side of his—two ardent hearts against one poor little conscience—that she tried to fortify her resolution by every means in her power." (Hardy, 1993A: 154) In following her own heart towards the destination of happiness, Tess finds her way blocked by excessive indecisiveness. The heart of Tess finds an antagonistic force in her conscience. She does not want Angel to suffer from the condemnation that the society has unjustly inflicted upon her. It is justifiable and necessary to build one's life and happiness upon conscience. Nonetheless, Tess fails to clearly realize that there is no inevitable conflict between her marriage to Angel and her conscience. She fails to clearly realize that there exist some constructive ways which could be found out for the resolution of the contradictions inflicted upon her life. In her indecisiveness, Tess loses much time which could be invested in making practical plans for a bright future on the basis of a constructive conscience. The loss of time and the failure in making practical plans in time contribute to the formation of Tess's disastrous conclusion. Intertwined with the indecision about whether to accept the marriage proposal from Angel, the indecision about whether to reveal her "disgraceful" past to Angel also plagues Tess.

From the perspective of Tess, she should reveal her past humiliation to Angel before her marriage to him. This revelation could provide the prerequisite for the continuous and stable mutual trust and mutual respect between Tess and Angel. It could lay a foundation for the lovers' clear understanding of their relationship out of their own views of life and views of the world. If the male protagonist could forgive the female protagonist, the life of Tess will be freed from potentially destructive factors, and if not, Tess will also be open to future chances of getting a worthier husband. However, excessive indecisiveness prevents Tess from making a timely decision about the revelation, or confession. Tess is always uncertain about whether to, when to and how to make the revelation. The failure of Tess to make the revelation before the wedding has manifold reasons. After much hesitation, she once slips a confession note under the door of her lover; however, the latter fails to notice it for it accidentally goes under the carpet. Afterwards, Tess wants to make the confession when she meets Angel upon the landing, but Angel dismisses that by saying there will be a mutual confession, but only after the wedding. Chance and the lack of interest on the part of Angel set in and block Tess's revelation. Nonetheless, in the final analysis, it is the indecisiveness on the part of Tess that determines her failure in making a pre-marriage revelation. "Her one desire, so long resisted, to make herself his, to call him her lord, her own—then, if necessary, to die—had at last lifted her up from her plodding reflective pathway." (Hardy, 1993A: 186) The excessive indecisiveness in Tess's disposition makes the revelation of the past before marriage a mission extremely difficult for Tess and leaves her mind in a weak and unsettled state. In that state, the mind of Tess fails to adhere to reason and succumbs to the glittering temptations of immediate happiness. In that way, the revelation of the past is postponed after the wedding. That makes it more difficult for Angel to accept Tess and helps bring about the breakup between the two, which finally results in the woman's disastrous conclusion.

Besides excessive indecisiveness, Tess also suffers from excessive rashness. "Tess's is a fragmented personality." (Keys, 1976: 181) The fragmentariness of

Tess's personality lies in, to a considerable extent, the discrepancy between excessive indecisiveness and excessive rashness. "Tess acts, on several occasions, from impulses". (Johnson, 1894: 190) Tess's actions facilitated by impulses constitute manifestations of the excessive rashness in her disposition. The excessive rashness in Tess is most conspicuously demonstrated in her killing of Alec which is the most direct and fiercest push upon her towards her execution, the disastrous conclusion. After being deserted by her husband Angel, the situations of Tess's life are in the process of deterioration. The financial conditions of Tess and her family are bad, which is later greatly worsened by the death of Tess's father and the eviction of the family from the original cottage. More devastating for Tess is the disillusionment that comes after the hope for the return of Angel has been repeatedly battered. Alec the persecutor takes advantage of the weaknesses of Tess and wins her back to him by cheating and temptation. When Angel realizes the unfairness in his treatment of Tess and suddenly appears before Tess, she is driven into extreme agonies. In a frenzy Tess quarrels bitterly with Alec and stabs him to death, resulting in her own execution, the disastrous conclusion. The killing of Alec by Tess has manifold causes, among which the excessive rashness in the disposition is an important one. Due to the excessive rashness, Tess does not spend enough time in considering the essence and consequences of the deed. With enough time invested in consideration, Tess would possibly have been saved from her ultimately destructive decision. In the novels of Thomas Hardy, "The [the] loss of mental control is a recurring problem for female characters, who are often overcome with passionate feelings." (Malane, 2003: 218) Tess is just the most typical one among those female characters. Overwhelmed by passionate feelings, Tess loses the control of her mind and kills Alec. In this process, Tess demonstrates the excessive rashness in her disposition. In Tess, the loss of mental control as a psychological condition and the excessive rashness as a dispositional trait are closely correlated with each other. Making the most horrible decision in the shortest time, Tess, by the excessive rashness in her disposition, is plunged into the unredeemable abyss of the disastrous conclusion.

2.4   The Idea about Disposition in *The Mayor* and Its Historical Significance

"His [Henchard's] inner strengths and weaknesses are so complex and powerful they create a wide psychological and emotional distance between him and the other characters." (Hanlon, 1983: 240) Moreover, Henchard's inner weaknesses, namely his dispositional defects the negative tendency and the mood-based aggressiveness, achieve a decisive role in the formation of the protagonist's death in despair—his disastrous conclusion, which differentiates the man markedly from other characters. In *The Mayor*, the negative tendency and the mood-based aggressiveness in the protagonist Henchard's individual disposition constitute the inappositeness of his individual cultural system. The inappositeness of Henchard's individual cultural system in the dimension of disposition, or from another perspective, the negative tendency and the mood-based aggressiveness, give rise to his disastrous conclusion. By demonstrating this condition, *The Mayor* develops the anxiety that disadvantageous qualities in the disposition may pose threats to individuals and the society.

The most conspicuous demonstration of the negative tendency in Henchard's disposition is achieved through the relationship between Henchard and Farfrae. In getting along with Farfrae, Henchard meets with some frustrations. Henchard hopes to cooperate with Farfrae in business. He also wants to keep Farfrae under his control and prevent him from overshadowing his master with his brilliant talents. However, Farfrae's advantages over Henchard gradually reveal themselves and the manager's unwillingness to be left in a state of complete subordination and submission grows more and more obvious along with the process of the revelation. In this situation, Henchard feels that his need is frustrated and his negative tendency shows itself. Henchard grows cold and unfriendly towards Farfrae. Instead of being cooperative, he tends to be challenging in their common business. At last, after being completely overshadowed by Farfrae in the organization of the activities for the celebration of a national event, Henchard publicly announces his dismissal of Farfrae. Henchard takes the dismissal of Farfrae as a solution to his frustrated condition. But in fact, it is not. "Henchard went home, apparently satisfied. But in the morning, when his jealous temper had passed away, his heart sank within him at what he had said and done." (Hardy, 1994: 84) After the careful consideration of his handling of the matter, Henchard regrets. The force of reason brings Henchard to a temporary recognition that his way of coping with the energy of his frustrated need is harmful. However, the negative tendency in his disposition has already stimulated a sequence of unwise deeds, which eventually leads to the irretrievable breakup of the cooperation between him and Farfrae. The negative tendency in Henchard's disposition involves his ability to manage his relationship with himself along the diachronic dimension. If a person's need is frustrated, it means that his self in the past or his self at the present does not live up to his expectations. The negative tendency means the failure to form a rational and positive assessment of his self in the past or his self at the present and the failure to construct a rational and optimistic scheme for the development of his self in the future. It also means the handling of the energy that the frustrated need creates by the utter negation of his self in the past or his self at the present and by the abandoning of the active governance of his self in the future. Henchard's negative tendency means he lacks the competence to manage his relationship with himself along the diachronic dimension. By showing the harm that the negative tendency does to Henchard's relationship with his important business partner Farfrae and to his life, the novel develops the anxiety about the possible threats of disadvantageous qualities in the disposition for individuals and the society.

The most conspicuous demonstration of the mood-based aggressiveness in Henchard's disposition is also achieved through his relationship with Farfrae. In Henchard's cooperation with Farfrae, disagreements and frictions arise. In dealing with the disagreements and frictions, Henchard often feels offended, easily loses control of his temper and grows hostile, which shows the mood-based aggressiveness, one of his major dispositional traits. Henchard's mood-based aggressiveness displayed in his relationship with Farfrae rushes to its summit in a wrestle between the two. One day, a Royal Personage passes through the town of Casterbridge. Henchard, drunken, waves his handmade flag in front of the carriage of the Personage, bringing shame to the town. Farfrae, out of a sense of responsibility, drags Henchard away from the scene. Henchard's resentment towards Farfrae is stimulated by this confrontation. Spurred by the resentment, Henchard challenges Farfrae to a wrestle, with the determination to settle accounts with him with sheer violence. This episode displays Henchard's mood-based aggressiveness in a very concentrated way. However, after the fight, Henchard again regrets. "Henchard took his full measure of shame and self-reproach. The scenes of his first acquaintance with Farfrae rushed back upon him—that time when the curious mixture of romance and thrift in the young man's composition so commanded his heart that Farfrae could play upon him as on an instrument." (Hardy, 1994: 213) Henchard regrets because as his resentment fades out, his former sentiments for Farfrae reappear. However, his mood-based aggressiveness has already irredeemably hurt his relationship with Farfrae. Henchard's mood-based aggressiveness entails his ability to manage his relationship with other individuals in the synchronic dimension. The mood-based aggressiveness in Henchard's disposition means that he could not peacefully and constructively manage his relationship with others in the synchronic dimension, being left in a disadvantageous position. By showing the harm that the mood-based aggressiveness does to Henchard's relationship with Farfrae and to Henchard's life, the novel further develops the anxiety about the possible threats of disadvantageous qualities in the disposition for individuals and the society. This anxiety is finally consummated in Henchard's death in despair, his disastrous conclusion.

The anxiety that disadvantageous qualities in the disposition may pose threats to individuals and the society in *The Mayor* corresponds to and achieves a literary interpretation of the emphasis on advantageous qualities of individuals in evolutionism. Evolutionism is originally a biological theory inaugurated by the British scientist Charles Darwin (1809 – 1882), but it transcends the sphere of biology and influences the whole system of ideological discourses of the Victorian age and the ensuing ages. Evolutionism exerts profound influence upon Hardy's literary career and constitutes a significant constituent of the intellectual atmosphere for the creation of *The Native.* The concept of natural selection is the basis of evolutionism. Moreover, the struggle for survival [namely the struggle for existence] constitutes a principle that is important for natural selection. (Jones, 1975: 194) In Darwin's theory of evolutionism, natural selection means the "preservation of favourable variations and the rejection of injurious variations" (Darwin, 2008: Chapter Ⅳ). Besides, Darwin "use[s] the term Struggle for Existence in a large and metaphorical sense, including dependence of one being on another, and including (which is more important) not only the life of the individual, but success in leaving progeny". (Darwin, 2008: Chapter Ⅲ) With limited resources in the environment, different species and different individuals of the same species have to compete with each other for existence and development and that constitutes the struggle for existence. "individuals [Individuals] having any advantage, however slight, over others, would have the best chance of surviving and of procreating their kind", whereas "any variation in the least degree injurious would be rigidly destroyed". (Darwin, 2008: Chapter Ⅳ) In the process of natural selection, species or individuals of species with advantageous qualities tend to win in the completion and survive, and the advantageous qualities tend to be passed on forward along the evolutionary route. In a similar manner, species or individuals of species with disadvantageous qualities tend to be defeated in the competition and deprived of the right of survival, and the disadvantageous qualities tend to die out in the evolutionary movement. Therefore, advantageous qualities are of vital significance for the existence of a species or a certain individual of a species. First, advantageous qualities of individuals are of decisive importance for the existence of individuals. Moreover, when the relevance between the advantageous qualities of a species and the existence of the species is assessed, the species is considered as an integrated whole and in that sense, it is also an individual. It can be said that in evolutionism, the advantageous qualities of individuals receive much emphasis.

In the literary interpretation of the emphasis on advantageous qualities of individuals in evolutionism, *The Mayor* chooses to show the harm of the negative tendency and the mood-based aggressiveness. It can be seen that *The Mayor* pays special attention to the dispositional fitness as a category of human qualities. The humankind are intelligent beings. The existence and the development of the humankind mainly depend upon the highly-developed intelligence. The disposition or the mode of psychology, as the inner context of intelligence operation, is of vital importance for the efficiency of the humankind's utilization of intelligence. Therefore, dispositional fitness is particularly meaningful for the humankind's existence and development. Therefore, it is reasonable for *The Mayor* to pay special attention to dispositional fitness in the interpretation of the emphasis upon advantageous qualities of individuals in evolutionism.

The Mayor shows the negative tendency and the mood-based aggressiveness in the protagonist's disposition. The former involves an individual's ability to manage his relationship with himself along the diachronic dimension, while the latter involves an individual's ability to manage his relationship with other individuals in the synchronic dimension. The treatment of the two qualities achieves an investigation into the dispositional fitness of the humankind from different temporal dimensions. For human beings who have a high level of intelligence and a complicated subjective world, the realization of dispositional fitness involves a crucial assembly of advantageous qualities. The negative tendency and the mood-based aggressiveness are both manifestations of the deficiency of dispositional fitness. In *The Mayor*, the negative tendency and the mood-based aggressiveness in the protagonist Henchard's disposition give rise to his disastrous conclusion and make him a failure in the struggle for existence. In other words, Henchard gets sifted out in natural selection. Of course, in the case of Henchard, the terms struggle for existence and natural selection have already extended from the purely natural sense to a social sense. *The Mayor*, through showing the negative tendency and the mood-based aggressiveness in the disposition of Henchard, and through showing how the two factors give rise to the protagonist's disastrous conclusion, demonstrates how the deficiency of dispositional fitness weakens one in the struggle for existence and handicaps one in natural selection.

2.5   The Idea about Disposition in *Tess* and Its Historical Significance

In *Tess,* the internal existence of the protagonist Tess's individual cultural system in the dimension of disposition is predominated by the imbalance of psychological rhythm, which comprises excessive indecisiveness and excessive rashness. The imbalance of psychological rhythm plunges the individual cultural system of Tess into inappositeness in the dimension of disposition. The imbalance of psychological rhythm, or from another perspective, the inappositeness of Tess's individual cultural system in the dimension of disposition, generates a force which is in part responsible for the engendering of the disastrous conclusion of Tess. By showing that the imbalance of psychological balance results in the disastrous conclusion of the protagonist, *Tess*, just like *The Mayor*, develops the anxiety that disadvantageous qualities in the disposition may pose threats to individuals and the society.

In *Tess*, the protagonist Tess suffers from the excessive indecisiveness and the excessive rashness which make up her imbalance of psychological rhythm. Facing the sexual harassment and sexual violence from Alec, Tess has not been able to escape from the danger and take protective measures in time. Caught by the excessive indecisiveness, she cannot timely put relative factors in order and shield herself against the threat. Because of the excessive indecisiveness, she loses the chance to save herself in time from the claws of Alec. When Tess falls in love with Angel, she considers revealing her humiliated past to her lover before their marriage. However, after rounds of hesitations, she misses the more advantageous circumstances to make a confession and conduct an exchange of views with Angel, again caught by excessive indecisiveness. Due to the excessive indecisiveness, Tess loses the chances which can possibly reduce the injustice that social institutions impose upon her. By showing the harm that excessive indecisiveness does to Tess and by showing the function that excessive indecisiveness accomplishes in the creation of Tess's disastrous conclusion, the novel develops the anxiety about the possible threats that disadvantageous qualities in the disposition may pose to individuals and the society. When Tess meets Angel again after returning to the claws of Alec, she does not give herself enough time to consider relative factors and work out a wise solution. Tess loses control of herself, stabbing Alec to death. After knowing that Tess has killed Alec, Angel "supposed [supposes] that in the moment of mad grief of which she spoke [speaks] her mind had [has] lost its balance, and plunged her into this abyss." (Hardy, 1993A: 339) The imbalance of mind, caused by the excessive rashness, does harm to Tess's life at this most critical moment. Excessive rashness is the dispositional trait that directly results in Tess's disastrous conclusion. By showing the harm that excessive rashness does to Tess and by showing the function that excessive rashness accomplishes in the creation of Tess's disastrous conclusion, the novel further develops the anxiety about the possible threats that disadvantageous qualities in the disposition may pose to individuals and the society. The imbalance of psychological rhythm, made up of the two disadvantageous dispositional qualities—the excessive indecisiveness and the excessive rashness, eventually results in Tess's disastrous conclusion. The disastrous conclusion of Tess consummates the anxiety about the threats that disadvantageous dispositional qualities may pose to individuals and the society.

The aforementioned anxiety in *Tess* also achieves a literary interpretation of the evolutionist emphasis upon the importance of advantageous qualities of individuals in the struggle for existence, like in *The Mayor*. The excessive indecisiveness, as a kind of disadvantageous quality, weakens Tess in the struggle for existence and the natural selection. The excessive rashness, as another kind of disadvantageous quality, further weakens Tess in the aforementioned processes. By showing the harms of disadvantageous qualities, the novel makes prominent the significance of the advantageous qualities of individuals in the struggle for existence and the natural selection. In the novel, dispositional qualities are chosen for the interpretation of the evolutionist idea. It can be seen that *Tess*, like *The Mayor*, pays special attention to dispositional fitness as a sequence of human qualities.

Chapter Three
Cultural Inappositeness in
the Dimension of Identity

"identity [Identity] is an essence that can be signified through signs of taste, beliefs, attitudes and lifestyles. Identity is deemed to be both personal and social. It marks us out as the same as and different from other kinds of people." (Barker, Jane, 2016: 260) Identity is the core of the individual cultural system and it constitutes a major dimension of the system. "So deep a human interest— in the renewed and renewable means of recognition, self-recognition and identity—can be practiced over a very wide range, from the most collective to the most individual forms." (Williams, 1995: 129) The dimension of identity, constantly capturing the attention of human intellect, is of pivotal importance for human existence and development. Identity and identification, lying at the core of the variety of human endeavors, exercise profound influence upon various aspects of individuals' lives. Therefore, the appositeness condition of the individual cultural system in the dimension of identity has the potential to significantly influence individuals' lives.

3.1   *Tess:* The Conflict Between the Identity of Explicit Equality and the Explicit Identity Inequality

Identity comprises explicit identity and implicit identity. Explicit identity is the identity that is explicitly approved and supported by social institutions. It gets verification in the explicit discourses of social institutions. Implicit identity is the identity that is implicitly approved and supported by social institutions, or in other words, it establishes itself in the acquiescence of social institutions. It gets verification in the implicit discourses of social institutions.

In *Tess*, the individual cultural system of the protagonist Tess is in inappositeness in the dimension of identity. This book will make analyses of the conditions of the fields of explicit identity and implicit identity respectively. In the field of explicit identity, the identity of explicit equality constitutes the internal existence of Tess's individual cultural system, and the explicit identity inequality constitutes the external existence of her individual cultural system. In the field of implicit identity, the identity of implicit equality constitutes the internal existence of Tess's individual cultural system, and the implicit identity inequality constitutes the external existence of her individual cultural system. The identity of explicit equality conflicts with the explicit identity inequality, and the identity of implicit equality conflicts with the implicit identity inequality. The conflict between the identity of explicit equality and the explicit identity inequality and the conflict between the identity of implicit equality and the implicit identity inequality plunge Tess's individual cultural system into inappositeness in the dimension of identity. The conflict between the identity of explicit equality and the explicit identity inequality and the conflict between the identity of implicit equality and the implicit identity inequality, or in other words the inappositeness of Tess's individual cultural system in the dimension of identity, fundamentally does harm to the life of Tess and results in her disastrous conclusion.

By the explicit identity inequality, Tess's self-defined identity of explicit equality is denied. The conflict between the identity of explicit equality and the explicit identity inequality experienced by Tess is mainly manifested in her relationship with her lover Angel Clare. There is a brief encounter between Tess and Angel almost without any communication at the May Day festivities beside the village of Marlott. Afterwards, Tess really gets to know Angel at the Talbothays Dairy. As she gets along with Angel, she discovers in him a learned, hard-working, pure and handsome youngster, the very epitome of ideal manhood. On the other side, Angel also finds that Tess is an exceedingly beautiful and kind girl, his deeply deposited craving for true love awakened. Because of the admiration from the depths of the girl's soul, escalating shows of love by Angel leave the heart of Tess reverberating with earnest longings for the belated happiness, although also at a loss about how to handle her past of humiliation. Before long Angle and Tess announce their love to their family members and fellow working people, after which a wedding is scheduled.

As a woman who places much emphasis on spiritual life and deems true love as indispensable to a happy existence, Tess feels hopes of resurrection in the bond between her and Angel, which is essentially different from that between her and Alec d'Urberville, her persecutor. The love from Angel promises a happy future for Tess. However, on the part of Angel, there is also a potential problem for Tess. "although [Although] he [Angel] sometimes reminds himself that she does have her own subjectivity, he inscribes her through the whole range from divine to vegetable." (Henson, 2011: 198) Angel once calls Tess by the names of goddesses, and he also tends to perceive Tess by the comparison between her and animals or even the vegetable with certain admirable qualities. Angel's way of addressing and perceiving Tess can show his admiration for her. However, on another level, that also shows that he does not view Tess as an equal human being. Angel views Tess more as an object of eulogy, admiration or the male gaze, than as an equal human being with the full subjectivity with whom authentic communication can be conducted. Angel's materialized conception of Tess, as a demonstration of the explicit identity inequality, gets more serious with the passage of time and "the closer he draws to sympathetic and sensuous participation in Tess's world, the more helplessly his unreconstructed visual bias renders Tess a spectacular object of lust" (Gussow, 2000: 455). Afterwards, Angel's failure to view Tess as an equal human being turns out to be a threat to her. The first turning point in the relationship between Tess and Angel is their mutual confession. In the evening that follows the wedding, Angel first confesses his past indiscretion, a short-lived affair with an older woman in London. A tolerant girl, Tess accepts the stain of the previously-assumed perfect man and forgives the fault of her husband. Giving her forgiveness to Angel, Tess expects that she could more easily get her husband's generosity reciprocally, based on her self-assumed identity of explicit equality. Tess revolts against the patriarchal society and its ethics and thereby pursues her spiritual independence. (刘磊, 2019:47) The spiritual independence and the self-assumed identity of explicit equality form a relationship of mutual interpretation. "Forgive me as you are forgiven!" (Hardy, 1993A: 200) Tess's appeal shows her view of identity equality. Nevertheless, contrary to her wish and anticipation, Angel shows reproaching anger at her confession. "Different societies, different manners" (Hardy, 1993A: 203), says Angel, describing Tess as "an unapprehending peasant woman, who have [has] never been initiated into the proportions of social things" (Hardy, 1993A: 203). While touching on his own fault lightly, Angel is "unable to disengage himself from his religious, social, and moral upbringing which defined a fallen woman as socially unacceptable". (Schoenfeld, 2005: 196) Angel's underestimation of the seriousness of his own fault and his overestimation of the seriousness of the fault of Tess, in a certain sense, derive from his upbringing. Moreover, the underestimation and overestimation, together with the upbringing of Angel, are in the final analysis products of the explicit identity inequality.

"Hardy reflects what would be likely to be the contemporary judgement of Tess through the male perspective of Angel Clare." (Ferguson, 2013: 120) Angel's view is representative of the judgement made through the explicit inequality in contemporary social institutions. One made out of the identity of explicit equality of a female, one made on the basis of the explicit identity inequality of the patriarchal society, the couple's interpretations of their respective slips and the relationship between two slips are in sharp contrast to each other. On the basis of explicit equality, social institutions would give explicit backing to the equal treatment of people as human beings rather than to the unequal treatment of people as entities from different classifications. In accordance with her identity of explicit equality, Tess regards her slip as of the same nature with that of Angel. According to her understanding, the contemporary social institutions should not and would not explicitly support the discriminating handling of the same deeds by people of different genders. Nevertheless, the patriarchal society then works in another way. Gender hierarchy is one of the hierarchies that make up patriarchy. In the social institutions of the patriarchal society, women are treated as inferior and subordinate to men. Gender hierarchy and gender discrimination receive explicit affirmation, rather than tacit permission, from the system of social institutions of patriarchy, constituting a demonstration of the explicit identity inequality. In this institutional context, sexual experience of a man before matrimony is understated as a mistake; nevertheless, that of a woman, no matter forced or of her own accord, is overstated as a felony.

Entirely different judgements of the errors of hers and Angel's and of the relationship between the two errors, as a demonstration of the conflict between the identity of explicit equality and the explicit identity inequality, leave Tess deeply anguished and stricken. She feels that her long-held faith in equality receives a heavy blow from Angel, her lover, much more devastating than one from ordinary people. Her dreams about love and happiness, which are closely related to the faith in equality, are relentlessly driven into disillusion. "For Hardy, confession and forgiveness are [...] a play of verbal forces and consequences, in which self and other find themselves helplessly involved." (Nishimura, 2005: 216) In the episode of mutual confessions, the cultural conflict in the dimension of identity deals material forces to Tess and works out material consequences to her mentality and her life. In an aimless walk outside of their lodging after her revelation of the humiliated past, Tess says to her husband: "I don't see how I can help being the cause of much misery to you all your life. The river is down there. I can put an end to myself in it. I am not afraid." (Hardy, 1993A: 204) At this point, spiritual disillusion causes her despair about life, together with doubts about or even denial of the necessity of continuing corporeal existence. From a certain perspective, the agony that Tess suffers in the episode of mutual confessions is even more bitter than the one that she suffers from in the first two Phases, for in this case agony is inflicted upon her by one who she loves instead of one who she finds repugnant. In the episode of mutual confessions, the conflict between the identity of explicit equality and the explicit identity inequality intensifies the miserable and pessimistic atmosphere in the psyche of Tess, which in turn erodes the foundation of her belief in the possibility of the construction of a bright future. More negative energy is generated in this second wave of adversities than in the first one; the negative energy accumulates in Tess's psyche and contributes much to the final breakdown and the ultimate stimulation of the tendency to take desperate and destructive measures in defense against miseries, which is the direct trigger of the protagonist's disastrous conclusion.

In the awkwardly-spent days which follow the mutual confessions, Angel continues to show the patriarchal judgement of the past of Tess which is dominant in his mind, and Tess continues to feel the bitterness and estrangement on the part of Angel. Gradually, it is revealed to Tess that Angel just stays together with her temporarily to avoid possible rumors. Angel gives every sign of the impossibility of forgiveness, and Tess "was [is] awe-stricken to discover such determination under such apparent flexibility". (Hardy, 1993A: 212) The "apparent flexibility" of Angel is a product of his kindness in nature, while his unshakeable determination takes shape under the control of social institutions. In the patriarchal framework of the explicit identity inequality, women are irreversibly and permanently deprived of virginity and integrity once they have sexual experience before marriage, with no attention paid to concrete circumstances. In that way, women are lowered to the status of male objects from the status of female subjects, with the identity of the human being weakened. As a result, Angel refuses to "countenance the equality of male and female virginity" (Lovesey, 2003: 926 – 927). Also in that patriarchal framework, women are considered the natural wives of the men who first have sexual relationships with them, with little attention paid to concrete circumstances. That is a notion which often haunts and tortures the heart of Angel. That notion is a direct factor which spurs him away from Tess. The patriarchal interpretation of the dishonor inflicted upon Tess is in conflict with and produces harm to her identity of explicit equality. This identity guarantees basic innocence and integrity after the disgrace which is inflicted upon the subject by external agents at an immature age. In conflict with the explicit identity inequality, the identity of explicit equality of Tess suffers from continuous tortures in the days after her confession. In those days, Tess is always in self-condemnation. Her self-condemnation does not signify the acceptance of or the assimilation by the patriarchal ideas of inequality, but demonstrates her ardent love for Angel, her husband. Tess is in deep love with Angel. Witnessing the pain of Angel, she is no longer in the mood to compare their respective errors and argue for the view that her error is as pardonable as that of his. Instead, she is overwhelmingly focused on how guilty she is for harming her husband's emotions.

Feeling it meaningless to continue living together with Angel, Tess offers to go home. In the conflict with the explicit identity inequality, the identity of explicit equality of Tess experiences suppression together with tortures and that wounded identity needs resurrection. Tess does not make many attempts to stop their parting, which would lower herself; instead she submits to the will of Angel in the handling of their relationship. "Pride [...] entered [enters] into her submission" (Hardy, 1993A: 222), and in that way Tess protects her pride and saves her identity of explicit equality. Driven by the conflict between the identity of explicit equality and the explicit identity inequality, Tess returns to her home in the village of Marlott. Tess's return to home provides space for identity resurrection, but that initial separation from Angel leads to the long-time and long-distance separation from him. Angel goes to Brazil which is far away from Britain; that desertion puts Tess in seriously unfavorable situations in economic and social terms, thus resulting in her disastrous conclusion.

After their separation, Angel decides to start a farm in Brazil, which places him completely out of the reach of Tess. "A product of Victorian culture, Angel cannot conceive of a relationship of equality with a woman; in his mind, his gender determines his superiority." (Stave, 1995: 111) As "the slave to custom and conventionality" (Hardy, 1993A: 232), Angel gets a decision which is brought about by the explicit identity inequality of the patriarchal society. Under the control of patriarchal ideas, Angel considers the erring Tess completely unacceptable. His journey to Brazil can take him far away from Tess, thus alleviating his suffering. Separated from her husband, Tess searches for work opportunities to support herself and her poor family. "She preferred [prefers] this to living on his allowance" (Hardy, 1993A: 239), because her identity of explicit equality requires her to rely on herself rather than her husband, especially in their misunderstanding and estrangement. In extremities of hardship, Tess refuses to give up. According to previous arrangements by Angel and the never-abrogated responsibility of mutual support between Angel and her, Tess could write to her husband for help. However, in the preservation of her dignity and equality, Tess could not easily persuade herself to write a letter to Angel. At last, tortured by the earnest yearning for Angel and the incessant harassment from Alec, Tess writes a letter to her husband. Instead of asking for financial support, she just expresses her unquenchable love for him and pleads for his quick reunion with her, her appeal for the identity of equality never abandoned. As a female suffering from attacks by the patriarchal society, it is exceedingly difficult for Tess to make a living alone for herself and her family, difficulties in life leaving her vulnerable to further hurt. In her self-dependent life, Tess sticks to the equal identity, even if at a high price. That condition eventually becomes something that Alec d'Urberville the persecutor successfully takes advantage of, finally resulting in the disastrous conclusion of

Tess. Under the despotic power of the explicit identity inequality, the self-assumed identity of explicit equality of Tess facilitates the creation of her disastrous conclusion. In that case, in essence, it is the conflict between the equal identity and the identity inequality in the explicit field that shall be held responsible for the creation of the disastrous conclusion.

3.2 *Tess*: The Conflict Between the Identity of Implicit Equality and the Implicit Identity Inequality

The destructive force generated by the inappositeness of Tess's individual cultural system in the dimension of identity is demonstrated in the conflict between the internal existence and the external existence of the individual cultural system in the fields of explicit identity and implicit identity respectively. Besides the identity of explicit equality, Tess also places herself at the identity of implicit equality. Accordingly, besides the explicit identity inequality, she meets with implicit identity inequality in her cultural setting. The identity of implicit equality is the equal identity in the field of implicit social coordination. Implicit identity inequality can also be called institutional inequality beyond institutions, realized outside of the institutional structure proper and tacitly affirmed by social institutions. The identity of implicit equality and the implicit identity inequality are in conflict and the equal identity of Tess is thus subjected to implicit oppression by social institutions. Tess is a female from the lower social stratum, deprived of the equal rights in the social activities and gender politics by the implicit identity inequality of the patriarchal-capitalist society then. Social institutions, as a part of culture, are in a certain sense determined by economic institutions which constitute the base of a society. In *Culture and Materialism*, Raymond Williams writes:

> [...] while [While] a particular stage of the development of production can be discovered and made precise by analysis, it is never in practice either uniform or static. It is indeed one of the central propositions of Marx's sense of history that there are deep contradictions in the relationships of production and in the consequent social relationships. (Williams, 2005: 33 - 34)

The economic relations in the society where Tess lives, in that era of transition, are especially permeated with profound contradictions and tremendous tension. The system of economic relations in society then is in fact made up of two sub-systems which, although often conspiring to achieve their common end, have fundamental conflicts. The two conflicting sub-systems are the sub-system of patriarchy and the sub-system of capitalism. The contemporary social institutions, as constituents of Tess's cultural setting, are in a certain sense determined by the system of economic relations. Like the economic relations, the contemporary social institutions are also permeated with contradictions and tension. The social institutions are governed both by patriarchy and capitalism. Both patriarchy and capitalism play their roles in the formation and functioning of the implicit identity inequality which implicitly deprives Tess of her equal rights in social activities.

The identity of implicit equality concerns the equal status in the field of implicit identity. Implicit identity inequality receives tacit permission, rather than public support, from social institutions. This kind of inequality is achieved not by the explicit functioning of social institutions, but by the implicit functioning of social institutions. In the individual cultural system of Tess, in the conflict between the identity of implicit equality and the implicit identity inequality, the protagonist suffers from further suppression from social institutions. The conflict between the identity of implicit equality and the implicit identity inequality, contributing to the destructive force of the cultural inappositeness in the dimension of identity, results in Tess's disastrous conclusion.

The conflict between the identity of implicit equality and the implicit identity inequality which Tess experiences is mainly shown in her relationship with Alec d'Urberville. The society in which Tess lives is not only a patriarchal society, but also a capitalist society. Both the patriarchal dimension and the capitalist dimension of the society are related to Tess's experience in the field of implicit identity, different from her experience in the field of explicit identity, which is primarily associated with the dimension of patriarchy. Tess does not want her equal status to sustain implicit harms from society and assumes the identity of implicit equality. Nonetheless, Alec always wants to sexually take advantage of her, against her own will. "Alec d'Urberville, the son of a 'colonizer' from the North [...], behaves like a slave owner, sexually exploiting the local girls." (Bownas, 2012: 129) Alec is a villain who often commits sexual harassment. After he meets Tess and is fascinated by her, this villainous aspect of him is brought under the spotlight by his treatment of Tess. Sexual offences like those committed by Alec upon Tess are also prohibited, condemned, or even considered as crimes in the public discourses of the patriarchal-capitalist society then. However, the status of a rich male provides convenience to Alec's infringement upon Tess as a poor female. In other words, the sexual offences committed by Alec against Tess, which are not allowed publicly by social institutions, get the society's acquiescence. Infringements by Alec receive backing from and constitute a demonstration of the implicit identity inequality of the patriarchal-capitalist society. The implicit identity inequality enables Alec to create a hierarchy of identity with himself as the superior one like a slave owner and the local girls including Tess as the inferior ones like slaves. In a certain sense, the image of Alec as a villain is just an epitome of the implicit identity inequality in the patriarchal-capitalist social institutions.

After claiming kin with the sham d'Urbervilles at Trantridge Parish, Tess accepts a job of keeping poultry at the d'Urberville estate, urged by her parents. The experience of keeping poultry at the d'Urberville estate is the beginning of Tess's career as a member of the proletariat. The acceptance of this job turns Tess into an agricultural worker who works for wages. (聂珍钊, 1992: 214 – 215) She is thus plunged into the sphere of influence of the capitalist institutions of the society. After Tess's acceptance of the job, Alec d'Urberville fetches her from her native village by a fancy vehicle. On the way, Alec drives the vehicle dangerously fast, in order to compel her to put her arms around his waist and even allow him a kiss. "Let me put one little kiss on those holmberry lips, Tess, or even on that warmed cheek, and I'll stop—on my honour, I will!" (Hardy, 1993A: 46) Alec says so. Why dare he say that and behave in that way? Because he is a male, a member of the more powerful gender, and more importantly and decisively, he is rich. Tess, a poor lass, together with her poor family, has to depend upon his sham d'Urberville family for income and for living. Based upon that, Alec never intends to "seeks [seek] her out as a loving, equal partner" (Stave, 1995: 111). The social institutions of patriarchy-capitalism do not explicitly allow him to behave in that way, and the explicit discourses of social institutions would label him as a villain. However, the same social institutions render him the force to do what he has done and he gets implicit approval for his sexual harassment from society. Backed by the implicit identity inequality, it is extremely difficult or utterly impossible for Alec to get due punishment. Driven by her identity of implicit equality, Tess feels incensed at Alec's sexual advances, and after some forced yielding, she decides to go to Trantridge on her own feet. The conflict between the identity of implicit equality and the implicit identity inequality leads to this initial confrontation between Tess and Alec, which leads to a sequence of sufferings that contribute to Tess's disastrous conclusion.

On the d'Urberville estate, Tess begins her management of a fowl-farm. Alec, taking advantage of his more powerful status in the patriarchal-capitalist society, continues to sexually harass Tess, plunging Tess into a vexing and helpless state. During a late night walk back from a market, Tess has a quarrel with some female companions because of their envy of her beauty and favor with men. In an irritated and extremely tired state, Tess accepts Alec's offer to give her a ride back. Alec purposefully drives off the normal path and into an ancient wood called The Chase, which is especially bewildering in the dense fog and dense night that day. Despite her extreme exhaustion and helplessness, Tess resolutely fends against the sexual advances of Alec and demands to walk home by herself. However, when Alec leaves her alone to search for directions, Tess falls asleep. When back, Alec uses this chance and takes advantage of her sexually. Afterwards, in great agonies, Tess returns to her own home, asserting her equal identity. This is the first summit of the suffering of Tess, which constitutes one of the critical links that lead to her disastrous conclusion. The narrator of Tess's story says, "why [Why] so often the coarse appropriates the finer thus, the wrong man the woman, the wrong woman the man, many thousand years of analytical philosophy have failed to explain to our sense of order." (Hardy, 1993A: 65) In this case, the implicit identity inequality leads to the appropriation of the finer by the coarse. The implicit identity inequality, compared to the explicit identity inequality, can more easily evade from people's observation and analytical power; therefore it is more dangerous. Alec and Angel are identical to each other in the sense that they both represent identity inequality. "Both accept in its totality the patriarchal dictum that women are somehow at fault, tainted, for being sexual beings." (Stave, 1995: 110) To be brief, both refuse to regard females as equal beings. Alec differs from Angel in that he represents the implicit identity inequality furtively rather than the explicit identity inequality openly.

By his superior status in the economic structure and the economic dependence of the Durbeyfields upon him and his family, Alec secures the social power to tightly keep Tess under his lustful claws. Once the chance comes, he can sexually take advantage of Tess unfairly. The sexual assault of Tess by Alec is not openly allowed by the social institutions then, and in the public discourses of the patriarchal-capitalist society then Alec's deed shall be classified as a disgraceful fault or even a felony. However, the patriarchal-capitalist social institutions then provide him with the resources and the guts to do that. Under the patriarchal-capitalist social institutions, it is difficult for Tess to seek the punishment of Alec, and besides, the seeking process itself can bring serious damage to herself in the ideological atmosphere of the society then. Therefore, it could be said that although the deed of Alec is not supported actively by social institutions, it is made possible tacitly by them and accepted passively by them. The unpunished sexual assault of Tess by Alec manifests the implicit identity inequality then. Tess cannot dwell in her world with her identity of implicit equality being socially supported. "For Hardy true or authentic dwelling in an existential sense in the second half of the nineteenth century is inaccessible, so removed have his characters become from their worlds, as a result of their modernity." (Wolfreys, 2009: 184) Tess is one typical Hardy-type character who is removed from her world in an alienated manner of dwelling. This alienation of dwelling consists in the confrontation between her identity of equality and the identity inequality in social institutions, which is realized both on the explicit level and on the implicit level. The identity of implicit equality of Tess does not allow her to accept the humiliation from Alec and compels her to return home. The severe conflict between the identity of implicit equality and the implicit identity inequality generates deep-rooted hatred in the heart of Tess, which, accumulating and stimulated, finally results in her killing of Alec, together with her own disastrous conclusion.

The conflict between Tess's identity of implicit equality and the implicit identity inequality is also shown in the later phase of Tess's relationship with Alec. Deserted by Angel Clare, the life of Tess sinks into mental agonies and economic difficulties. Alec again appears, setting in motion another round of sufferings for Tess, which more evidently shows "the ever-widening circles of Alec's power as Tess vainly strives to outstrip it" (Musselwhite, 2003: 93). Alec, formerly converted by Reverend Clare, Angel's father, and devoting himself to missionary work, gives up his faith and renews his harassment of Tess, his lustful side re-stimulated by Tess's beauty. Tess repeatedly fends off his advances. Later, Tess's father dies and leaves the family in direr conditions. They are no longer qualified to live in their old house and have to look for some alternative shelter. At last, they settle their bed in an aisle of the church of Kingsbere, the ancestral place of the d'Urbervilles. The more serious the difficulties of the Durbeyfield family are, the more advantages over Tess Alec gathers at his claws. Beside the ancestral tombs of the d'Urbervilles, Alec boasts of his power towards Tess, "The little finger of the sham d'Urberville can do more for you than the whole dynasty of the real underneath..." (Hardy, 1993A: 320) The power of which Alec boasts comes from the capitalist social institutions. His economic advantages over Tess put him in a powerful social position which enables him to drag Tess back to him. With a homeless family, and with highly limited economic resources at her disposal, Tess is left in a social position with little freedom to make a choice out of her own accord. Besides, the patriarchal social institutions then, although do not encourage a man to use his economic resources as the primary means to gain advantages in the pursuit of a woman's emotions or the settlement of a marriage, acquiesce in this kind of behavior and tacitly consider it a natural occurrence. However, the patriarchal social institutions hold the same matter in the opposite direction, namely that done by a woman to a man, in much ridicule. In brief, social institutions of the capitalist-patriarchal society, without public approval, give inactive and tacit consent to Alec's "re-enslavement" of Tess against her own will by economic means. In this process, the implicit identity inequality shows itself. Again left in the grip of Alec, Tess finds that Angel comes back to look for her, out of all expectations and absolutely contrary to Alec's prediction. Finding that Alec again ruins the hope of her life and permanently deprives her of the chance for love, Tess plunges into a crazy state. She says, "My little sisters and brothers and my mother's needs—they were the things you moved me by ... O, you have torn my life all to pieces..." (Hardy, 1993A: 335) Treating the needs for survival of Tess's family members as her weakness which can be exploited, Alec maximizes his social advantage over Tess and eventually fulfills his purpose. Tess feels her life has been torn all to pieces; the most important cause of this feeling is that her identity of implicit equality suffers bitterly under the weight of implicit identity inequality. In the fierce conflict between the identity of implicit equality and implicit identity inequality, Tess loses control of herself and stabs Alec to death, which results in her execution, the disastrous conclusion.

3.3 *The Mayor:* The Conflict Between the Identity as a Patriarch and the Modernized Identity Mechanism

Michael Henchard, the protagonist in *The Mayor*, identifies himself as a patriarch. He is a "patriarch who holds fast to the traditional patriarchal society". (鲁春芳, 2006: 91) Nevertheless, in Henchard's cultural setting, the modernized identity mechanism is in a dominant position. The conflict between the identity as a patriarch and the modernized identity mechanism plunges Henchard's individual cultural system into inappositeness in the dimension of identity. The conflict between the identity as a patriarch and the modernized identity mechanism gives rise to Henchard's death in despair, his disastrous conclusion. From another perspective, it can also be said that the inappositeness of the individual cultural system in the dimension of identity exerts a negative influence upon Henchard's life and gives rise to his disastrous conclusion. From Raymond Williams's perspective, in the development of society, there is "a cultural struggle about ways of life and between ways of life" (Eldridge, Eldridge, 1994: 66). In Henchard's individual cultural system, the struggle "between ways of life" is embodied in the conflict between the identity as a patriarch and the modernized identity mechanism and it powerfully influences the protagonist's course of life. With his identity in conflict with the requirements of the cultural setting, Henchard is plunged into the status of an outcast. "As an outcast, Henchard gains identification with the alienated figure of Sisyphus who knew that he was fated to be destroyed." (Pandey, 2001: 138) Like Sisyphus, a figure in Albert Camus's works, Henchard gets alienated from his surroundings. Henchard suffers from pains which originate from identity conflict and in alienation he is moved towards a disastrous conclusion by the conflict.

The conflict between the identity as a patriarch and the modernized identity mechanism experienced by Henchard is first revealed in the relationship between him and his wife Susan. He does not treat his wife as an equal family member. Instead, he treats her as a subordinate and inferior person who is possessed by him like an inanimate object. This mentality proves his self-defined identity as a patriarch. Henchard's identity as a patriarch in his marital relationship is most evidently found in the initiating episode of his story. In the beginning of the novel, Henchard and Susan walk shoulder by shoulder on the way towards Weydon-Priors. However, rather than conduct some communication with his wife or at least make communication possible, Henchard "was reading, or pretending to read, a ballad sheet" (Hardy, 1994: 1), just ignoring her. From this manner of Henchard it can be seen that he lacks the respect for Susan, which is a reflection of his self-defined identity as a patriarch. Later in a porridge tent, under the stimulation of the liquor mixed in the porridge, Henchard endlessly complains about his marriage and his wife and even offers to sell his wife by auction. " 'For my part I don't see why men who have got wives, and don't want 'em, shouldn't get rid of 'em as these gypsy fellows do their old horses,' said the man in the tent. 'Why shouldn't they put' em up and sell 'em by auction to men who are in want of such articles? Hey? Why, begad, I'd sell mine this minute if anybody would buy her!'" (Hardy, 1994: 5–6) The stimulation of alcohol is only a minor one among the factors that cause Henchard's complaint of his wife and his offer to sell her by auction, while the self-defined identity as a patriarch is one of the major and decisive factors that cause such behavior of Henchard. It can be said that the selling of the wife by Henchard clearly shows ideas of patriarchy. (高万隆, 2009: 175) In line with the identity as a patriarch, Henchard occupies a superior position in the marital hierarchy. In that way, his wife is inferior to him, subordinate to him, and even possessed by him as a piece of property. Henchard compares wives to horses and lists them among articles; from that it can be seen that Henchard holds strong patriarchal ideas upon which his identity as a patriarch is based. That way of comparison and denotation reveals the seriousness and stubbornness of Henchard to place himself at the identity as a patriarch.

The society in *The Mayor* is going through a process in which patriarchy gives way to modernism. (In this book, the term modernism refers to a kind of social paradigm and the worldview that validates the social paradigm; the social paradigm and the worldview appeared and developed after the Enlightenment. The modernism discussed in this book shall be differentiated from the modernism as a school of literary creation and literary criticism which appeared at the end of the nineteenth century and flourished in the first half of the twentieth century.) Charles E. Bressler writes, "For many historians and literary theorists alike, the Enlightenment or the Age of Reason (18th century) is synonymous with modernism." (Bressler, 2004: 96) He also writes, " At the center of this view of the world lie two prominent features: a belief that reason is humankind's best guide to life, and that science, above all other human endeavors, could lead humanity to a new promised land." (Bressler, 2004: 96) Modernism, drawing upon the intellectual resources of the Enlightenment, attaches much importance to reason and science. The spirit of reason lies at the core of modernism. Due to the worship of reason, modernism tends to identify human beings by their common role as possessors of reason rather than by their different social status. Therefore, in modernism, the worship of reason naturally leads to the approval and advocacy of equality. The approval and advocacy of equality in modernism are also promoted by the development of modern commercialism. Modern commercialism is one of the major aspects of the modernism as a social paradigm. Modern commercialism pays much attention to the spirit of reciprocity and the reciprocity of different parties on an equal basis is much valued. As a consequence, in the modern social paradigm, reciprocity replaces hierarchy and equality replaces subordination. In the society where Henchard lives, modernism has gained obvious advantages over traditional patriarchy. Under the conspicuous influence of the modernized identity mechanism, Susan has developed some ideas about the equality of identity. The unreasonable complaint about her and the offer to sell her by her husband are really repugnant to her and they profoundly hurt her feelings. Incensed by her husband's inquiry about whether or not anybody will buy her, Susan expresses her indignation. "'I wish somebody would,' said she firmly. 'Her present owner is not at all to her liking!'" (Hardy, 1994: 7) Driven by the modernized identity mechanism, Susan's dissatisfaction with her husband's attitudes and practices based upon the self-defined identity as a patriarch is on the increase. Finally, the sailor Newson accepts the offer and buys Susan. The woman, together with her little daughter Elizabeth-Jane, leaves with him.

The conflict between the identity as a patriarch and the modernized identity mechanism drags Susan, together with the little daughter, away from Henchard. That is the first major blow to Henchard in his life and the source for all later blows which conspire in bringing about the man's death in despair, his disastrous conclusion. In a broader sense, the conflict between the identity as a patriarch and the modernized identity mechanism in the relationship between Henchard and Susan plunges the marital life of the couple into a distorted state, which constitutes a source of Henchard's disastrous conclusion.

The conflict between the identity as a patriarch and the modernized identity mechanism is also demonstrated in the relationship between Henchard and Farfrae. Farfrae once helps Henchard resolve the problem of the grown wheat. Out of gratitude and admiration, also out of the hope to bring his business to greater prosperity, Henchard insistently invites Farfrae to stay and assume the office of the manager of the corn branch of his business. At first, the two get along well and cooperate well with each other. However, as time elapses, problems reveal themselves. There is an employee named Abel Whittle in the corn business. Whittle always oversleeps and comes late for work, keeping others waiting for him. One day, Henchard commands that Whittle must be in time the next morning, but the young man still comes late. Henchard flies into a rage and swears that if Whittle is late again, he will drag him out of bed. The next day, however, the young man still does not appear when then time comes. Enraged, Henchard goes to Whittle's home and shouts at him, "Out of bed, sir, and off to the granary, or you leave my employ today! 'Tis to teach ye a lesson. March on; never mind your breeches!" (Hardy, 1994: 76) Henchard forces

Whittle to go to work without giving him enough time to dress himself decently. In a disadvantaged position, Whittle has no choice but to obey the command of his boss. Nevertheless, the young man feels much humiliated and claims that he will kill himself. The tyrannical treatment of Whittle by Henchard is based upon his self-defined identity as a patriarch. This identity is extended by Henchard into the sphere of commerce. According to his identity as a patriarch, Henchard commands absolute superiority over his employees who are personally affiliated with and subordinated to him. Henchard believes that there is a hierarchy of identity among the boss and the employees which authorizes him to blame Whittle and command him to do things without paying heed to his self-esteem and dignity. Seeing the humiliated Whittle, Farfrae as the manager tells him to return home and dress decently for work. He says, "Get back home, and slip on your breeches, and come to wark like a man!" (Hardy, 1994: 76) Under the influence of the modernized identity mechanism, Farfrae holds the view that employees have the right to dignity and the right to an equal identity. Employees work for the boss in return for payment, and the process does not involve the affiliation of individuality or the subordination of identity. As a consequence, Farfrae takes the resolution to free Whittle from the shame which he deems unreasonable. Moreover, he emphasizes that the demeanor of Whittle shall be becoming for a man. That is a recognition of his identity as an unsubordinated man with unalienable decency. In contrast to that, driven by the self-assumed identity as a patriarch, Henchard insists that Whittle instantly rush to work. Afterwards Henchard says, "Why did you speak to me before them like that, Farfrae? You might have stopped till we were alone." (Hardy, 1994: 77) In this incident, the conflict between the identity as a patriarch and the modernized identity mechanism is not only projected upon the treatment of Whittle but also projected upon the requirement for the behavioral pattern of Farfrae as the manager in the business. According to the self-assumed identity as a patriarch, Henchard thinks that Farfrae shall show unconditioned obedience to him, especially in public. Nevertheless, Farfrae, driven by the modernized identity mechanism, holds the opinion that he can challenge the command of Henchard as long as he has a well-established reason. The focus of the difference is still the equality and inequality of identity. Disappointed with Farfrae, Henchard even thinks Farfrae's daring challenge of the hierarchy in the business is a result of the fact that he has confided in him his top secret. He does not realize the crisis of his self-assumed identity as a patriarch and the crisis of patriarchy itself. Although Henchard shows regrets for the confrontation with Farfrae, the conflict between the identity as a patriarch and the modernized identity mechanism is not resolved and does not show any prospect of resolution.

After the unpleasant experience about Abel Whittle, Henchard and Farfrae enter into another clash as the news comes that a festive day is to be observed in celebration of a national event. Farfrae organizes amusements which overwhelmingly surpass those organized by Henchard. Irritating to the ears of Henchard are jests like "Cut ye out quite, hasn't he?" and "he's beat you" (Hardy, 1994: 83), etc. In accordance with his self-defined identity as a patriarch in his business, Henchard can keep Farfrae in an inferior position; in that case, the employee's accomplishments which overshadow the boss would be considered as improper. Due to the sense of failure which is intensified by jokes about the superiority of the employee, the mind of Henchard plunges out of balance. Contrary to Henchard's expectations, influenced by the modernized identity mechanism, Farfrae tries his best to bring success to the amusements without paying any attention to the possibility of any displeasure on the part of his boss. Eventually, Henchard dismisses Farfrae. As discussed before, the negative tendency in Henchard's disposition plays a role in the dismissal of Farfrae. Nevertheless, the conflict between the identity as a patriarch and the modernized identity mechanism also constitutes an agent in precipitating that decision. Under the influence of the modernized identity mechanism, Farfrae considers the intense reaction by Henchard is especially unreasonable. Thinking and acting according to the self-assumed identity as a patriarch, Henchard cannot really understand Farfrae, either. In the conflict between the identity as a patriarch and the modernized identity mechanism, Henchard loses his valuable business cooperator. Gradually, Henchard gets into business competition with Farfrae and the newcomer gets the upper hand in the confrontation and leaves his former boss in bankruptcy. After his business failure, Henchard still wears his merchant garments, which are already quite old and frayed. "the [The] clothes Henchard chooses to wear imply a complex appreciation of his situation and what he means by his appearance." (Gatrell, 2011: 46) The clothes function as a token of the upper social stratum and meet Henchard's psychological need for the dignity of a patriarch. The retained old clothes constitute another demonstration of Henchard's self-defined identity as a patriarch. The conflict between the identity as a patriarch and the modernized identity mechanism stubbornly haunts Henchard's life and does harm to his relationship with Farfrae. The chasm between Henchard and Farfrae is brought into being by the conflict and is ever widened. Moreover, due to the conflict, the antagonism between the two men increases. These results of the conflict in the dimension of identity lead to Henchard's downfall in business and eliminate his chance of resurrection in business, giving rise to his death in despair, his disastrous conclusion.

3.4   The Ideas about Identity in *Tess* and Their Historical Significance

Tess demonstrates the conflict between the identity of explicit equality and the explicit identity inequality and the conflict between the identity of implicit equality and the implicit identity inequality which result in the protagonist Tess's disastrous conclusion. In this process of demonstration, two layers of information can be found. On the first layer, it is shown that the identity of explicit equality and the identity of implicit equality contribute to the development of Tess as a human being. Thereby the novel achieves the approval of the identity of equality. On the second layer, it is shown that the explicit identity inequality and the implicit identity inequality do harm to the identity of explicit equality and the identity of implicit equality as well as the development of Tess as a human being. Moreover, it is emphasized that the oppression of the identity of explicit equality by the explicit inequality and the oppression of the identity of implicit equality by the implicit inequality, eventually realize their respective functions in the creation of the disastrous conclusion of Tess. Thereby the novel develops the anxiety that unfavorable conditions in society may jeopardize the identity of equality and pose threats to individuals and the society.

In *Tess*, the protagonist Tess defines herself both by the identity of explicit equality and by the identity of implicit equality. Through thus defining herself, she epitomizes the identity of explicit equality and the identity of implicit equality. By virtue of the identity of explicit equality and the identity of implicit equality, Tess realizes the importance of her own dignity, which is of essential importance for her development as a human being. The self-defined identity of explicit equality of Tess is mainly embodied in her relationship with her husband Angel, and the self-defined identity of implicit equality of Tess is mainly embodied in her relationship with her persecutor Alec. At the Talbothays Dairy, Tess meets Angel. With the days passing by, they fall in love with each other. In getting along with Angel, Tess thinks that her identity of equality should be explicitly guaranteed by social institutions. That constitutes an assertion of the right of a human being with a full character. In the evening of their wedding, Tess and Angel confess their former missteps to each other. Based upon her identity of explicit equality, Tess expects that her forgiveness of Angel's misstep could be requited by his forgiveness of that of hers. However, out of Tess's expectation, Angel bitterly condemns her and eventually discards her by going to Brazil alone. Being put on the basis of equal identity, the misstep of Tess is much less serious than that of Angel's. Angel makes his judgement and decision under the control of the explicit identity inequality in social institutions. The patriarchal social institutions explicitly establish a hierarchy between men and women, imposing much more seriousness upon Tess's misstep than upon that of Angel. Urged by social institutions explicitly, he refuses to give a just assessment of their respective faults on an equal basis. That is in essence a refusal to admit Tess as one human being with the full character. After being abandoned by Angel, Tess occupies herself with the long wait for her husband's return. In this process which tortures her much, Tess feels the indifference and cruelty of Angel, and she experiences the tremendous pressure that the explicit inequality imposes upon her identity of explicit equality. The explicit identity inequality has been doing harm to Tess's identity of explicit equality and her development as a human being.

At the beginning of the novel, Tess's father John Durbeyfield learns from a person that he is a descendant of a noble family called the d'Urbervilles. Overjoyed at their august lineage, the parents of Tess urge their daughter to visit Mrs. d'Urberville to claim kin and make use of the kinship to solicit financial aid for the family. At the d'Urberville estate, Tess meets Alec. Tess upholds the self-defined identity of implicit equality and does not expect her equal identity to be impinged upon implicitly by social institutions. This attitude of Tess helps her to gain the dignity of a human being with the full character. However, Alec harasses her and finally takes advantage of her sexually. Alec's deeds are not supported or allowed explicitly by the patriarchal-capitalist social institutions then. Nevertheless, the patriarchal-capitalist social institutions equip Alec with the power and convenience to carry out his deeds and make the punishment of Alec difficult or even impossible. In other words, the patriarchal-capitalist social institutions acquiesce in Alec's deeds and implicitly support his unfair treatment of Tess. Backed by the social institutions implicitly, Alec contrives to take advantage of Tess sexually in an unfair way. That is a humiliation of Tess's character as a human being with the inalienable right to dignity. Suffering the abuses from Alec, Tess feels the tremendous pressure that the implicit identity inequality inflicts upon her identity of implicit equality. The implicit identity inequality does harm to her identity of implicit equality and her development as a human being.

Receiving unfair treatments from Angel as a representative of the explicit identity inequality and from Alec as a representative of the implicit identity inequality, Tess feels her self-defined identity of equality is in difficult circumstances. After a long wait for Angel, which seems endless, Tess again falls into the scope of power of Alec, who tries to regain her, taking advantage of the difficulties that haunt Tess and her family. One day, Tess steps into the ancestral sepulcher of her noble family. "she [She] bent down upon the entrance to the vaults, and said—'Why am I on the wrong side of this door!'" (Hardy, 1993A: 320) Being tortured both in the explicit way and in the implicit way, Tess feels her identity of equality cannot possibly prop up some space for its own continuous existence. Living in this world, she has to give up her identity of equality or at least modify it considerably; if she sticks to the identity of equality, maybe she can only go to the other side of the door of the vaults. On the one hand, by manifesting the benefits that the identity of equality brings to Tess's development as a human being, the novel achieves the approval of the identity of equality. On the other hand, the identity inequality in social institutions does harm to the identity of equality of Tess and her development as a human being. Finally, the oppression of the identity of equality by the identity inequality realizes its function in the creation of Tess's disastrous conclusion. Thereby the novel *Tess* develops the anxiety that unfavorable conditions in society may jeopardize the identity of equality and pose threats to individuals and the society. The approval of the identity of equality and the anxiety about the vulnerable position of this identity in the society which could be perceived in *Tess* correspond to Matthew Arnold's cultural notions which advocate the equality among people. The approval of the identity of equality and the anxiety about the vulnerable position of this identity in society constitute a literary interpretation of the idea of equality in Matthew Arnold's cultural notions.

The idea of equality is one key element in Matthew Arnold's cultural notions. Arnold says, "Certainly equality will never of itself alone give us a perfect civilisation, but with such inequality as ours, a perfect civilisation is impossible." (Arnold, 1993: 238) In Arnold's view, the English society of his time is plagued by the belief in inequality among human beings. He holds the opinion that inequality undermines the basis of the civilization of England and on the contrary equality could pave the way for that civilization's redemption and development. Due to the inequality in England, the upper class gets preoccupied with materiality, the middle class gets immersed in vulgarity and the lower class gets lost in brutality. (Arnold, 1993: 236) In contrast to that, in France, equality has admirably and enviably advanced humanization, the emancipation of humanity. (Arnold, 1993: 226,221) From the perspective of Arnold, inequality in England places aristocracy in possession of enormous wealth, immense luxury and unparalleled secular prosperity. Indulging in and preoccupied with material interests, the upper class, or the aristocracy, is deprived of the ability to devote adequate energy to the cause of humanization. In the social context of inequality, the middle class, disappointed by the insurmountable difficulties of obtaining the material interests of aristocracy, abandons itself in vulgarity. The middle class gives up the pursuit of refinement and elegance, and in the end the pursuit of humanization. Moreover, the lower class, or the working class, suffers from a kind of disillusion from the utter impossibility of obtaining the material interests of the aristocracy. The lower class thus abandons itself in brutality, opposite to refinement and elegance, incompatible with the ideal of humanization. As a result, it can be said that in the view of Arnold, the aforementioned classes are all driven away from the ideal of humanization, making the perfect civilization impossible in England. Only by following the example of France and aspiring after the ideal of equality, can the three classes in England solve their respective problems and be restored to a satisfactory state in which adequate preparation can be made for the process of humanization.

The idea of equality is closely related to the ideal of culture in Arnold's cultural notions. Matthew Arnold places much emphasis upon the ideal of culture and in fact the ideal of culture constitutes the core of his cultural notions and social propositions. For Arnold, the ultimate salvation shall be achieved by culture, in social, economic and political ways. From the perspective of Matthew Arnold, the ideal of culture is inevitably linked to equality. The ideal of perfection means the perfection of all people, and the universal perfection constitutes an authentic guarantee of equality. (Lewis, 2002: 116) Arnold hopes that with the function of culture fully exercised, a civilized state of society could be realized. In that state, all members of society could get enlightened by the best knowledge and wisdom available during the contemporary period. In other words, all citizens are vouchsafed the equal right to enjoy the best knowledge and wisdom of the society at a certain time. Matthew Arnold advocates the promotion of an advanced culture which crosses the boundaries between different social strata and unites them in a communal happy life. That constitutes the negation of the justifiability of the inequality between different social strata and a practical proposition to overcome the inequality. Thus, the idea of equality penetrates Arnold's ideal of culture and is placed at a critical place in Arnold's cultural notions.

Arnold places the hope for the realization of his cultural ideal upon the proper exercise of the function of cultural leadership. Cultural leadership means that a group of cultural missionaries shall be chosen and this group of cultural missionaries shall undertake the task of enlightening the common people and bringing best knowledge and wisdom to them. Matthew Arnold classifies people in the society into three groups, the aristocracy, the middle class and the working class. He calls them the Barbarians, the Philistines, and the Populace respectively. In Arnold's view, all the three social groups, weakened by their own disadvantages, cannot satisfactorily administer cultural leadership. "But in each class there are born a certain number of natures with a curiosity about their best self, with a bent for seeing things as they are, for disentangling themselves from machinery, for simply concerning themselves with reason and the will of God, and doing their best to make these prevail; —for the pursuit, in a word, of perfection." (Arnold, 1993: 109) Arnold does not regard any social group as superior to the other two and entrust the cultural leadership entirely to that group. Instead, he proposes to search for cultural missionaries from all three social groups. It can be seen that Arnold considers the three groups as equal social existences. The three social groups play roles of equal significance in the administering of cultural leadership and the promotion and development of culture. The equal roles that are assigned to the three social groups in the matter of culture and culture leadership constitute another perspective from which one can get a glimpse of the idea of equality in Matthew Arnold's cultural notions.

By emphasizing the significance that equality has for civilization and humanization, by advocating the ideal of culture which calls for equality, and by assigning equal roles to the three social classes in the administering of cultural leadership, the cultural notions of Matthew Arnold show the idea of equality. The novel *Tess* interprets the idea of equality in Arnold's cultural notions with its approval of the identity of equality and its anxiety that unfavorable conditions in the society may jeopardize the identity of equality and pose threats to individuals and society. In Arnold's cultural notions, there is a dissatisfaction with the lack of equality in the contemporary society of England. However, there is also the confidence that equality can be established in due course for the development of civilization and humanization, as well as for the realization of the ideal of culture. In contrast to that, *Tess* interprets the idea of equality by the identity of equality which is under threat and the anxiety about the vulnerability of this identity under unfavorable social forces. A gloomy atmosphere is created in the literary interpretation of the idea of equality advocated by Matthew Arnold's cultural notions. There arises an earnestness to remind readers of the grim situation in the promotion of equality in the contemporary era. In the novel, the matter of equality is treated with urgency and there is also the calling for readers to take actions to protect equality against threats and make contributions to the implementation of the idea of equality which is in difficulties.

3.5 The Idea about Identity in *The Mayor* and Its Historical Significance

The Mayor demonstrates the conflict between the identity as a patriarch and the modernized identity mechanism which gives rise to the protagonist Henchard's disastrous conclusion. In this process of demonstration, the justifiability of the identity as a patriarch and patriarchy as a whole is shown. The justifiability of the modernized identity mechanism and modernism as a whole is shown too. Thereby, *The Mayor* develops the inquietude that the entangled relationships between patriarchy and modernism in the era of transition may endanger individuals and the society. (The entangled relationships between patriarchy and modernism have two layers of meanings. First, patriarchy and modernism have disagreements with each other. Therefore, the conflict between the two sides is possible. Second, patriarchy and modernism have their respective justifiability in the era of transition. There is no sign of definite supremacy of one over the other. Therefore, both patriarchy and modernism can easily appeal to people and exert stable influence upon their followers. As a consequence, the probability of the formation of the conflict between the two sides will be greater. Moreover, once the conflict is formed, the difficulty of its resolution will also be greater.)

In the demonstration of the conflict between the identity as a patriarch and the modernized identity mechanism in *The Mayor*, the identity as a patriarch and the modernized identity mechanism, together will the patriarchy and modernism behind them, show their respective justifiability at the same time. First, the advantages of the modernized identity mechanism and the modernism behind it over the identity as a patriarch and the patriarchy behind it are shown in the novel. Thereby the modernized identity mechanism and modernism are justified. According to his self-determined identity as a patriarch, Henchard assumes the right of disposing of his wife at his own discretion and announces that he will sell his wife for his own good. His wife Susan, backed by the arising modernized identity mechanism, first urges him not to do that, then retorts upon him, and at last indignantly goes away with her buyer, a sailor named Newson. The modernized identity mechanism instills in the mind of Susan the idea of identity equality which shields her against the insults from the patriarchal hierarchy of identities. The modernized identity mechanism helps Susan protect the dignity of herself. Spurred by his identity as a patriarch, Henchard bitterly humiliates Abel Whittle for his lateness. Supported by the modernized identity mechanism, Farfrae severely condemns Henchard for his improper handling of the matter. He says, "It is tyrannical and no worthy of you." (Hardy, 1994: 77) Encouraged by the modernized identity mechanism, Farfrae holds the view that the relationships between people with different identities should be built upon the principle of reciprocity and people of different identities are all entitled to the right of equality. As a result, Farfrae regards Henchard's humiliating treatment of Whittle as tyrannical and totally unacceptable. Backed by the modernized identity mechanism, Farfrae helps in the protection of Whittle's dignity. The modernized identity mechanism and the modernism behind it return to people the right to equality which is abolished by the identity as a patriarch and the patriarchy behind it. Thereby the modernized identity mechanism and the modernism behind it protect the dignity of people in lower social strata. In that way, the modernized identity mechanism and the modernism behind it demonstrate their advantages and justifiability.

Second, the advantages of the identity as a patriarch and the patriarchy behind it over the modernized identity mechanism and the modernism behind it are also shown in *The Mayor*. The identity as a patriarch and patriarchy are thus justified in a certain sense Henchard fixes himself at the identity as a patriarch. The self-determined identity as a patriarch pushes him to treat his wife Susan unfairly. According to his identity as a patriarch, Henchard regards his wife as someone subordinate to him. Therefore, he holds the view that he has the right to sell his wife when he wants to do so and he actually does that. His patriarchal view and his deeds worked out accordingly bring much pain to his wife.

However, in another sense, patriarchy also provides a source of stability for the bonds between Henchard and his wife. After their separation, Susan, also influenced by patriarchal ideas to some extent, is always concerned about Henchard and their marriage. On the other side, for a very long time Henchard has always been cherishing the hope of his reunion with Susan and does not consider marrying another woman. It is only after many years when the chance of his first wife being still alive has become very slight that he proposes to another woman Lucetta Templeman, but then Susan appears unexpectedly. Henchard himself comments, "I feel I should like to treat the second, no less than the first, as kindly as a man can in such a case." (Hardy, 1994: 61) But he also says, "My first duty is to Susan—there's no doubt about that." (Hardy, 1994: 61) Henchard is determined to reunite himself with his wife Susan after so many years of wait. Regarding himself as a patriarch, Henchard always retains his sense of duty towards Susan. The identity as a patriarch of Henchard distorts his relationship with his wife in a certain sense, but in another sense, the identity also substantiates the bonds between him and her. In accordance with the doctrines of patriarchy, different identities are placed along a hierarchy. In this case, people with the identities in lower positions are deprived of equality, but interpersonal bonds among identities are unconditionally set and are relatively stable. In accordance with the doctrines of the modernism of which modern commercialism constitutes one major ingredient, different identities are placed upon a reciprocal basis. In this case, people with the identities in lower positions could better enjoy the right to equality and dignity, but interpersonal bonds, as conditioned entities, can more easily break or change along with the development of the concrete conditions of reciprocity. The advantageous aspect of Henchard's identity as a patriarch is also shown in his treatment of Abel Whittle, the employee at his corn business. Whittle is always late for work and he is reprimanded by Henchard mercilessly. In line with his self-determined identity as a patriarch, Henchard does not pay any attention to the dignity of Whittle, treating the employee as a person without self-esteem who is subordinated and affiliated to him. However, in contrast to his humiliating reprimand of Whittle, Henchard also cares for this employee very much. In fact, it is Henchard who "had kept Abel's old mother in coals and snuff all the previous winter" (Hardy, 1994: 77). Due to his identity as a patriarch, Henchard is ready to do benefactions to others beyond the requirement of the principle of reciprocity which receives much emphasis in the modernized social paradigm. Showing the advantages of the identity as a patriarch and the patriarchy, the novel justifies them in a certain sense and expresses tender sentiments towards the rural patriarchal society in Wessex which is on the decline. In this society, the building and maintenance of the bonds between different identities are to a large extent independent of interest relationships. However, in the modernized society, people of different identities build and maintain their bonds according to the principle of reciprocity and interpersonal relationships depend upon material interests to a large extent.

As discussed above, *The Mayor* shows the justifiability of the identity as a patriarch and the patriarchy behind it. At the same time, the novel also shows the justifiability of the modernized identity mechanism and the modernism behind it. In this process, *The Mayor* establishes itself as "a narrative which juxtaposes different historical perspectives" (Tandon, 2003: 474) and becomes the embodiment of "Hardy's skill in juxtaposition" (Tandon, 2003: 474). By virtue of the juxtaposition the novel is endowed with rich historical significance. The society of Wessex, portrayed in the novel as a literary embodiment of the southwestern rural region of England in the late Victorian era, is just experiencing a transition from patriarchy to modernism. In the Wessex depicted by Hardy one can perceive "the process by which the pre-railway world of his [Hardy's] childhood became [becomes] the rapidly mobility of later Victorian England" (Gatrell, 2003: 233). However, "Wessex is a place where pre-Victorian ways of life survive with more than usual tenacity" (Gatrell, 2003: 230). On the one hand, in the society of Wessex, modernism has gained the upper hand over patriarchy and patriarchy is plunged into the process of decline. On the other hand, the problems brought out by modernism also begin to appear. Along with the appearance of those problems, the justifiability of patriarchy becomes visible. Depending upon its justifiability in some respects, patriarchy refuses to totally give up its grip upon humanity. Commenting upon Thomas Hardy, Raymond Williams writes, "Within the major novels, in several different ways, the experiences of change and of the difficulty of choice are central and even decisive." (Williams, 2011B: 197) *The Mayor* just emphasizes the experience of change from patriarchy to modernism. Furthermore, by showing the respective justifiability of patriarchy and modernism, the novel also emphasizes the difficulty of choice between patriarchy and modernism.

Because patriarchy and modernism have disagreements with each other, the conflict between the two sides is possible. Moreover, the respective justifiability of the two sides enables them to appeal to different people and consolidate their grip upon people. Then the conflict between the two sides will be more likely to take place and that conflict, once formed, will be more difficult to resolve. In other words, the conflict between the two sides can more easily take shape and last. The conflict in the dimension of identity in Henchard's individual cultural system, namely the conflict between the identity as a patriarch and the modernized identity mechanism is just precipitated and stabilized by the respective justifiability of patriarchy and modernism. Through showing how the conflict between the identity as a patriarch and the modernized identity mechanism gives rise to Henchard's disastrous conclusion, *The Mayor* develops the inquietude that the entangled relationships between patriarchy and modernism may endanger individuals and the society. This inquietude corresponds to the twofold ideas about the relationship between patriarchy and modernism in Matthew Arnold's cultural notions.

The twofold ideas about the relationship between patriarchy and modernism in Matthew Arnold's cultural notions are based upon the idea of equality and idea of anti-industrialism. The central feature of patriarchy is the abolishment of equality and the idea of equality establishes the justification of modernism as advantageous to patriarchy. The central social embodiment of modernism is industrialism and the idea of anti-industrialism establishes the justification of patriarchy as advantageous to modernism. The idea of equality in Arnold's cultural notions has already been discussed in the previous section and this section will directly go to the discussion of the idea of anti-industrialism. Faced with the moral and spiritual decadence brought about by the industrial revolution, Matthew Arnold hopes that the redemption of humanity and society could be accomplished by the advocacy of culture. "Faith in machinery is, I said, our besetting danger." (Arnold, 1993: 63) Arnold comments upon his contemporaries' firm belief in machinery in this way. Arnold's criticism of the English society of his contemporary period is focused upon the faith in machinery. Machinery, the technological basis for industrialism, makes up a symbol for the era of modernism. Arnold's worry about the faith in machinery and his criticism of that faith provide us with a glimpse of his negative views about industrialism and his anxiety about the era of modernism. "culture [Culture] begets a dissatisfaction which is of the highest possible value in stemming the common tide of men's thoughts in a wealthy and industrial community, and which saves the future, as one may hope, from being vulgarised, even if it cannot save the present." (Arnold, 1993: 65) In the era of modernism, there appears an unprecedented craze for wealth. Industrialism establishes itself as the material basis and an accelerating agent for the modern mania for wealth. From Arnold's view, industrialism, aggravating the faith in machinery and the fanaticism for wealth, can vulgarize the society and cause a lot of social problems. Thus, Arnold protests against industrialism and proposes the promotion of culture as a remedy for the problems brought about by industrialism.

Arnold believes that the cultural system in the contemporary English society is out of balance, with Hebraism being relatively strong and Hellenism being relatively weak. Arnold longs for the revitalization of the relatively weak Hellenism and places his hope for the solving of the problems of industrialism mainly on the re-energized Hellenism and the regained balance between Hebraism and Hellenism. "Matthew Arnold praises highly the quintessence of the culture of wisdom (the culture of ancient Greece), whereby he hopes the perfection of humanity and the harmonious development of society could be achieved and the disorder in the development of the industrial society could be overcome."(肖滨, 2010: 165) The industrial revolution which took place in the West in the 18th and 19th century drastically changed the mode of production and the mode of life. After that, an industrialized society takes shape. In the industrialized society, mechanized mass production, instead of manual operation, functions as the mainstream of the mode of production. The efficiency of production is greatly enhanced and by virtue of that the creation and accumulation of social wealth could be conducted at an unprecedentedly high speed. Promoting the creation and accumulation of social wealth, the industrialized society improves the overall level of the material life of the humankind. However, along with the advantages, the industrialized society also brings about its disadvantages. In that society, the attention of people is focused on the material side of life. Instrumental rationality, as a puissant promoter of material interests, comes to prevail in society. As an ideological catalyst, instrumental rationality in turn worsens people's preoccupation with material interests and the acquisition of material interests. The materialized tendency establishes itself among people. On the microscopic level people become indifferent to spiritual value and on the macroscopic level a kind of spiritual barrenness and spiritual crisis take shape. The spiritual barrenness and spiritual crisis constitute an important feature of the industrialized society. Faced with the spiritual barrenness and spiritual crisis, Matthew Arnold hopes to rejuvenate Hellenism and thereby reach the harmony between Hebraism and Hellenism in English culture. Arnold hopes that by the harmony between Hebraism and Hellenism an ideal culture could be created and from the ideal culture a force of redemption could be attained for the industrialized society. It can be said that the faith in the rejuvenated Hellenism and the regained balance between

Hebraism and Hellenism in Matthew Arnold's cultural notions shows the idea of anti-industrialism from a particular perspective.

While patriarchy abolishes equality, modernism supports equality. The idea of equality in Matthew Arnold's cultural notions naturally leads to the justification of modernism as advantageous to patriarchy. Industrialism is the central social embodiment of modernism. The idea of anti-industrialism in Matthew Arnold's cultural notions naturally leads to the justification of patriarchy as advantageous to modernism. Matthew Arnold's cultural notions are lost between patriarchy and modernism which are in disagreements with each other; those cultural notions implicitly express twofold ideas about the relationship between patriarchy and modernism.

The inquietude that the entangled relationships between patriarchy and modernism may endanger individuals and the society developed in *The Mayor* corresponds to and makes up a literary interpretation of the twofold ideas about the relationship between patriarchy and modernism which are implicitly expressed in Matthew Arnold's cultural notions. In the development of the aforementioned inquietude about the relationship between patriarchy and modernism, the respective justifiability of patriarchy and modernism is demonstrated together with the harmful conflict between the two sides. The conflict between patriarchy and modernism and the personal disaster which arises thereby are clearly shown. In other words, the novel presents an explicit demonstration of the inherent clash between patriarchy and modernism and its unfavorable effects upon individuals and the society. In the interpretation of the twofold ideas about the relationship between patriarchy and modernism, *The Mayor* develops a strong sense of crisis. The novel directly faces the social problems of the period of transition and achieves an analysis of the harmful internal tension of the contemporary social structure. There is an awareness of the imminent dangers in the society then with the disputes between patriarchy and modernism unresolved, and there is also the deliberately worked out cautiousness in handling the relationship between the two social paradigms.

Chapter Four
Cultural Inappositeness in the
Dimension of Value Concept

"Value concept is a general term for the faith, conviction, cognition, emotion and will of an individual or an organization about whether or not things at the present and things in the future possess worth, about what amount of worth they possess, and about what type of worth they should possess." (晏辉, 2009: 34) The value concept determines what an individual pursues in life and it forges an individual's pattern of personal pursuit. The value concept is the orientation of the individual cultural system and it constitutes a major dimension in the system. The inappositeness of the individual value concept, the social mechanism of value or the relationship between the individual value concept and the social mechanism of value will plunge the individual cultural system into inappositeness in the dimension of value concept. The inappositeness of the individual value concept, the social mechanism of value or the relationship between the individual value concept and the social mechanism of value, or in other words, the inappositeness of the individual cultural system in the dimension of value concept, can generate a conspicuous destructive force for the individual's life.

4.1   *Jude:* The Conflict between the Value Concept of Knowledge and the Synchronic Value Hegemony

In the novel *Jude*, the theme of pursuit is made especially prominent. "There is a perpetual sense of rootlessness, of almost trancelike drifting", and accordingly "Motifs [motifs] of wandering and searching dominate the tale". (Vigar, 2013: 192) The actions of the novel are scattered over a wide range of localities. The lack of geographical stability—the frequent shift of geographical settings along with the unfolding of the plot gives rise to the sense of rootlessness. The sense of rootlessness naturally calls for the pursuit of roots in life. The theme of pursuit shown by the protagonist Jude is magnified and strengthened by the sense of rootlessness and its call for roots in life. The value concept determines what one pursues in life and the theme of pursuit corresponds to the theme of value concept in the novel *Jude*. "In his literary creation", Hardy "eulogizes the natural and beautiful emotions and love of human beings, and passionately extols the humanitarian spirits of activeness, enterprise, and freedom" (马弦, 2003: 118). These two elements in the thematic aspect of Hardy's literary creation are epitomized by the value concept of love and the value concept of knowledge in *Jude*. In the internal existence of Jude's individual cultural system, the value concept of knowledge and the value concept of love are obviously manifested. Besides, in the external existence of Jude's individual cultural system, there are the synchronic value hegemony and the diachronic value hegemony. In Raymond Williams's cultural vision, hegemony "involves relations of domination and subordination produced with and as part of multiple and concrete relationships and processes" (O'connor, 1989: 115), which are certain manifestations of social institutions. The synchronic value hegemony and the diachronic value hegemony, as manifestations of certain social institutions in the social environment where Jude lives, constitute important parts of the external existence of Jude's individual cultural system. In the individual cultural system of the protagonist

Jude, there is the conflict between the value concept of knowledge and the synchronic value hegemony and moreover there exists the conflict between the value concept of love and the diachronic value hegemony. The two kinds of conflicts, from their respective angles, together constitute the inappositeness of the relationship between the internal existence and the external existence of the individual cultural system of Jude in the dimension of value concept, which plunges the system into inappositeness in that dimension. The conflict between the value concept of knowledge and the synchronic value hegemony and the conflict between the value concept of love and the diachronic value hegemony, engender a destructive force that brings about Jude's death in disillusion, his disastrous conclusion. It can also be said, from another perspective, that the inappositeness of Jude's individual cultural system in the dimension of value concept generates a destructive force, which brings about the protagonist's disastrous conclusion.

Jude loves reading and study. He hopes that he could enrich his knowledge by his own efforts and then attend the University of Christminster one day. He wishes that, as a person from a humble origin, he could get the recognition of the upper society in that way. Jude craves for knowledge and the social recognition on the basis of knowledge; that constitutes a value concept of knowledge. Nevertheless, in accordance with the social pattern for the allocation of value concepts in which Jude lives, the value concept of knowledge belongs to the upper strata, not the stratum of working people, of which Jude himself is a member. Jude's upholding of the value concept of knowledge, which is expected to belong to the upper social strata exclusively poses a threat to the allocation pattern of values and meets with resistance from the synchronic value hegemony, a significant constituent part of the social mechanism of value then. Under the ruthless attacks from the synchronic value hegemony, Jude appears as "an inspired but naïve dreamer whose only fault is that he lives for a non-existent ideal" (Vigar, 2013: 200). The conflict between Jude's value concept of knowledge and the synchronic value hegemony thus arises. In that conflict, Jude encounters a series of failures in his search for knowledge. Jude's wish to be admitted into the University of Christminster has never been realized and he has never been accepted by the upper social strata. Jude's value concept of knowledge suffers from rounds of blows and the frustration and bitterness arising therefrom eventually drive the protagonist to his disastrous conclusion.

After ten years of hard study and after being freed from the unhappy marriage with Arabella, Jude eventually sets out upon his pilgrimage to the long-dreamed-of Christminster. Once there, he tries to find employment so as to get settled down. Although already in the city of Christminster, there are obstacles virtually insurmountable before Jude's ambition for the university education. In the pursuit of a university education, to try to get qualified for a scholarship seems a good choice for Jude. However, it is exceedingly difficult. "It was next to impossible that a man reading on his own system, however widely and thoroughly, even over the prolonged period of ten years, should be able to compete with those who had passed their lives under trained teachers and had worked to ordained lines." (Hardy, 1993B: 97 – 98) As a youngster who has been raised up in the social stratum of working people, Jude's access to basic education is highly limited. He does not have the opportunity to get the professional guidance which is necessary for the enhancement of his competitiveness for higher education scholarships. The status of Jude in the society deprives him of the equal rights in the competition for a university scholarship. There is still another alternative scheme for Jude, namely to pay for his higher education by himself. Nonetheless, it is extremely difficult for him to deposit enough money. "at [At] the rate at which, with the best of fortune, he would be able to save money, fifteen years must elapse before he could be in a position to forward testimonials to the Head of a College and advance to a matriculation examination." (Hardy, 1993B: 98) As a working-man, Jude has few financial resources at his proposal. He only has a meager income, which is exceedingly insufficient to support his ambition of university education. The economic conditions of Jude do not place him in a social position which can provide him with the material resources to finance his study in the University of Christminster. In the society where Jude lives, there is a synchronic value hegemony which serves for the stabilization of the synchronic pattern for the allocation of value concepts among different social strata. Due to the synchronic value hegemony, embodied in the afore-discussed social conditions facing Jude, the protagonist can utilize neither one of the two alternatives to get admitted into the University of Christminster. The synchronic value hegemony blocks the two alternative ways to the admittance of Jude into the university.

After some hesitation, Jude makes up his mind to initiate the application for getting admitted into the university. He selects five from the heads of the institutions of the university and sends letters to them. However, for a long time, no reply comes. After a long wait, the reply from the head of one of the colleges reaches Jude, however, only to his disappointment. It says, "judging [Judging] from your description of yourself as a working-man, I venture to think that you will have a much better chance of success in life by remaining in your own sphere and sticking to your trade than by adopting any other course." (Hardy, 1993B: 99) On the superficial layer, these words present an unbiased understanding of the aforementioned social conditions that bar Jude from entering the university. On the essential layer, these words are a demonstration of the ideological institutions through which the synchronic value hegemony works. Besides the organizational social institutions, the synchronic value hegemony also functions through the ideological social institutions. In the mind of the college leader, certain values belong to people from certain "spheres" and "trades". The value concept of knowledge, although admirable and respectable when held by a person from the upper strata like himself, can only constitute a kind of arrogation when it is fostered by a person from the lower strata. Members of the upper strata perceive members of the lower strata like Jude in a distracted way, showing blindness to their creativity in the matter of value. The Christminster constitutes "the very symbol of the corrupt exclusiveness of a visionless ruling class, a manifestation of the distracted gaze in its collective rather than its individual form" (Wotton, 1985: 104). In the novel, Christminster is the focus of the functioning of the synchronic value hegemony. The synchronic value hegemony, functioning through the exclusiveness of the ruling class, denies people from lower social strata the right to uphold values which are considered to belong to upper social strata exclusively. In the conflict between his value concept of knowledge and the synchronic value hegemony, Jude suffers from severe "intellectual disappointment" (Hardy, 1993B: 99) and emotional blows, which bring about his mental and physical breakdown and disastrous conclusion.

The ideological functioning of the synchronic value hegemony can not only affect people from the higher social strata but also affect people from the lower social strata. In other words, people from Jude's own social stratum can also demonstrate derogative conceptions of Jude's ambition for the university education and the associated ambition of a clerical life. Immersed in the disappointment at his academic failure, Jude goes to a tavern, abandoning himself in alcohol all day long. In the evening, some frequenters of the tavern appear one after another. Some of these people are from the laboring stratum like Jude himself and some others are undergraduates from the upper strata. They either show disbelief in Jude's academic ability or hold negative opinions about his inordinate ambitions. In a largely ridiculing manner, they challenge Jude to say the Creed in Latin. Although successfully demonstrating his talents and academic achievements by saying the Creed, Jude still could not control his mounting anger and leaves the scene of vanity. "Only don't hate me and despise me like all the rest of the world!" (Hardy, 1993B: 104) Jude later says to Sue. Dominated by the synchronic value hegemony, both people from the higher social strata and people from the lower social strata show misunderstandings of or even contempt for Jude's ambition for the knowledge-centered lifestyle. Tracy A. Ford writes, "Perhaps part of Jude's tragedy is his unwillingness to be what he was, to be satisfied being a stone mason instead of a Doctor of Divinity." (Ford, 2008: 173) However, through the analysis in this section it can be seen that the unwillingness itself cannot bring about Jude's disastrous conclusion. Only when the unwillingness is set in certain social circumstances can Jude's disastrous conclusion be brought into being. In the conflict between the value concept of knowledge and the synchronic value hegemony, Jude is driven to increasing depression and agonies which are an important agent for the triggering of his mental and physical breakdown and disastrous conclusion.

4.2　*Jude*: The Conflict Between the Value Concept of Love and the Diachronic Value Hegemony

In *Jude*, the protagonist Jude's disastrous conclusion also has much to do with the conflict between the value concept of love and the diachronic value hegemony. In the novel, "aspirational desire coheres around and in the body of a Lady" (Thomas, 2013: 97), namely Sue. Moreover, more importantly, the aspirational desire of Jude also focuses upon the spirituality of Sue. Some time after Sue is married to Phillotson, she begins to regret her decision of the marriage. At Sue's invitation, Jude goes to visit her at Shaston. Jude plays upon a piano in the schoolroom. "the [The] vibrating chords of the piano momentarily allow both he and Sue to explore their feelings for one another without the encumbrance of words." (Asquith, 2005: 155) Here, "emotional fulfilment" is embodied "in the quavering chords". (Asquith, 2005: 155) In this case which is of certain significance for the interpretation of Jude's emotional sphere, music provides a chance for the protagonist to probe, demonstrate and communicate his love for Sue. For the greater part of the novel's plot, Jude earnestly pursues the love of Sue and considers love as a spiritual prop which is essential to human happiness. From the perspective of Jude, for love, inner emotion is the embodiment of the essential value and the value of outward form (procedures of marriage) depends on the value of inner emotion. Inner emotion occupies more significance than outward form; and therefore, outward form could be sacrificed for inner emotion if it is necessary. That is Jude's value concept of love. In line with this value concept of love, Jude pursues love together with Sue and following Sue's opinion he lives with her without any procedures or ceremony of marriage. However, in the society where Jude lives, the pursuit of love is required to be carried out within the confines stipulated by social norms and conventions. In the field of love, outward form is considered more important than inner emotion. Inner emotion is regarded as something that can be sacrificed and outward form is regarded as something that can by no means be sacrificed. In that society, love without the procedures and ceremony of matrimony can only receive severe condemnation. Jude's value concept of love challenges the diachronic stability of social values and is thus placed in the conflict with the diachronic value hegemony which serves for the diachronic stability of social values. In this conflict, Jude suffers from the suppression from society and his life is moved towards a disastrous conclusion.

When Jude and Sue find they could only find true love in each other they decide to live together. After their divorces and the farewell to their respective unsuccessful previous marriages, Jude and Sue could get formally and lawfully united in wedlock, and that is a quite natural choice in common eyes. However, Sue appears reluctant to do that. She always tries to elude from or postpone the procedures of marriage. She describes herself as "being proof against the sordid conditions of a business contract again." (Hardy, 1993B: 252) Sue previously had an unsuccessful marriage. She fears that the vow and all the solemnity at the wedding with Jude would be in conflict with those at the wedding with her ex-husband Phillotson. From Sue's perspective, the new solemnity of matrimonial procedures would constitute a negation and total deconstruction of the matrimonial solemnity that she has previously experienced. More importantly and more essentially, the matrimonial procedures, in Sue's view, are just like a "business contract". The adding of a mandatory quality to love constitutes the alienation of love and the abolishment of its value. Thus, according to Sue's value concept of love, the outward form of love not only holds less importance than the inner emotion, but also hampers the inner emotion of love. The sacrifice of love's outward form for inner emotion, in her case, is not only acceptable but also necessary.

Of course, the value concept of love that constitutes the focus of discussion here is that of Jude's. However, the submission of Jude to Sue in the matter of the arrangement of their marriage makes Sue's value concept of love a window from which a glimpse of Jude's value concept of love could be caught. "The intention of the contract is good, and right for many, no doubt; but in our case it may defeat its own ends because we are the queer sort of people we are—folk in whom domestic ties of a forced kind snuff out cordiality and spontaneousness." (Hardy, 1993B: 252) Under the directing of Sue who dismisses the necessity and even the justifiability of matrimonial procedures, Jude develops a somewhat negative view about those procedures. Nevertheless, from Jude's perspective, the reason why their matrimonial procedures can be dispensed with mainly lies in their special characters, which is different from the understanding of Sue. Jude's submission to Sue, his view that matrimonial procedures are not compulsory, and his understanding of the reason why he and Sue can dispense with matrimonial procedures define and reveal his value concept of love. In contrast to Jude's understanding, the society then considers the procedures of marriage as sacred and compulsory, and more significant than the inner emotion for a couple's love. Thus, Jude's value concept of love and the diachronic value hegemony which protects the diachronic stability of social values are driven into direct conflicts. Sue says, "We are a little beforehand, that's all. In fifty, a hundred, years the descendants of these two will act and feel worse than we. They will see weltering humanity still more vividly than we do now, as 'shapes like our own selves hideously multiplied' and will be afraid to reproduce them." (Hardy, 1993B: 252) Sue gets the essence of their condition. Their attitude towards and treatment of matrimonial procedures are untimely rather than wrong. Jude's value concept of love collides with social values along the axis of time. The conflict between the value concept of love and the diachronic value hegemony exerts tremendous pressure upon Jude and moves him towards the disastrous conclusion step by step.

The conflict between the value concept of love and the diachronic value hegemony makes it difficult for Jude to reside in the community. Neighbors show indifference, unfriendliness or even hostility to Jude and his wife Sue. It is difficult for the couple to endure the negative attitudes from others. What's worse, it becomes difficult for Jude to get enough work to make a living. Jude and Sue have to "grapple with the real 'rules' which society has laid down for them" (Vigar, 2013: 203). One time, Jude attains a piece of work for church restoration in a nearby place and undertakes the job together with his wife. However, people there seem to find out something about their history and present conditions. They talk in subdued voices about Jude and his wife's unaccepted mode of life and moreover, the churchwarden tells an anecdote alluding to the inauspiciousness of the couple working there. In the end, the employer of Jude is pressed by the public opinions there to fire Jude. In this incident, Jude together with his wife could feel the suppressive force from the diachronic value hegemony. Later, Jude gets elbowed out from an artisans' mutual help association for the advancement of learning, also because of his unconventional marital life with Sue. "Jude's acquaintances among upwardly mobile members of the working class regard his sexual nonconformity as a slur on their respectability" (Dellamora, 2014: 251); these acquaintances of Jude incarnate the diachronic value hegemony in their own way and deal a further blow to Jude. In accordance with his value concept of love, Jude chooses a lifestyle which, although acceptable some years later, cannot get recognized by his contemporary society. In the conflict between the value concept of love and the diachronic value hegemony, life becomes difficult for Jude both in the material sense and in the spiritual sense, and a gloom is cast upon the protagonist's life. In that way, Jude is driven towards his disastrous conclusion.

The climax of the conflict between the value concept of love and the diachronic value hegemony comes in the last part of the novel. Driven by the needs of life and lured by the university complex, Jude again takes his family to Christminster. Not formally married, it's difficult for Jude and his wife to find lodging in the same place. Jude and Sue "refuse to impose either a legal or a religious sanction upon their union, which they hope to keep free of the misunderstandings and antagonisms that such sanctions appear to precipitate". (Luten, 1992: 293) Under the guidance of the value concept of love, Jude makes the unconventional choice together with Sue. The challenge to the diachronic stability of values incurs punishment from the diachronic value hegemony. The family have to live separately, Sue and the three children being kept away from Jude. Even in this way, they are not popular with the landlord. Sue and the children are refused long-term housing in the place where they first get settled down. Among the three children, there is one boy who is nicknamed Little Father Time because of his precocious and melancholy traits. He is the son of Jude and his first wife Arabella and he is left in the care of Jude and Sue. Little Father Time, in his gloomy and twisted mentality, attributes all those difficulties to the presence of so many children in the family. When the parents are away, the boy commits a horrible deed—he hangs the other two younger children and himself to death. This incident is overwhelmingly destructive for Jude and Sue. From the conversation between the two piteous creatures the magnitude of the devastation of the incident could be felt: " 'Yes ... O my comrade, our perfect union—our two-in-oneness—is now stained with blood!' 'Shadowed by death—that's all.'" (Hardy, 1993B: 300) In line with his value concept of love, Jude pursues and organizes the lifestyle of himself and his wife Sue. The lifestyle is perfect for him, a crystallization of happiness itself. However, the perfect life arrangement comes hand in hand with the bloodiest and cruelest happening to him. The best and the worst become inseparable twins for him. This perverse combination is a devastating shock to the psyche of Jude. In the aggravated conflict between the value concept of love and the diachronic value hegemony, Jude is thrown into excessive bewilderment and agony which add to the momentum towards his mental and physical breakdown and disastrous conclusion.

　　The unnatural death of the children is devastating for Jude, but what's even more devastating is the betrayal by Sue of their love and shared mode of life which is an aftermath of the children's death. Sue thinks that the killing of her children born out of wedlock by the son of Arabella born in wedlock is the punishment from God. She develops the view that her challenge to matrimonial conventions and social values incurs the doom. As a result, Sue chooses to turn her back upon Jude and returns to her ex-husband Phillotson. After that, Jude is also cheated into marrying Arabella again. In depression, Jude develops serious inflammation of lungs. In his serious disease, Jude's only hope is to see Sue once again even at the cost of his life. With the malicious disease which attempts to grab at his life and in the rampant rain which shows no mercy at his situation, Jude trudges to Marygreen to look for Sue. Although Sue does not deny her unchanged love for Jude, she refuses to return to Jude. With her original view about love and marriage overthrown, Sue changes herself into a forced yet stubborn representative of the diachronic value hegemony which wreaks havoc upon the psyche of Jude. "I would never come to see you again, even if I had the strength to come, which I shall not have any more. Sue, Sue, you are not worth a man's love!" (Hardy, 1993B: 343) Once Jude's ally in the pursuit of love, Sue has been completely tamed by the diachronic value hegemony. The diachronic value hegemony deprives Jude of his beloved one and tortures his heart together with his value concept of love. In the aggravated conflict between the value concept of love and the diachronic value hegemony, Jude is driven to complete disillusion at last. The trudge in the rain takes away the last drop of vitality in Jude and his life soon withers. In the conflict between the value concept of love and the diachronic value hegemony, Jude goes to the final mental and physical breakdown, and to the death in disillusion, his disastrous conclusion.

4.3   *The Native:* The Conflict Between the Exterior-Oriented Value Concept and the Interior-Oriented Value Mechanism

In *The Native*, the individual value concept of the protagonist Clym is an exterior-oriented value concept. He regards his service for others as the source of value. Nevertheless, the cultural setting in which he lives demonstrates an interior-oriented value mechanism. Under the control of the interior-oriented value mechanism, people regard the advancement of one's own prosperity as the source of value, showing indifference to others. The conflict between the exterior-oriented value concept and the interior-oriented value mechanism plunges the individual cultural system of Clym into inappositeness in the dimension of value concept. The inappositeness of the individual cultural system in the dimension of value concept generates a negative force which leads to Clym's ending in rejection, his disastrous conclusion. It can also be said that the conflict between the exterior-oriented value concept and the interior-oriented value mechanism leads to the disastrous conclusion of Clym.

Clym returns from Paris to Egdon Heath, supposedly for the celebration of Christmas. However, after some days have elapsed he does not show any intention to go back to Paris, which is quite unnatural. Clym reveals to the villagers at Egdon Heath that he will not go to Paris again and he intends to found a school for the heath. He says, "[...] my [My] business was the idlest, vainest, most effeminate business that ever a man could be put to. [...] I would give it up and try to follow some rational occupation among the people I knew best, and to whom I could be of most use." (Hardy, 1995: 144) The position as the manager of a diamond business in Paris means higher social status for Clym. In that position, he can lead a wealthy life. People around him will regard him as someone capable and successful, and pay their respect and admiration to him. However, Clym is by no means satisfied with this position. This position cannot provide what he pursues in life. He considers the service that he can do to others instead of the advancement of his own prosperity as the source of value and the target of his lifelong pursuit. As a consequence, he chooses to stay on the heath and start a school, which he deems as a proper way to serve his fellow villagers. The fellow villagers themselves, under the control of the interior-oriented value mechanism, hold a view contrary to that of Clym's about the same matter. Hearing that Clym plans to stay and start a school, one villager says, "He'll never carry it out in the world." (Hardy, 1995: 144) Another says, "I think he had better mind his business." (Hardy, 1995: 144) Under the control of the interior-oriented value mechanism, villagers at Egdon Heath hold the view that the source of one's value is the advancement of one's own prosperity. They believe that one shall naturally concentrate upon the pursuit of one's own prosperity in life, and a choice harmful for one's own prosperity is not understandable or natural for him or her. Therefore, they either think that Clym would change his mind or think that he has made a mistake in his choice. The exterior-oriented value concept and the interior-oriented value mechanism are in conflict and that conflict sets the development of the relationship between Clym and his fellow villagers in a direction which is not so favorable.

The conflict between the exterior-oriented value concept and the interior-oriented value mechanism is also revealed in the relationship between Clym and his mother Mrs. Yeobright. Clym resolves to stay on Egdon Heath and serve the residents there, but Mrs. Yeobright cannot accept his son's decision. Clym says, "[...] I hate that business of mine, and I want to do some worthy thing before I die. As a schoolmaster I think to do it—a schoolmaster to the poor and ignorant, to teach them what nobody else will." (Hardy, 1995: 147) Clym regards the founding of a school and the education and enlightenment of the local residents as a worthy thing which he must do before he dies. He considers this cause as the way towards the achievement of value. Due to the harsh natural environment of Egdon Heath, residents there could only lead a meagre life both in the material sense and in the spiritual sense. By receiving education in the school that Clym plans to found for the heath, the local residents may get a new chance and acquire new abilities to pursue a more prosperous material life. More important for Clym, they, by virtue of the enlightenment they may attain in the school, can possibly enrich themselves and get rid of the ignorance that they have already got accustomed to and deemed as nothing unnatural. Then they can also lead an intellectually prosperous life. As a result, Clym holds the view that the local residents are really in need of his service. Clym thinks, by rendering service to the folks at Egdon Heath, he can realize his value. The value that Clym pursues consists in the service that he renders to others instead of the advancement of his own prosperity. Therefore, the individual value concept of Clym is an exterior-oriented value concept. Clym's mother Mrs. Yeobright says, "After all the trouble that has been taken to give you a start, and when there is nothing to do but to keep straight on towards affluence, you say you will be a poor man's schoolmaster. Your fancies will be your ruin, Clym." (Hardy, 1995: 147) Mrs. Yeobright thinks that Clym shall persistently pursue his own affluence which is the really valuable thing in his life. Many efforts have been made for setting Clym on the route towards personal prosperity. In the view of Mrs. Yeobright, the aim of personal prosperity is worthy of all these efforts and the efforts have been set in a justifiable direction. However, out of all her expectations, Clym resolves to deviate into another direction, sacrificing his personal prosperity for the interests of others. From the perspective of Mrs. Yeobright, Clym's choice is not understandable and totally wrong. By his new course of life, Clym's value will collapse and he can only go to ruin. It can be inferred that Mrs. Yeobright is under the influence of the interior-oriented value mechanism. Under that value mechanism, Mrs. Yeobright regards the advancement of Clym's own prosperity rather than the service to others as the source of his value. As a result, the choice to bid farewell to his way towards personal affluence and start a trudge towards the service for others, in Mrs. Yeobright's view, constitutes the destruction of value rather than the construction of value. Therefore, Mrs. Yeobright is resolutely against Clym's choice and plan. The conflict between the exterior-oriented value concept and the interior-oriented value mechanism generates an ever-widening crack in the relationship between Clym and Mrs. Yeobright. Thereby unpleasantness and estrangement increase between the mother and the son.

　　The conflict between the exterior-oriented value concept and the interior-oriented value mechanism reveals itself in the relationship between Clym and Eustacia too. "The perspective of Clym's psychic world differs from Eustacia's from the outset. His characterization is based on idealistic intentions of speeding up social change, but he lacks the connotations of mystery and slumbering power of Eustacia that are developed through 'Queen of Night.'" (Kramer, 1975: 51) The mind of Clym is focused upon the change of the society and the betterment of others, which shows an exterior-oriented value concept. In Eustacia, there are "the connotations of mystery and slumbering power". These connotations originate from Eustacia's egoistic stance and egoistic charm and constitute a manifestation of her interior-oriented value concept. After their marriage, Clym plans to stay on the heath, while Eustacia wishes that Clym would bring her to Paris. Their future plans are totally different and clash with each other.

   In the novel, Hardy writes: "[...] Yeobright was an absolute stoic in the face of mishaps which only affected his social standing; and, apart from Eustacia, the humblest walk of life would satisfy him if it could be made to work in with some form of his culture scheme." (Hardy, 1995: 207) Upholding the exterior-oriented value concept, Clym is not interested in his own prosperity, thus indifferent to what kind of social standing he can acquire. If an unfortunate happening only affects his social standing, although it may be considered rather disastrous by others, Clym does not deem it as a major blow. What draws Clym's attention is the service that he can do to others. Whether or not Clym remains cheerful and happy utterly depends upon whether or not he is still in possession of certain abilities that can enable him to render service to others. When his eyesight is harmed by overdue study in preparation for his schoolmaster career and his life meets with inconvenience and uncertainty, Clym still remains rather happy. The reason lies in the fact that he can still continue his philanthropist plan by keeping a night-school. Later, Clym undertakes the job of a furze-cutter which does not pose a strict requirement for eyesight. Although this job means a social ranking which is much lower than his former one, Clym is still quite happy and sings joyously. Commenting upon Clym's work as a furze-cutter and the relationship between Clym and the

Egdon landscape, Andrew Radford writes, "Clym's rapt immersion in the terrain and his response to Egdon as a numinous presence entails not so much a prelapsarian rapport with the creatures around him but a frightening loss of individuality." (Radford, 2003: 93) From the perspective of the conditions of the individual cultural system, what Clym loses is not individuality, but the interior-oriented feature of the individual value concept. The Egdon landscape, the variety of life forms on Egdon, and more importantly the human residents on Egdon, function as the focus of Clym's pursuit of value, providing a manifestation of his exterior-oriented value concept.

　　Hardy writes in the novel: "It was bitterly plain to Eustacia that he did not care much about social failure; and the proud fair woman bowed her head and wept in sick despair at thought of the blasting effect upon her own life of that mood and condition in him." (Hardy, 1995: 210) Under the control of the interior-oriented value mechanism, Eustacia develops her interior-oriented value concept and considers the advancement of her own prosperity as the source of her value. She wishes to flee from the gloomy Egdon Heath and go to the glittering Paris. She wishes to enjoy all the comforts and luxuries there and the social superiority which could be attained there. Her self-belief, her self-esteem, and her pride are all closely associated with the prospects of her own prosperity. Eustacia refuses to stay subordinate to the will and arrangements of her husband and her family and she shows the "failure to conform to the expectations of womanhood" (Malton, 2000: 159). The failure in terms of the observance of patriarchal conventions manifests Eustacia's interior-oriented value concept in a special and dramatic way. Contrary to Eustacia's expectations, the exterior-oriented value concept of Clym and the plan for the future which he develops accordingly undermine the prospects of the prosperity of her. Thus, she sinks into sadness and grievance, fostering doubts about the future. In the novel, Eustacia is portrayed "as a frustrated woman living out an empty existence on Egdon Heath" (Stave, 1995: 49). Her existence gives the impression of emptiness because she cannot successfully implement her interior-oriented value concept. Eustacia appears as "a mildly neurotic hedonist" (Mehta, 2013: 101). The hedonist tendency of Eustacia derives from her interior-oriented value concept and constitutes an embodiment of this kind of value concept. Moreover, her mild neuroticism originates from the frustrations in her implementation of the interior-oriented value concept, and thus the neuroticism also constitutes an embodiment of this kind of value concept in an indirect way. The conflict between the exterior-oriented value concept and the interior-oriented value mechanism brings about frictions in the relationship between Clym and his wife Eustacia. They hold different values, develop different plans for the future, and make efforts in different directions. The conflict of value concepts gradually draws them away from each other.

As has been discussed, the conflict between the exterior-oriented value concept and the interior-oriented value mechanism exerts an unfavorable influence upon the relationship between Clym and his fellow villagers, the relationship between Clym and his mother, and the relationship between Clym and his wife. The value concept of Clym and the value concepts of Mrs. Yeobright and Eustacia are embodied in their different ambitions in life. The ambitions of the two sides contradict each other and the different types of pathos which arise therefrom are also in disagreement with each other. There develops the collision of two opposite types of pathos and the tragedy of ambition shows itself in the process. (Seimiya, 2005: 70) The conflict of value concepts produces discord between Clym and Mrs. Yeobright, also between Clym and Eustacia, which eventually leads to the enhancement of estrangement and even the mounting up of hostility. By the estrangement and hostility, Eustacia and Mrs. Yeobright are both placed in dangerous situations. Eustacia, taking a risk by fleeing away from the heath at a stormy night, drowns in a weir. Mrs. Yeobright, failing to get admission into his son's house, accidentally dies on the heath with a broken heart. Deprived of his mother and his wife in such a way, Clym falls into irredeemable agonies. He is rejected both physically and spiritually by his most close family members. Clym goes to his ending in rejection, his disastrous conclusion. Moreover, when Clym eventually becomes a solitary preacher on the heath, his fellow villagers, in the conflict between the exterior-oriented value concept and the interior-oriented value mechanism, do not render him enough understanding and support. Although somewhat sympathizing with him, they do not give him the recognition of his value concept. The mode of treatment by the fellow villagers adds to Clym's sense of rejection.

4.4　*Tess:* The Conflict Between the Spiritualized Value Concept and the Materialized Value Mechanism

In the novel *Tess*, the individual value concept of the protagonist Tess is a spiritualized value concept, while the social mechanism of value in which Tess lives is a materialized value mechanism. The conflict between the spiritualized value concept and the materialized value mechanism plunges the individual cultural system of Tess into inappositeness in the dimension of value concept. The creation of the disastrous conclusion of Tess is partly due to the destructive force of the cultural inappositeness in the dimension of value concept, which is demonstrated in the aforementioned cultural conflict. The materialized value mechanism that Tess faces is concentratedly embodied in Alec d'Urberville. As a result, the conflict between the spiritualized value concept and the materialized value mechanism experienced by Tess is mainly revealed through the conflict between her spiritualized value concept and the materialized value concept of Alec.

At the first meet with Tess, Alec d'Urberville marvels at and gets fascinated by her physical charms. From then on, he looks for every way to approach and win favor with Tess. His flirtation with and seduction of Tess are for one common purpose—the physical possession of her. What Alec pursues in a male-female relationship is all physical possession and what directs him is a materialized value concept. Contrary to Alec, Tess has the spiritualized value concept. Tess "often carries out philosophical meditation about life and about society" (马弦, 2004: 76). She is always in pursuit of spiritual meanings both in her personal life and in the broad society under the guidance of the spiritualized value concept. Moreover, Tess is in pursuit of the love that is independent of material possessions. That reveals her spiritualized value concept in the most concentrated way. The conflict between Tess's spiritualized value concept and Alec's materialized value concept engenders mental shocks and mental agonies to the girl and develops the hatred and antagonism towards Alec in her bosom, thereby producing a strand of thrust which results in her disastrous conclusion.

Several weeks after being taken advantage of sexually during a night ride in the Chase, Tess bitterly retreats to her own home at the village of Marlott. Alec drives a vehicle and catches up with her on the way. Alec says, "I am ready to pay to the uttermost farthing. You know you need not work in the fields or the dairies again. You know you may clothe yourself with the best, instead of in the bald plain way you have lately affected, as if you couldn't get a ribbon more than you earn." (Hardy, 1993A: 68) However, Tess responds, "I have said I will not take anything more from you, and I will not—I cannot!" (Hardy, 1993A: 68) Here the conflict between the spiritualized value concept and the materialized value concept is quite obvious. For Alec, the relationship with Tess is directed towards the material sphere. He gets along with Tess in the purpose of physically occupying her and his way to requite Tess is to put her in control of material possessions. Dominated by the materialized value concept, Alec understands the relationship between lovers totally in the material sense. Essentially different from him, Tess understands the relationship between lovers in the spiritual sense. Directed by the spiritualized value concept, she really regards love as the defining feature of the relationship between lovers. Confronted with a fake lovers' relationship laden with material possessions while devoid of spiritual meanings, Tess makes her final choice to leave. In the conflict with the materialized value concept, or in other words with the materialized value mechanism, Tess feels that her spiritualized value concept is negated, harmed and insulted. From the perspective of Tess, she is not only physically possessed but also spiritually hurt by Alec the persecutor. Under such circumstances, hatred intensifies in Tess's heart and adds to the momentum of hostility towards Alec. The momentum of hostility, stimulated and heightened by other incidents, finally results in the killing of Alec by Tess which constitutes the last and most critical straw that breaks the girl's life and brings about her disastrous conclusion.

After the failure in retrieving her joys at her native village Marlott, Tess goes to Talbothays Dairy to work as a dairymaid. There she finds her true love Angel Clare and marries him. However, after the revelation of Tess's humiliated past made after the wedding, Angel deserts her and later goes to Brazil. In the difficult days after the desertion, Alec unexpectedly reappears and begins to harass Tess again. In their confrontation, Tess "resists Alec's advances" with a slap on his face. In doing so, Tess puts up her resistance and asserts the agency as a female through physical actions. (Youngkin, 2002: 127) Through the assertion of agency, Tess emphasizes her independent pursuit of value. Focused upon spirituality, Tess's value concept shows repugnance at the material lure. However, in her own hopeless sufferings and her family's helpless conditions, Tess is eventually won back by Alec through temptation and cheating. When Angel, realizing the unfairness in his treatment of Tess, unexpectedly comes back and appears before Tess's eyes, the weather-beaten woman eventually collapses. From the attire and words of Tess, the conflict between the spiritualized value concept and the materialized value concept could be perceived. "She was loosely wrapped in a cashmere dressing-gown of grey-white, embroidered in half-mourning tints, and she wore slippers of the same hue." (Hardy, 1993A: 332) "These clothes are what he's put upon me: I didn't care what he did wi' me!" (Hardy, 1993A: 333) After winning Tess back, Alec provides financial aid to her impoverished family and gives Tess an affluent material life. He dresses Tess with resplendent attire and feeds her with delicacies while depriving her of the right for love and spiritual value. Alec reciprocates the physical possession of Tess by placing her in the physical possession of material wealth. In accordance with the materialized value concept of Alec, he is treating Tess fairly, of which he is fairly proud. Nonetheless, from the "half-mourning tints" of her attire it can be inferred that Tess is not happy with this lifestyle. The conflict between the spiritualized value concept and the materialized value concept, or in other words the conflict between the spiritualized value concept and the materialized value mechanism, does harm to the personality of Tess and brings miseries to her life. With love quenched permanently and spiritual value destructed mercilessly, Tess is left in utter depression. When Angel again appears before her and she finds out that she has been cheated again and jeopardized permanently by Alec, the emotional effects of the conflict between the spiritualized value concept and the materialized value mechanism are greatly magnified and the hatred and hostility towards Alec in Tess's psyche come to their summit. The conflict between the spiritualized value concept and the materialized value mechanism constitutes one of the forces that result in the killing of Alec by Tess and the execution of Tess herself, her disastrous conclusion.

4.5   The Ideas about Value Concept in *Jude* and Their Historical Significance

As discussed before, *Jude* demonstrates the conflict between the value concept of knowledge and the synchronic value hegemony and the conflict between the value concept of love and the diachronic value hegemony, which together bring about the disastrous conclusion of the protagonist Jude. In this process of demonstration, two layers of meanings can be perceived. On the first layer, it is shown that the value concept of knowledge and the value concept of love have their benefits for Jude's development as a human being. Thereby the novel achieves the approval of the value concept of knowledge and the value concept of love. On the second layer, it is shown that the synchronic value hegemony and the diachronic value hegemony impair the value concept of knowledge and the value concept of love, thus hindering Jude's development as a human being. Furthermore, it is emphasized that the oppression of the value concept of knowledge by the synchronic value hegemony and the oppression of the value concept of love by the diachronic value hegemony eventually fulfill their roles in the formation of Jude's disastrous conclusion. Thereby the novel develops the anxiety that unfavorable conditions in the contemporary society may jeopardize the value concept of knowledge and the value concept of love, thus posing threats to individuals and the society.

Jude has long cherished the value concept of knowledge. The value concept of knowledge is one of the two pillars that prop up his palace of values. Jude works hard to accumulate knowledge and holds the conviction that knowledge could change his life one day. He believes that knowledge could help him get admitted into the University of Christminster and eventually qualify himself as a minister. One day, someone comments upon Christminster as a common place, basing his judgment upon the outward appearance of the city. Jude, however, totally disagrees with him. He says, "there [There] is more going on than meets the eye of a man walking through the streets. It is a unique center of thought and religion—the intellectual and spiritual granary of this country. All that silence and absence of goings-on is the stillness of infinite motion—the sleep of the spinning-top, to borrow the simile of a well-known writer." (Hardy, 1993B: 96) The remark shows that Jude regards the value of knowledge as superior to the value of material wealth and glittering appearance. Jude's eulogy of Christminster carries his eulogy of knowledge and it is the value concept of knowledge that frames his understanding of Christminster and his cognition of the world. The value concept of knowledge renders an ideal to Jude. By virtue of the value concept of knowledge, Jude no longer wanders in the world without a direction and wastes his life in repeating the lives of his ancestors aimlessly and mechanically. Therefore, the value concept of knowledge is beneficial for the development of Jude as a human being. Unfavorable for Jude's value concept of knowledge, Jude's cultural setting demonstrates the synchronic value hegemony which hinders people from lower social strata from upholding values which are expected to belong to higher strata exclusively. The hegemony refuses to grant Jude, a stonemason from a humble family, the right to uphold the value concept of knowledge which is synchronically attributed to the upper social strata. The synchronic value hegemony impairs Jude's value concept of knowledge and hinders his development as a human being.

The value concept of love is another one of the two pillars that prop up Jude's palace of values. Jude harbors the value concept of love in his heart and projects his conviction in this value concept upon his lover Sue. With his value concept of knowledge driven into great difficulties, the value concept of love appears especially important for him. Jude cares for and supports Sue, and in their shared daily life, Jude upholds the value concept of love. The value concept of love provides Jude's life with meanings. The value concept of love functions as a harbor for Jude to rest his heart and pacify his feelings. In the value concept of love, Jude finds a source of the sense of happiness. Therefore, the value concept of love is beneficial for Jude's development as a human being. One day, after the funeral of Jude and Sue's aunt, the two say farewell to each other. Withholding the impetus for a kiss, Jude and Sue part ways. Nevertheless, after an instant, they simultaneously cast glances back at each other. "That look behind was fatal to the reserve hitherto more or less maintained. They had quickly run back, and met, and embracing most unpremeditatedly, kissed close and long. When they parted for good it was with flushed cheeks on her side, and a beating heart on his." (Hardy, 1993B: 188) From this episode, the intensity of Jude's love for Sue can be felt. At the same time, the social pressure upon the love could also be perceived. As discussed before, Jude's value concept of love holds the inner aspect of love as more important than the outward aspect of love. In line with Jude's value concept of love, the outward aspect of love could be sacrificed for the inner aspect of love if necessary. As a result, Jude follows Sue's opinion and lives with her without matrimonial procedures or a wedding. Jude's value concept of love infringes upon the diachronic stability of social values and challenges the diachronic value hegemony. Therefore, Jude's value concept of love and the diachronic value hegemony are driven into conflict.

Facing the oppression of the diachronic value hegemony, it is very difficult for Jude to uphold his value concept of love. The diachronic value hegemony impairs the value concept of love and hinders Jude's development as a human being. In *Jude*, "It [it] is not transgression of conventional sexual mores that Hardy locates at the center of his construction of perversion, but conformity to them", and "the legal bond of marriage is itself consistently represented as a perverse bondage" (O'malley, 2000: 650). The value concept of love is placed upon the positive side as beneficial to individual development. In contrast to that, the diachronic value hegemony, epitomized by the formal bond of marriage, is placed upon the negative side as perverse and detrimental to individual development.

Jude has "a hunger for something that transcends immediate experience" and he cannot get satisfied with "immediate wants and needs: food, clothing and sexual pleasure" (Bullen, 2013: 186). It can be said that the value concept of knowledge and the value concept of love help Jude to break through the confinements of immediate experience and in that way bring benefits to his development as a human being. Moreover, "the novel establishes Jude as one of the exceptional heroes who seek oneness and harmony with the universe through spirit". (Vidas, 1973: 86) In a certain sense, the value concept of knowledge and the value concept of love also boosts Jude's personal development by promoting his spiritual pursuit of oneness and harmony. By showing the benefits of the value concepts of knowledge and love for Jude's development, the novel achieves the approval of the two kinds of value concepts. On the other hand, in *Jude*, the synchronic value hegemony and the diachronic value hegemony impair the protagonist's value concept of knowledge and his value concept of love, thus hindering his development as a human being. In the end, the oppression of Jude's value concepts by the contemporary value hegemonies fulfills its role in the formation of the protagonist's disastrous conclusion. (The two concrete value concepts—the value concept of knowledge and the value concept of love—make up his individual value concept.) Thereby, the novel develops the anxiety that unfavorable conditions in the society may jeopardize the value concept of knowledge and the value concept of love, thus posing threats to individuals and the society. The approval of the value concept of knowledge and the value concept of love and the anxiety about the two kinds of value concepts' vulnerability in unfavorable social conditions correspond to Matthew Arnold's cultural notions which accomplish the emphasis of the value concept of knowledge and the value concept of love by the advocacy of the Hellenistic spirit. The aforesaid approval and anxiety constitute a literary interpretation of the Hellenistic value concepts of knowledge and love in Arnold's cultural notions.

In Hellenism, which is much emphasized in Matthew Arnold's cultural notions, there is also the advocacy of the value concept of knowledge and the value concept of love. "The uppermost idea with Hellenism is to see things as they really are." (Arnold, 1993: 127) Hellenism attaches importance to the unification of the subjective sphere and the objective sphere which could be denoted, from a certain perspective, by the term knowledge. It can be said that knowledge and the value concept of knowledge occupy a central place in the ideological system of Hellenism. The Hellenistic spirit evaluates highly and eulogizes "the lover of pure knowledge, of seeing things as they really are" (Arnold, 1993: 130). In line with the Hellenistic view, lovers and pursuers of knowledge are the most qualified undertakers of the mission of humanity's perfection and salvation.

The Hellenistic advocacy of the value concept of knowledge is first a product of the emphasis laid upon "the wholeness of the human personality" (Trilling, 1954: 257), which is made up by a variety of aspects. The humankind leads a kind of highly intelligent existence, and the intellectual aspect is the central aspect of the wholeness of humanity. All other aspects of the humanity revolve around the intellectual aspect and get their meaning and interpretation by aid of the reference to the intellectual aspect. Therefore, knowledge, as the crystallization of the intellectual aspect of the humanity, receives special emphasis in the ideological framework of Hellenism. Secondly, the Hellenistic advocacy of the value concept of knowledge also results from the specific role that Hellenism assigns to reason. Both Hebraism and Hellenism lay stress upon reason. However, they assign different roles to reason in their respective ideological frameworks. The Hebraistic view regards reason as something outside humanity, serving as an outward guidance for the humankind. Therefore, in the Hebraistic ideological context, the reason is an external criterion for the value of the humankind rather than a source and guarantee of that value. In contrast to that, the Hellenistic view holds reason as an inherent and intrinsic strength of humanity, in which the value of the humankind lies. The direct outcome of the reason as the inherent and intrinsic strength of humanity is just knowledge. Knowledge derives from humanity's intrinsic reason and the attainment and accumulation of knowledge depend upon the strength of the subjectivity of the humankind. Based upon the celebration of reason, Hellenism eulogizes knowledge which is the epitome and proof of the inherent and intrinsic strength of humanity. In that way, in the Hellenistic ideological field, the value concept of knowledge is developed.

Hellenism advocates the value concept of love and the value concept of love advocated by Hellenism first involves the love of humanity. The Hellenistic love for humanity originates from and is based upon a particular view about humanity. According to Heine, all people "are either Jews or Greeks—either men who ascetically question life and nourish their apocalyptic visions, or men who love life with a realism generated by their personal integration". (Qtd. in Trilling, 1954: 256) In the Hellenistic ideological context, the human being as an integrated whole constitutes a solid foundation for the creation of meanings and a reliable guarantee for the validity of meanings. People regard humanity as something that contains original value and something that is endowed with the original force to create happiness, beauty and brightness. Holding this view, people naturally cherish an ardent love for humanity and human life. In *Culture and Anarchy*, Matthew Arnold writes:

> As one passes and repasses from Hellenism to Hebraism, from Plato to St. Paul, one feels
> inclined to rub one's eyes and ask oneself whether man is indeed a gentle and simple being, showing
> the traces of a noble and divine nature; or an unhappy chained captive, labouring with groanings that
> cannot be uttered to free himself from the body of this death. (Arnold, 1993: 131)

In the Hebraistic ideological context, humans are deemed as passive beings. They cannot define themselves and identify themselves freely. They cannot, with their own strength, guarantee their happiness and salvation. Surrounded by a sense of weakness and uncertainty, human beings are lost in the depths of pain and deprived of happiness and joy. Nevertheless, in the Hellenistic ideological context, humans are viewed as active beings. Human beings take initiative and command a constructive and decisive force in their existence and development. Therefore, human beings are perceived, in a Hellenistic light, as innocent creatures and the embodiment of nobility and divinity. The high status that Hellenism renders to humanity provides a basis for the love for humanity and naturally leads to that love.

Besides the love of humanity as a whole and as an abstract concept, the Hellenistic value concept of love also entails the love among human individuals for each other. As a matter of fact, the love among human individuals as a second element in the Hellenistic value concept of love is a derivative of the love for humanity. Mankind is a highly-socialized species. Collective existence and collective development make up one of the essential aspects of humanity. Therefore, the interpersonal communication and interpersonal interactions between human individuals constitute an essentially important facet of human life. As a consequence, the love among human individuals for each other is developed in the Hellenistic ideological field and makes up a crucial part of the value concept of love.

According to Matthew Arnold's cultural notions, in the culture of the England of his time, the spirit of Hellenism has already withered, with the value of knowledge and the value of love much neglected. However, in those cultural notions, there is the confidence for the rejuvenation of Hellenism together with its value concept of knowledge and its value concept of love. There is also the confidence for a balanced relationship between Hebraism and Hellenism which can be created through the rejuvenation of Hellenism. In *Jude*'s literary interpretation of the Hellenistic values of knowledge and love, a gloomy atmosphere takes shape. In the novel, the value concept of knowledge and the value concept of love meet with unfavorable social conditions. Jude's implementation of the values of knowledge and love is hindered by the synchronic value hegemony and the diachronic value hegemony and it is not successful. The novel develops a sense of crisis about the value concept of knowledge and the value concept of love. It treats the difficulties of the value concepts of knowledge and love with more urgency than Matthew Arnold's cultural notions.

4.6　The Ideas about Value Concept in *The Native* and *Tess* Together with Their Historical Significance

As discussed before, *The Native* demonstrates that the conflict between the exterior-oriented value concept and the interior-oriented value mechanism leads to the disastrous conclusion of the novel's protagonist Clym. In this process of demonstration, the novel justifies both the exterior-oriented value concept and the interior-oriented value concept. (The interior-oriented value mechanism can form the interior-oriented value concepts of individuals and the interior-oriented value mechanism is the social form of the interior-oriented value concept.) Thereby *The Native* develops the inquietude that the entangled relationships between the exterior-oriented value concept and the interior-oriented value concept may endanger individuals and the society. (The entangled relationships between the exterior-oriented value concept and the interior-oriented value concept have two layers of meanings. First, there is disagreement between the exterior-oriented value concept and the interior-oriented value concept. Therefore, the conflict between the two sides is possible. Second, both the exterior-oriented value concept and the interior-oriented value concept have certain justifiability. Therefore, they can both easily appeal to people and continuously affect their respective followers. As a result, the probability of the formation of conflict between the two sides will be greater. Moreover, once the conflict is formed, the difficulty of the resolution of the conflict will also be greater.)

In the demonstration of the conflict between the exterior-oriented value concept and the interior-oriented value mechanism, *The Native* justifies both sides of the conflict. Through the upholding of the exterior-oriented value concept, Clym gets a direction in life. Facing the lure of the material possessions of the modern world, he has not got lost, just by virtue of the exterior-oriented value concept. It is shown that the exterior-oriented value concept is beneficial for his development as a human being. Thereby the novel justifies the exterior-oriented value concept. Mrs. Yeobright and Eustacia, together with the residents at Egdon Heath, show the interior-oriented value mechanism. Upholding the interior-oriented value concept, Eustacia "rebels against" her "social position" (Ferguson, 2012: 101). She "symbolizes radical energies associated with the French Revolution and seeks a revolutionary figure in both Clym and Wildeve" (Ferguson, 2012: 101). The interior-oriented value concept directs Eustacia in the revolt against patriarchal oppression, and it aligns itself with and justifies itself by the sense of justice in the rebellion against patriarchal oppression. In that way, the novel justifies the interior-oriented value concept. From another perspective, controlled by the interior-oriented value mechanism, Mrs. Yeobright, Eustacia and the residents at Egdon Heath think that Clym shall give priority to his own prosperity rather than to the prosperity of others. According to their design, Clym shall return to Paris and continue to pursue his career as a manager. If Clym follows the opinions of these people, he will certainly attain his personal success. Having achieved his own success, Clym can better protect his own life and make efforts to facilitate the welfare of others in a more sustainable way. It is suggested by the novel that the interior-oriented value concept, if adopted by Clym, can also pave the way for the implementation of the exterior-oriented value concept. Then both the interior-oriented value concept and the exterior-oriented value concept can be implemented successfully and the coexistence of the two sides may be accomplished. Thereby the novel justifies the interior-oriented value concept and the interior-oriented value mechanism.

Because the exterior-oriented value concept and the interior-oriented value concept are in disagreement with each other, the conflict between the two sides is possible. Because the exterior-oriented value concept and the interior-oriented value concept have their respective justifiability, the two sides can both easily appeal to people and continuously influence people. Therefore, the conflict between the two sides will be more likely to take shape. Furthermore, once the conflict takes shape, it will be more difficult to resolve it. The conflict between the exterior-oriented value concept and the interior-oriented value mechanism in Clym's individual cultural system is just precipitated and made more difficult to resolve by the respective justifiability of the exterior-oriented value concept and the interior-oriented value concept. The protagonist Clym "is ineffective, a failure" (Natarajan, 2006: 857). In him, one can perceive "the mundane reality of the nineteenth-century male" (Natarajan, 2006: 857). In his pursuit of an effective mode of modernity by his exterior-oriented value concept which is frustrated, Clym goes to his disastrous conclusion. By demonstrating the conflict between the exterior-oriented value concept and the interior-oriented value mechanism, *The Native* develops the inquietude that the entangled relationships between the exterior-oriented value concept and the interior-oriented value concept may endanger individuals and the society. This inquietude corresponds to the conviction in the harmonious coexistence of the exterior-oriented value scheme and the interior-oriented value scheme in Matthew Arnold's cultural notions, which is reflected in the advocacy of the combination of Hebraism and Hellenism.

From the perspective of Matthew Arnold, England of the Victorian Era had placed its attention solely upon Hebraism, ignoring the value of Hellenism.

Therefore, the value scheme of that period is out of balance. In *Culture and Anarchy*, Matthew Arnold writes:

> while [While] Hebraism seizes upon certain plain, capital intimations of the universal order, and rivets itself, one may say, with unequalled grandeur of earnestness and intensity on the study and observance of them, the bent of Hellenism is to follow, with flexible activity, the whole play of the universal order, to be apprehensive of missing any part of it, of sacrificing one part to another, to slip away from resting in this or that intimation of it, however capital. (Arnold, 1993: 128)

Both Hebraism and Hellenism aspire for the universal order. Nevertheless, the two spiritual disciplines demonstrate different tendencies in the handling of the matter of the universal order. Hebraism attaches great importance to the intimations of the universal order and deem them as the foundation of the aspirations for and pursuit of the universal order. Focused upon the intimations of the universal order which are outside of human subjectivity, Hebraism represents a kind of exterior-oriented value scheme. Different from Hebraism, Hellenism relies on the strength of humanity to attain an unbiased understanding of the universal order. Turning away from the intimations of the universal order, Hellenism regards the subjectivity and intelligence of human beings as the basis for the access to the universal order. Thereby Hellenism manifests a kind of interior-oriented value scheme. "Though both seek the same end—the perfection of man—and at times even use the same language, Hebraism is concerned primarily with conduct and with obedience to a law of conduct—with strictness of conscience—whereas Hellenism is concerned primarily with seeing things as they are—with spontaneity of consciousness." (Trilling, 1954: 257) Hebraism is directed towards the conduct and the principle of conduct. According to Hebraism, the realization of value depends upon the conduct and the principle of conduct. Conduct links the subject and the object and reflects the particular relationship between the subject and the object. By conduct, the subject makes contact with and establishes relationships with objects and the external world as a whole. The emphasis that Hebraism places upon conduct is essentially a product of the emphasis upon the external world in the establishment and promotion of human value. The principle of conduct, as the outcome of an endeavor to put conducts in order, is an existence outside of the subject. The emphasis upon the obedience to the principle of conduct is essentially an embodiment of the tendency to pursue the value of the subject outside of the subject. Therefore, it can be said that Hebraism manifests an exterior-oriented value scheme. In contrast to Hebraism, Hellenism attaches the focus of attention to the perception of things in their original state. Among the things that are anticipated to be perceived in the original state, the subject counts as the central and most significant one. From the perspective of Hellenism, the subject shall, in the pursuit of value, preserve and demonstrate the original self. Therefore, the "spontaneity of consciousness" receives much emphasis. In the framework of Hellenism, the subjectivity of the subject constitutes an essential source of value which is indispensable to human existence and human endeavors. As a consequence, it can be said that Hellenism demonstrates an interior-oriented value scheme.

"Hellenism is chiefly occupied with the beauty and rationality of the ideal and tends to keep difficulties out of view", but "Hebraism lacks this sunny optimism" and it is "marked by the sense of sin, pessimistic of perfection". (Trilling, 1954: 257) On the basis of the exterior-oriented value scheme, there is a lack of confidence in the human subject's merit and strength in Hebraism. The hope for the realization of value is placed upon the external world, but the external world apparently goes beyond the certain reach of the subject. Perceived from the angle of the subject, the pursuit of value is accompanied by human passivity and human weakness. Lack of command over the prospects of the pursuit of value undermines optimistic views about the future. Furthermore, the role of spontaneous human subjectivity in the pursuit of value is largely ignored and the independent merit of human subjectivity is largely discarded. Different from Hebraism, Hellenism is fully aware of the merit and strength of human subjectivity. Moreover, it preserves human subjectivity as a reliable foundation for the realization of value. Hellenism focuses itself upon "the beauty and rationality of the ideal" (Trilling, 1954: 257). Besides, it regards the ideal as something inside the subject and realizable only by the original strength of the subject. Therefore, Hellenism also focuses itself upon the "beauty and rationality" of human subjectivity. With the confidence in humanity and the passion attached to the confidence, Hellenism harbors the optimism about the future.

From the standpoint of Matthew Arnold, Hellenism better meets the requirement of the conditions of the 19th century and could create more promising prospects for the development of a nation. England, unlike other European countries, is too much confined to the ideas of Hebraism, while ignoring the value of Hellenism. Therefore, Arnold proposes a revival of Hellenism in England as a remedy for contemporary social problems. Of course, this proposition is made in view of the particular conditions of England in the Victorian era. In the final analysis, Matthew Arnold holds the harmonious coexistence of Hebraism and Hellenism as the ultimate perfect condition. From the perspective of Arnold, the realization of value depends both on the obedience to a law of conduct and the stimulation of inner strength, both in the external sphere and in the internal sphere. Putting forward the harmonious coexistence of Hebraism and Hellenism as a perfect cultural condition, the cultural notions of Matthew Arnold fuse together the exterior-oriented value scheme and interior-oriented value scheme and advocate their harmonious coexistence.

The Native, with its inquietude that the entangled relationships between the exterior-oriented value concept and the interior-oriented value concept may endanger individuals and the society, corresponds to and achieves the literary interpretation of the conviction in the harmonious coexistence of the exterior-oriented value scheme and the interior-oriented value scheme in Matthew Arnold's cultural notions. In the literary interpretation of that conviction, the harmonious coexistence between the exterior-oriented value concept and the interior-oriented value concept is disrupted, and the exterior-oriented value concept and the interior-oriented value mechanism are driven into conflict. Moreover, the conflict between the exterior-oriented value concept and the interior-oriented value mechanism leads to the protagonist Clym's disastrous conclusion. In her discussion of the elemental forces in *The Return of the Native*, Rosemarie Morgan says, "It happens thus: the clash, or opposition lies between Hellenistic polytheism and the pursuit of happiness, of Greek joyousness—and Christian monotheism and the pursuit of godliness, of self-redemption through self-denial." (Morgan, 1988: 64 - 65) The exterior-oriented value concept and the interior-oriented value mechanism, together with the Christian ideas (Christian ideas and Hebraistic ideas are closely related to each other) and the Hellenistic ideas behind them, have not achieved the harmony proposed by Matthew Arnold's cultural notions. In the literary interpretation of the conviction in the harmonious relationship between the exterior-oriented and the interior-oriented value schemes, the focus is placed upon the harms of the disruption of the harmony rather than the benefits of the establishment and preservation of the harmony. Therefore, in the novel, a basically negative attitude is suggested about the condition of the relationship between the exterior-oriented and interior-oriented values in the contemporary British society. There is an urge to improve the relationship between the exterior-oriented value concept and the interior-oriented value concept and thereby avoid the harms that confrontations between the two sides may do to individuals and the society.

Tess demonstrates that the conflict between the spiritualized value concept and the materialized value mechanism results in the disastrous conclusion of the protagonist Tess. In this process of demonstration, two layers of meanings can be found. In the first layer, it is shown that the spiritualized value concept brings benefits to the protagonist Tess's development as a human being. Thereby the novel achieves the approval of the spiritualized value concept. In the second layer, it is shown that the materialized value mechanism impairs the spiritualized value concept of Tess and her development as a human being. Moreover, it is emphasized that the oppression of the spiritualized value concept by the materialized value mechanism eventually realizes a function in the creation of the disastrous conclusion of the protagonist Tess. Thereby the novel develops the anxiety that unfavorable circumstances in the society may jeopardize the spiritualized value concept and thus pose threats to individuals and the society. The approval of the spiritualized value concept and the anxiety about the fragility of the spiritualized value concept in unfavorable social circumstances correspond to the emphasis upon the Hellenistic spiritual development in Matthew Arnold's cultural notions. The aforementioned approval and anxiety achieve a literary interpretation of Matthew Arnold's emphasis upon the Hellenistic spiritual development.

Hellenism involves "the intelligence driving at those ideas which are, after all, the basis of right practice, the ardent sense for all the new and changing combinations of them which man's development brings with it, the indomitable impulse to know and adjust them perfectly" (Arnold, 1993: 126). The intelligence, the ardent sense and the indomitable impulse constitute elements of the humankind's spiritual development. With these three elements, human beings can investigate into the intellectual basis of their existence and development. Backed by these three agents, the humanity does not stay satisfied with being informed of and complying with standards of practice. Instead, the humanity dedicates itself to the perseverant probing into the standards themselves. Driven by the three elements, the humanity establishes behavioral standards, questions them, revises them and even replaces them with new and more justifiable ones. The humanity persists in renewing the organizations and combinations of behavioral patterns. In that process, fundamental ideas behind those patterns also undergo the processes and cycles of construction, destruction and reconstruction. In that process, the spiritual development of humanity is pushed forwards.

Matthew Arnold "wishes to reconcile and improve the excessive rationality and moral self-control in the Hebraism of British culture, by Hellenism which holds the pursuit of active and free thoughts and the love of beauty as basic characteristics". (范一亭, 2014: 104) Of the spiritual development of the humanity in Hellenism, "the pursuit of active and free thoughts" and "the love of beauty" are two critical aspects. "The pursuit of active and free thoughts", mainly consisting in free aspirations for knowledge, occupies a primary position in the Hellenistic spiritual development of the humanity. Hellenism places great emphasis upon the "spontaneity of consciousness" (Trilling, 1954: 257). Therefore, from the perspective of Hellenism, the natural conditions of consciousness and the free development of subjectivity are something of much significance. "Active and free thoughts" are embodiments of the undisturbed consciousness and the unconstrained subjectivity, commanding critical significance for the guarantee of the "spontaneity of consciousness". By "active and free thoughts", human beings can stimulate and exercise the original interior force and effectively lead their spiritual existence and spiritual development. "The love of beauty" is also of vital importance for the spiritual development of the humanity. "Hellenism speaks of thinking clearly, seeing things in their essence and beauty, as a grand and precious feat for man to achieve." (Arnold, 1993: 131) "The pursuit of active and free thoughts", embodied in the voluntary investigation into the essence of things, naturally leads to the pursuit of beauty. The need for truth and wisdom corresponds to the need for beauty; and one side of the spiritual development should advance at an equal pace with the other side of the spiritual development. The orientation of beauty constitutes one of the axes of human subjectivity. With "the love of beauty", the humanity could realize itself and enrich itself spiritually. Through "the love of beauty", the spiritual world of the humanity could be greatly expanded and the spiritual value of the humanity could be further multiplied.

The approval of the spiritualized value concept and the anxiety about its fragility under unfavorable social circumstances in *Tess* achieve a literary interpretation of the emphasis upon the Hellenistic spiritual development in

Matthew Arnold's cultural notions. In *Tess*, the spiritualized value concept of the protagonist suffers from the suppression by the materialized value mechanism. In the suppression, the protagonist Tess eventually goes to her disastrous conclusion. Thus, in the novel there develops a basically negative attitude towards the condition of people's spiritual development. There arises the calling for readers to promote the humanity's spiritual development against unfavorable social circumstances and thereby bring benefits to individuals and the society.

Chapter Five
The Historical Significance of the Overall Format
of Cultural Inappositeness Leading to Tragedies

Driven by cultural inappositeness, the protagonists in Hardy's novels advance towards their disastrous conclusions with inevitableness in a certain sense. The cultural inappositeness which is directed at tragedies and the sense of inevitableness of the protagonists' fates correspond to the fatalism and pessimism of Arthur Schopenhauer and achieve their literary interpretation. Moreover, the overall format of cultural inappositeness leading to tragedies in the novels of Thomas Hardy fosters ideas of reformism, accomplishing the literary interpretation of the ideas of reformism of John Ruskin and Auguste Comte.

5.1 Literary Interpretation of the Fatalism and Pessimism of Arthur Schopenhauer

In the novels of Thomas Hardy, cultural inappositeness leads to the tragedies of the protagonists. The protagonists, caught in the inappositeness of their individual cultural systems, go to their disastrous endings with a certain sort of inevitableness. In the creation of tragic novels, Thomas Hardy receives the literary heritage of the genre of tragedy both in Europe and in Britain. There are rich resources of tragedies in the literary histories of Europe and Britain. Ancient Greek tragedies and Shakespearean tragedies can serve as examples. In

Shakespeare's most renowned tragedy *Hamlet*, "the tragic ending of him (the protagonist Hamlet) is inevitable and linked conflicts of the interest life space and the moral life space are the origin of Hamlet's fate" (刘磊, 2012: 25). In *Hamlet*, the interest life space and the moral life space involve complicated factors in the protagonist's cultural individuality and cultural setting. Similar to that, in the novels of Hardy, unfavorable conditions of the individual cultural system inevitably lead to the tragic endings of the protagonists. The overall format of cultural inappositeness leading to tragedies in the novels of Thomas Hardy achieves the interpretation of the fatalism and pessimism of German philosopher Arthur Schopenhauer (1788 – 1860). In *The World as Will and Representation* (1819) and other works, Schopenhauer interprets the world and all things existing in it as will and its representation. According to Schopenhauer, will is the origin of the universe. All existents in the universe, including human beings, are only representation or phenomena through which will shows itself. Different from thing-in-itself in the theories of Immanuel Kant (1724 – 1804), which cannot be perceived or understood by human intellect, will can enter the view of human intelligence. To acknowledge the inheritance Schopenhauer acquires from Kant, it can also be put in this way: "Schopenhauer retained the thing-in-itself, but identified it with will." (Russell, 1945: 755) In a certain sense, it can be said that Schopenhauer extends the sphere of application of the free will in Kantian theories from practice and morality to all human activities; free will functions as the essence of the world in Schopenhauer's philosophy, and a counterpart for Kant's thing-in-itself. (谢地坤, 2005: 46) According to Schopenhauer's argumentation, human intelligence itself is just a spark from the energy of will and a tool with which will strives for survival. Human intelligence, exerting inner energies, can perceive bustling actions in the human psyche, which are just will, as well as human intelligence itself.

The fundamental will in the universe is a primary force striving for survival. It is blind and unconscious, with no mercy towards individual existents. The magnetic needle of a compass always points to the north; stones always fall down vertically if not held by force. These phenomena are the show of will in inorganic sphere. Plants always strive for sunshine with their branches and leaves and strive for water with their roots. Animals always develop their respective advantageous physical features to assist them in striving for their food. These phenomena are the show of will in organic sphere. Human beings, harboring their impulses, wishes, demands and ambitions, and developing their physical and intellectual strengths, always strive for their survival and all other things that they want.(梯利,伍德,2013：529－532) Schopenhauer says, "I do not have cognition of my will as a whole, in its unity, in perfect accordance with its essence; rather I cognize it only in its individual acts, which is to say in time, time being the form in which my body (like every other object) appears：this is why the body is the condition of cognition of my will." (Schopenhauer, 2010：126) The subject recognizes his or her intrinsic will through bodily actions and psychological embodiments; he or she experiences the supremely abstract existence through supremely concrete existents. Will becomes conscious in human beings, utilizing intelligence as a tool and weapon reserved exclusively for humans, and struggles for its aim of survival and prosperity.

The perception of the world as will and its representation by Schopenhauer leads to fatalism and pessimism at both macroscopic and microscopic levels. At the macroscopic level, the fundamental will in the universe is blind and unconscious, striving for survival and its inherent aims without mercy towards individual existents, including human beings. The blind fundamental will, without care, engenders happenings ruthlessly and at random around human beings and inside human beings, always leading to individuals' disastrous endings. "A wish may be granted; but it is succeeded by another and we have ten times more desires than we can satisfy." (Kenny, 2019：305) Therefore, at the microscopic level, individuals cannot exempt themselves from the everlasting pain of frustrated ambitions. Moreover, individual human beings, driven by the will which is the original force embedded intrinsically in them, fight for their own survival and flourishing without mercy towards each other. In the web of interpersonal relationships, which is woven by will in the final analysis, there is cheat, hurt, betrayal and various embodiments of cruelty. In the merciless fight against each other, individuals go to disastrous endings with a certain type of inevitableness. At both macroscopic level and microscopic level, the interpretation of the world as will and its representation leads to fatalism and pessimism. The protagonists in the novels of Thomas Hardy, driven by cultural inappositeness, go to their disastrous endings. The overall format of cultural inappositeness leading to tragedies in the novels achieves the interpretation of the fatalism and pessimism of Arthur Schopenhauer in the literary sphere.

5.2 Literary Interpretation of the Ideas of Reformism of John Ruskin and Auguste Comte

In the four novels under discussion in the book, there are altogether ten cases of cultural inappositeness in major dimensions leading to tragedies of the protagonists. Among the ten cases of cultural inappositeness, two cases derive from the inappositeness of the internal existence of the individual cultural system, while eight cases derive from the inappositeness of the internal-external relationship of the individual cultural system. "The reason proposed by humanism renders humans considerable support in the worldly sphere and makes humans more enterprising" (刘磊, 迟欣, 2013: 140). However, the protagonists in Hardy's novels, somewhat exposed to the influence from Renaissance humanism, still suffer from obvious problems in the development of cultural individuality and need considerable improvement. Among the eight cases of cultural inappositeness that derive from the inappositeness of the internal-external relationship, three cases do not involve the negation and criticism of either side. Modifications and improvements should be made on both the individual side and the social side to ameliorate the internal-external relationship. For the majority of the eight cases of cultural inappositeness that derive from the inappositeness of the internal-external relationship, namely five cases, the external existence faces negation and criticism. It is implied that disadvantages and weaknesses in social conditions constitute the key factor that engenders the inappositeness of the internal-external relationship. On an overall basis, it can be seen that both the improvement of individuals and the improvement of society play roles in the redemption of humanity; it can also be seen that the novels of Hardy place the hope of the redemption of humanity more upon the improvement of the society than upon the improvement of individuals. From another perspective, it can be found out that none of the ten cases of cultural inappositeness derives from the inappositeness of the external existence. The arrangement shows that the social criticism in Hardy's novels is relatively moderate, not harboring the claim for radical changes of social mechanisms. Through these arrangements, the overall format of cultural inappositeness leading to tragedies in the novels of Thomas Hardy fosters ideas of reformism.

The ideas of reformism in Hardy's novels can be viewed from manifold perspectives, among which the overall format of cultural inappositeness leading to tragedies is an important one. Different perspectives from which the ideas of reformism can be viewed support each other and form a relationship of mutual interpretation. "Hardy's tragic heroes suffer for their impulses and desires inherited from their natural existence, and for their inability to carry them out in an acceptable way in a civilized society." （张成萍, 2016: 106）Conflicts between natural aspects and social aspects of humanity call for endeavors of reform to better reconcile the two sides. The process of the reforming and improvement of the society does not go along a smooth linear route which is exempt from setbacks and frustrations. "Gains will be partial. Temporary reversal is to be expected. Further advance will have to wait until new conditions come round." （Reid, 2017: 182）Progress through frustrations is a keynote in the novels of Thomas Hardy.

Sympathy and Support for the weak and the oppressed in contemporary society is an important angle from which Hardy's novels accomplish their reformist stance. For instance, the image of new women in Hardy's novels is characterized by rebelliousness, independence and bravery. They revolt against the oppression from patriarchal society and strive for independent value and equality with men. (马弦, 2019: 118 – 131) The novels of Hardy treat new women with sympathy and justify their efforts as a force to realize social reform and improvement. Although Hardy's novels are not completely immune from the influence of patriarchal ideas and are sometimes ambiguous about the value criteria and moral principles concerning gender roles, the tendency of reformism and progressivism is still fairly clear and set as the mainstream in the ideological construction of the novels. For example, the novel *Tess* "affirm[s] the value of Tess's unique consciousness" and "defend[s] her against any social condemnation".(Shaw, 2017: 143) Embedded in complex historical context and associated with nuanced social implications, the novels of Thomas Hardy speak for the weak and the oppressed in terms of gender, economic and social statuses, etc., and thereby prop up their reformist and progressive stance.

Awareness of timeis another dimension along which Hardy's novels develop a sense of progressivism and reformism. *The Mayor* is immersed in complicated and even contradictory historical implications, both reminiscent of the past and anticipant of the future. While favoring certain aspects of the past, "[...] Hardy acknowledges the mistake—embodied in the figure of Henchard—of refusing to adapt and embrace the modern world" (Salmons, 2017: 66) and establishes a recognition of the justifiability of the transformation of social norms, both in terms of custom and in terms of economic and social institutions. "However, Hardy's point is that far from following a linear, progressive route, history is based upon a recycling and reconstitution of folklore and myth, which is reinvented to suit its environment." (Salmons, 2017: 66) *The Mayor* presents a belief in the necessity and inevitability of reforming the society with the passage of time. However, the reformist tendency in the novel consists not in linear progression but in recycling patterns and intertwined endeavors. In *The Mayor* there are "local materials which emphasise rural oppression, rebellion, capital punishment and exile" (Jackson, 2017: 172). In the novel, accounts of history and descriptions of contemporary society intermingle with each other and together point to the reforming of the society which is directed at better and more harmonious social relationships.

In *The Native*, Clym fails in implementing his educational campaign and thereby enriching the spirituality of the local villagers. That arrangement shows the impracticability of the utilization of education as a means to culturally unite lower classes with upper classes.(罗影, 2020: 190) However, through the earnest endeavors and fearless pursuits by the protagonist, the novel still clearly demonstrates the estimable aspect of the impulse to improve the society, including its structure and inner relations, by education. The novel fosters an everlasting hope for the possibly feasible mode of education for remote area lower classes. The novel *Tess* puts forward Hellenism as a remedy for contemporary social ills. It advocates the overcoming of reason and self-constraint in Hebraism and the development of spontaneousness, sensuousness and enterprising ego in Hellenism. Viewed from a certain angle, the novel presents a proposition that, only in the aforementioned way, instead of people trying to reconcile the two conflicting cultural stances in vain, can the harmonious society that Matthew Arnold craves for be realized. (王智敏, 吴亭静, 2018: 135) Therefore, in the novel, surveyed from a certain perspective, the blueprint for social reform and improvement is closely related to the belief in Hellenism.

The overall format of cultural inappositeness leading to tragedies in the novels of Thomas Hardy fosters ideas of reformism, accomplishing the interpretation of the ideas of reformism of contemporary British social and artistic theorist John Ruskin (1819 – 1900) and French philosopher Auguste Comte (1798 – 1857) from a literary perspective.

In *Modern Painters* (five volumes, 1843 – 1860), *The Seven Lamps of Architecture* (1849), *The Stones of Venice* (1851 – 1853), and other works, John Ruskin puts forward his reformist ideas. Reformist ideas of Ruskin consist in his ideas about art and his ideas about society. Ruskin's artistic ideas are the focus of his reformism while his social ideas are the frame of his reformism. His artistic ideas can function only within the frame of reference provided by his social ideas while his social ideas can be established only by virtue of the support provided by his artistic ideas. Ruskin views art as a part of society and also as an organic element that interacts with society. Art is a part of society, and it can only search for its origin and source of inspiration in society and achieve its function in society. Moreover, art, together with beauty which is closely associated with it, interacts with society. On the one hand, art is determined by society. Different genres and different styles of art are determined by different historical and social conditions, and also by different national temperaments. Gothic architecture, for example, acquires its vitality from the enterprising spirit of the northern peoples.(朱立元, 陆扬, 张德兴, 2009: 1098) On the other hand, art shall be directed at society. In other words, art shall serve the society. According to Ruskin, "the demands made by art could be justified only by the seriousness of its moral purpose: namely, to reveal fundamental features of the universe". (Kenny, 2007: 263) Revealing the fundamental features of the universe, art paves a way for the improvement of individuality and society.

In *Modern Painters*, Ruskin says, "the noblest pictures [...] are always orderly, always one, ruled by one great purpose throughout, in the fulfilment of which every atom of the detail is called to help, and would be missed if removed; this peculiar oneness being the result, not of obedience to any teachable law, but of the magnificence of tone in the perfect mind [...]" (Ruskin, 1900: 139 – 140) Art, holding painting as a representative, could, led by a perfect mind with a great purpose, vitalize individuality and society with its moral strength. Art shall assist in improving individuals' morality and dispositions, and in improving conditions of values in society. On both the microscopic level and the macroscopic level, art helps in ameliorating the society. By virtue of endeavors in the realm of art and in other realms, society can achieve continuous improvement. The afore-mentioned aspects constitute the basic stance of the reformism of John Ruskin. Ruskin criticizes the industrial society and wishes for overcoming the evils in the industrial society and thereby improving the society. Criticism of industrialism constitutes one constituent of Ruskin's reformism which is directed at contemporary historical conditions. The reformism of Ruskin is a kind of social theory with the temperamental aspect enlarged while with the institutional aspect compressed. Ruskin's hope for the improvement of society lies more on reformation of morality and transformation of individuality, while less on institutional and political reconstruction (Anthony, 1983: 188). In contrast to that, the overall format of cultural inappositeness leading to tragedies in the novels of Thomas Hardy places the hope of the redemption of humanity more upon the improvement of the society than upon the improvement of individuals. That arrangement accomplishes the effect of highlighting the institutional aspect against the background of the temperamental aspect. The overall format interprets the reformist ideas of John Ruskin in contemporary ideological context, while also achieves a kind of counteraction towards the tendency of individualization of social development in the reformism of John Ruskin.

In *The Course on Positive Philosophy* (*1830 - 1842, six volumes*), *The System of Positive Polity*, *or Treatise on Sociology*, *Instituting the Religion of Humanity* (*1851 - 1854, four volumes*), and *The Early Writings* (*1820 - 1829*), etc., Auguste Comte establishes and elaborates on positivism. Positivism is a comprehensive interpretation of human society and its evolution, centering around positive philosophy. The positivism of Comte is directed at the establishment of more harmonious social institutions. (刘放桐, 2009: 529) The ideal of Comte is just to reconstruct the society. (梯利, 伍德, 2013: 553) In essence, Comte's positivism is a type of reformism. "No real order can be established, and still less can it last, if it is not fully compatible with progress: and no great progress can be accomplished if it does not tend to the consolidation of order." (Comte, 2009: 3) In light of positive social sciences, in the reconciliation and balance between order and progress, the society can achieve a mechanism bound for continuous improvement.

In accordance with positive philosophy, only the knowledge gathered from experience or experiments, namely the knowledge that can be proved by positive sciences, is valid. Knowledge that is not provable by positive sciences is lacking in essential validity and meaning. Under the world-view of positivism, human spirituality has three successive phases: theology, metaphysics and positivism. Correspondingly, human society also has three successive phases: absolute monarchy, democracy and industrial institutions. Human spirituality and human society evolve along the successive and progressive scale. Along the succession of phases, human spirituality and human society are set in a continuous process of refinement and amelioration. In the last phase, a society with universal love as the basis is possible. (邓晓芒, 赵林, 2005: 288) These ideas constitute the reformism of Auguste Comte, or in other words, the reformist connotations of Comte's positivism. Comte also fabricates a progressive scale of sciences, namely mathematics, astronomy, physics, chemistry, biology and sociology. Later, he adds ethics to the scale. The sciences that come later on the scale enter the stage of positivism later, but show higher degrees of sophistication and represent higher achievements of human spirituality. Sociology and ethics come last on the scale and they are of the most essential significance for the development of human spirituality and human society. The sciences culminate in ethics, which is directed at a religion of benevolence, a religion in the positive sense. In the development of sciences under the guidance of positivism, and along the progressive scale of human spirituality and human society, the world can achieve continuous improvement and betterment, conducted both on the individual level and on the social level while focused on the social level. The overall format of cultural inappositeness leading to tragedies in the novels of Thomas Hardy shows reformist ideas which especially emphasize transformation of social institutions, achieving the interpretation of the ideas of reformism of Auguste Comte from the literary perspective.

Conclusion

    As discussed before, the inappositeness of the individual cultural system achieves a decisive function in the formation of the protagonists' disastrous conclusions in Thomas Hardy's novels. The origin of the protagonists' tragedies in these novels consists in the inappositeness of the individual cultural system. In *The Native*, the cultural inappositeness which is responsible for the protagonist Clym's disastrous conclusion involves the dimension of morality and the dimension of value concept. Clym's cultural inappositeness in the dimension of morality consists in the conflict between the sufficiency of altruism and the moderation of altruism, as well as the conflict between the affirmative morality and the negative morality mechanism. Clym's cultural inappositeness in the dimension of value concept consists in the conflict between the exterior-oriented value concept and the interior-oriented value mechanism. The conflict between the sufficiency of altruism and the moderation of altruism, the conflict between the affirmative morality and the negative morality mechanism and the conflict between the exterior-oriented value concept and the interior-oriented value mechanism together lead to the disastrous conclusion of Clym. In *The Mayor*, the cultural inappositeness which is responsible for the protagonist's disastrous conclusion involves the dimension of disposition and the dimension of identity. The protagonist Henchard's cultural inappositeness in the dimension of disposition consists in the negative tendency and the mood-based aggressiveness. His cultural inappositeness in the dimension of identity consists in the conflict between the identity as a patriarch and the modernized identity mechanism. The negative tendency, the mood-based aggressiveness and the conflict between the identity as a patriarch and the modernized identity mechanism together give rise to the disastrous conclusion of Henchard. In *Tess*, the cultural inappositeness which is responsible for the protagonist's disastrous conclusion involves all the four major dimensions of the individual cultural system, namely the dimension of morality, the dimension of disposition, the dimension of identity and the dimension of value concept. The protagonist Tess's cultural inappositeness in the dimension of morality consists in the conflict between the spiritualized morality and the materialized morality mechanism. Tess's cultural inappositeness in the dimension of disposition consists in the imbalance of psychological rhythm. Tess's cultural inappositeness in the dimension of identity is comprised of the conflict between the identity of explicit equality and the explicit identity inequality, and the conflict between the identity of implicit equality and the implicit identity inequality. Tess's cultural inappositeness in the dimension of value concept consists in the conflict between the spiritualized value concept and the materialized value mechanism. The conflict between the spiritualized morality and the materialized morality mechanism, the imbalance of psychological rhythm, the conflict between the identity of explicit equality and the explicit identity inequality, the conflict between the identity of implicit equality and implicit identity inequality, and the conflict between the spiritualized value concept and the materialized value mechanism together result in the disastrous conclusion of Tess. In *Jude*, the cultural inappositeness which is responsible for the protagonist Jude's disastrous conclusion involves the dimension of morality and the dimension of value concept. Jude's cultural inappositeness in the dimension of morality consists in the conflict between the content-directed morality and the form-directed morality mechanism. Jude's cultural inappositeness in the dimension of value concept is comprised of the conflict between the value concept of knowledge and the synchronic value hegemony and the conflict between the value concept of love and the diachronic value hegemony. The conflict between the content-directed morality and the form-directed morality mechanism, the conflict between the value concept of knowledge and the synchronic value hegemony, and the conflict between the value concept of love and the diachronic value hegemony together bring about the disastrous conclusion of Jude.

Through demonstrating the cultural inappositeness which causes the protagonists' disastrous conclusions, the novels of Thomas Hardy develop certain ideas about morality, disposition, identity and value concept. These ideas correspond to, in certain ways, utilitarianism, evolutionism and the cultural notions of Matthew Arnold. The ideas about morality, disposition, identity and value concept, developed through the demonstration of the cultural inappositeness which causes disastrous conclusions, achieve literary interpretations of utilitarianism, evolutionism and the cultural notions of Matthew Arnold.

In the dimension of morality, the novels of Thomas Hardy echo and interpret certain aspects of utilitarianism. *The Native* develops the inquietude that the entangled relationships between the sufficiency of altruism and the moderation of altruism may endanger individuals and the society. This inquietude corresponds to and accomplishes a literary interpretation of the twofold ideas about the relationship between the principle of the sufficiency of altruism and the principle of the moderation of altruism which are implied in utilitarianism. *The Native* also develops the inquietude that the entangled relationships between the affirmative morality and the negative morality may endanger individuals and the society, and that inquietude corresponds to and interprets the twofold ideas about the dynamics of morality which are implied in utilitarianism. *Tess* develops the approval of the spiritualized morality and the anxiety that unfavorable social conditions can jeopardize the spiritualized morality and freedom, thus posing threats to individuals and the society. The approval and the anxiety correspond to the idea of liberty in utilitarianism and achieve a literary interpretation of that idea. The novel *Jude* accomplishes the approval of the content-directed morality and develops the anxiety that the unnecessary and overelaborate formalities may jeopardize people's practical interests, thus posing threats to individuals and the society. This approval and this anxiety correspond to the conviction in practical interests in utilitarianism and function as a literary interpretation of the conviction.

In the dimension of disposition, the novels of Thomas Hardy echo and interpret certain aspects of evolutionism. By showing the roles that the negative tendency and the mood-based aggressiveness play in forming the protagonist Henchard's disastrous conclusion, *The Mayor* develops the anxiety that disadvantageous qualities in the disposition may pose threats to individuals and the society. By showing the role that the imbalance of psychological imbalance plays in creating the protagonist Tess's disastrous conclusion, *Tess* also develops the anxiety that disadvantageous qualities in the disposition may pose threats to individuals and the society. The aforementioned anxiety in the two novels corresponds to and achieves a literary interpretation of the evolutionist emphasis upon the importance of advantageous qualities of individuals in the struggle for existence.

In the dimension of identity, the novels of Thomas Hardy echo and interpret certain aspects of the cultural notions of Matthew Arnold. The novel *Tess* achieves the approval of the identity of equality and develops the anxiety that unfavorable conditions in society may jeopardize the identity of equality and pose threats to individuals and the society. The approval and the anxiety correspond to and constitute a literary interpretation of the idea of equality in Matthew Arnold's cultural notions. *The Mayor* develops the inquietude that the entangled relationships between patriarchy and modernism in the era of transition may endanger individuals and the society. This inquietude corresponds to and interprets the twofold ideas about the relationship between patriarchy and modernism in Matthew Arnold's cultural notions.

In the dimension of value concept, the novels of Thomas Hardy also echo and interpret certain aspects of the cultural notions of Matthew Arnold. The novel *Jude* achieves the approval of the value concept of knowledge and the value concept of love. Moreover, the novel develops the anxiety that unfavorable conditions in the contemporary society may jeopardize the value concept of knowledge and the value concept of love, thus posing threats to individuals and the society. The aforementioned approval and anxiety correspond to and constitute a literary interpretation of the Hellenistic values of knowledge and love in Arnold's cultural notions. *The Native* develops the inquietude that the entangled relationships between the exterior-oriented value concept and the interior-oriented value concept may endanger individuals and the society. This anxiety corresponds to and interprets the conviction in the harmonious coexistence of the exterior-oriented value scheme and the interior-oriented value scheme in Matthew Arnold's cultural notions. *Tess* develops the approval of the spiritualized value concept and the anxiety that unfavorable circumstances in the society may jeopardize the spiritualized value concept and thus pose threats to individuals and the society. The aforementioned approval and anxiety correspond to and interpret Matthew Arnold's emphasis upon the Hellenistic spiritual development.

In these novels of Thomas Hardy, there are altogether ten cases of cultural inappositeness. Among them, two cases derive from the inappositeness of the internal existence of the individual cultural system. These are the two cases of cultural inappositeness in the dimension of disposition in *The Mayor* and *Tess*. The former results from the negative tendency and the mood-based aggressiveness; the latter results from the imbalance of psychological rhythm. All other eight cases of cultural inappositeness in the novels derive from the inappositeness of the relationship between the internal existence and the external existence. It can be seen that the novels of Thomas Hardy place more importance upon the individual-society relationship rather than upon the individual characteristics as the factor that can influence and determine people's lives.

For three of the eight cases of cultural inappositeness which derive from the inappositeness of the internal-external relationship, namely the conflict between the internal existence and the external existence, the novels do not take sides with either of the two parties in conflict. The first is the cultural inappositeness which results from the conflict between the sufficiency of altruism and the moderation of altruism and the conflict between the affirmative morality and the negative morality mechanism in *The Native*. The second is the cultural inappositeness which results from the conflict between the identity as a patriarch and the modernized identity mechanism in *The Mayor*. The third is the cultural inappositeness which results from the conflict between the exterior-oriented value concept and the interior-oriented value mechanism in *The Native*. By showing the disastrous effects of the conflict between the internal existence and the external existence without taking sides with either party, the novels develop the view that in some situations it may be difficult, unrealistic or even impossible to reestablish the harmony between the individuals and the society by endeavors to approve of and preserve one side and disapprove of and change the other side. For these cases, the novels place the hope for the redemption of individuals and the development of the society upon the reestablishment of the harmony between individuals and the society without negating either side. Modifications on both sides and more efficient communication and interactions are implied in these novels as methods for the reestablishment of individual-society harmony. For the majority (five cases) of the eight cases of cultural inappositeness which derive from the conflict between the internal existence and the external existence, the novels take sides with and approve of the internal existence. It can be seen that, the novels uphold the view that in most situations in the British society of the Victorian era, the reconstruction and reformation of the external existence constitute the proper and effective method for harmonizing the relationship between individuals and the society. In that way, positive qualities in individuals can be protected and the society can get a better chance for development. The novels place the hope for the redemption of individuals and the society more upon the macroscopic sphere than upon the microscopic sphere, more upon the amelioration of the society than upon the amelioration of individuals. From another perspective, it can be seen that none of the ten cases of cultural inappositeness derive from the inappositeness of the external existence. That arrangement shows that the social criticism in Hardy's novels is relatively moderate, not harboring the claim for radical changes of social mechanisms. The overall format of cultural inappositeness leading to tragedies in the novels of Thomas Hardy accomplishes the literary interpretation of the fatalism and pessimism of Arthur Schopenhauer. The overall format shows reformist ideas which especially emphasize transformation of social institutions, achieving the interpretation of the ideas of reformism of John Ruskin and Auguste Comte from the literary perspective.

Bibliography

Abrams, M. H., and Geoffrey Galt Harpham. *A Glossary of Literary Terms*. 9th ed. Boston, USA: Wadsworth Cengage Learning, 2009.

Alexander, Anne. *Thomas Hardy: The "Dream-Country" of His Fiction*. London: Vision Press Limited, 1987.

Anthony, P D. *John Ruskin's Labour: A Study of Ruskin's Social Theory*. Cambridge: Cambridge University Press, 1983.

Arnold, Matthew. *Culture and Anarchy and other Writings*. Ed. Stefan Collini. Cambridge: Cambridge University Press, 1993.

Asquith, Mark. *Thomas Hardy, Metaphysics and Music*. Houndmills, Basingstoke, Hampshire: Palgrave Macmillan, 2005.

Barker, Chris, and Emma Jane. *Cultural Studies: Theory and Practice*. 5th ed. Los Angeles: Sage, 2016.

Bentham, Jeremy. *An Introduction to the Principles of Morals and Legislation*. Kitchener: Batoche Books, 2000.

Beran, Carol Louise. "Thomas Hardy's Tragic Forms." Diss. University of California, Berkeley, 1977.

Bownas, Jane L. *Thomas Hardy and Empire: The Representation of Imperial Themes in the Work of Thomas Hardy*. Farnham, Surrey, England: Ashgate, 2012.

Bressler, Charles E. *Literary Criticism: An Introduction to Theory and Practice*. Beijing: Higher Education Press; [S.l.]: Pearson Education, 2004.

Bullen, J. B. *Thomas Hardy: The World of His Novels*. [S.l.]: Frances Lincoln Limited, 2013.

Chew, Samuel. *Thomas Hardy: Poet and Novelist*. New York: Alfred A. Knopf, Inc., 1928.

Cohn, Elisha. "'No insignificant creature': Thomas Hardy's Ethical Turn." *Nineteenth-Century Literature* 64. 4 (2010): 494 – 520.

Comte, Auguste. *Cambridge Library Collection The Positive Philosophy of Auguste Comte Volume 2*. translated by Harriet Martineau. Cambridge: Cambridge University Press, 2009.

Darwin, Charles. *On the Origin of Species*. Ed. Gillian Beer. Oxford: Oxford University Press, 2008.

Davis, Philip. *The Oxford English Literary History. Vol. 8/1830 – 1880 The Victorians*. Oxford: Oxford University Press; Beijing: Foreign Language Teaching and Research Press, 2002.

Dellamora, Richard. "Male Relations in Thomas Hardy's Jude the Obscure." *Papers on Language and Literature* 50. 3/4(2014): 245 – 268.

Dutta, Shanta. *Ambivalence in Hardy: A Study of his Attitude to Women*. Hampshire: Macmillan Press Ltd, 2000.

Eagleton, Terry. "Base and Superstructure in Raymond Williams." *Raymond Williams: Critical Perspectives*. Ed. Terry Eagleton. Boston: Northeastern University Press, 1989: 165 – 175.

Eldridge, John, and Lizzie Eldridge. *Raymond Williams: Making Connections*. London: Routledge, 1994.

Essex, Ruth. "A Study of the Role of the Woman in Thomas Hardy's Novels." Diss. New York University, 1976.

Fan, Yiting. *Capital, Culture, and the Heroine: Reconfiguring Gender in the Victorian Novel*. Beijing: Peking University Press, 2014.

Ferguson, Trish. "Bonfire Night in Thomas Hardy's *The Return of the Native*." *Nineteenth – Century Literature* 67. 1(2012): 87 – 107.

Ferguson, Trish. *Thomas Hardy's Legal Fictions*. Edinburgh: Edinburgh University Press, 2013.

Ford, Tracy. "Thomas Hardy: Timely Exits." Diss. The University of

Mississippi, 2008.

Gatrell, Simon. *Thomas Hardy Writing Dress*. Oxford: Peter Lang, 2011.

Gatrell, Simon. *Thomas Hardy's Vision of Wessex*. Houndmills, Basingstoke, Hampshire: Palgrave Macmillan, 2003.

Gussow, Adam. "Dreaming Holmberry-Lipped Tess: Aboriginal Reverie and Spectatorial Desire in *Tess of the d'Urbervilles*." *Studies in the Novel* 32. 4 (2000): 442 – 463.

Hanlon, Bettina Louise. "Supporting Characters and Rural Communities in the Novels of George Eliot and Thomas Hardy." Diss. The Ohio State University, 1983.

Hardy, Thomas. *Jude the Obscure*. Ware, Hertfordshire: Wordsworth Editions Limited, 1993B.

Hardy, Thomas. *Tess of the d'Urbervilles: A Pure Woman*. Ware, Hertfordshire: Wordsworth Editions Limited, 1993A.

Hardy, Thomas. *The Mayor of Casterbridge: A Story of a Man of Character*. Ware, Hertfordshire: Worthsworth Editions Limited, 1994.

Hardy, Thomas. *The Return of the Native*. Ware, Hertfordshire: Wordsworth Editions Limited, 1995.

Harvey, Geoffrey. *The Complete Critical Guide to Thomas Hardy*. London: Routledge-Taylor & Francis Group, 2003.

Henson, Eithne. *Landscape and Gender in the Novels of Charlotte Bronte, George Eliot, and Thomas Hardy: The Body of Nature*. Farnham, Surrey, England: Ashgate, 2011.

Ireland, Ken. *Thomas Hardy, Time and Narrative: A Narratological Approach to His Novels*. Houndmills, Basingstoke, Hampshire: Palgrave Macmillan, 2014.

Jackson, Lisa Hartsell. "Wandering Women: Sexual and Social Stigma in the Mid-Victorian Novel." Diss. University of North Texas, 2000.

Jackson, Rena. "Metropolitan Dissent in Thomas Hardy's Fiction: Class, Gender, Empire." Diss. Manchester: The University of Manchester

(United Kingdom), 2017.

Johnson, Lionel. *The Art of Thomas Hardy* . London: Elkin Mathews, 1894.

Jones, W. T. *A History of Western Philosophy: Kant and the Nineteenth Century* . 2nd ed. New York: Harcourt Brace Jovanovich, Inc., 1975.

Karin, Koehler. *Thomas Hardy and Victorian Communication: Letters, Telegrams and Postal Systems* . London: Palgrave Macmillan, 2016.

Kateb, George, David Bromwich, and John Stuart Mill. *On Liberty* . New Haven: Yale University Press, 2003.

Kenny, Anthony. *A New History of Western Philosophy: Volume IV Philosophy in the Modern World* . Oxford: Clarendon Press, 2007.

Kenny, Anthony. *An Illustrated Brief History of Western Philosophy: 20th Anniversary Edition. 3rd ed* . Hoboken, USA: Wiley Blackwell, 2019.

Keys, Romey Thomas. "Psychology of Character in Thomas Hardy and D. H. Lawrence." Diss. The Johns Hopkins University, 1976.

King, Jeannette. *Tragedy in the Victorian Novel: Theory and Practice in the Novels of George Eliot, Thomas Hardy and Henry James* . Cambridge: Cambridge University Press, 1978.

Kramer, Dale, ed. *The Cambridge Companion to Thomas Hardy.* Cambridge: Cambridge University Press; Shanghai: Shanghai Foreign Language Education Press, 2000.

Kramer, Dale. *Thomas Hardy: The Forms of Tragedy* . Detroit, Michigan: Wayne State University Press, 1975.

Langbaum, Robert. *Thomas Hardy in Our Time* . Houndmills, Basingstoke, Hampshire: Macmillan Press Ltd, 1995.

Law, Jules. "A 'Passing Corporeal Blight': Political Bodies in 'Tess of the d'Urbervilles'. " *Victorian Studies* 40. 2 (1997): 245–270.

Lewis, Jeff. *Cultural Studies—The Basics* . London: Sage Publications, 2002.

Lovesey, Oliver. "Reconstructing Tess. " *Studies in English Literature, 1500–1900* 43. 4 (2003): 913–938.

Luten, Karen Ann. "Different Countries: A Study of Unrequited Love in the

Novels of Charles Dickens, Anthony Trollope, and Thomas Hardy." Diss. Columbia University, 1992.

Malane, Rachel Ann. "'Sex in Mind': The Gendered Brain in Nineteenth-Century Literature and Mental Sciences." Diss. The University of Notre Dame, 2003.

Malton, Sara A. "'The Woman Shall Bear Her Iniquity': Death as Social Discipline in Thomas Hardy's *The Return of the Native*." *Studies in the Novel* 32. 2 (2000): 147 – 164.

Mehta, Naveen K. "A Critical Study of Character of Thomas Hardy's Tess." *Studia Universitatis Petru Maior. Philologia*. 17 (2014): 115 – 122.

Mehta, Naveen K. "A Study of the Character Eustacia Vye in Thomas Hardy's *The Return of the Native*." *Studia Universitatis Petru Maior. Philologia*. 15 (2013): 99 – 104.

Mill, John Stuart. *Utilitarianism*. [S.l.]: The Floating Press, 2009.

Miller, J Hillis. *Thomas Hardy: Distance and Desire*. Cambridge, Massachusetts: The Belknap Press of Harvard University Press, 1970.

Millgate, Michael. *Thomas Hardy: A Biography Revisited*. Oxford: Oxford University Press, 2004.

Morgan, Rosemarie. *Women and Sexuality in the Novels of Thomas Hardy*. London: Routledge, 1988.

Musselwhite, David. *Social Transformations in Hardy's Tragic Novels: Megamachines and Phantasms*. Houndmills, Basingstoke, Hampshire: Palgrave Macmillan, 2003.

Natarajan, Uttara. "Pater and the Genealogy of Hardy's Modernity." *Studies in English Literature, 1500 – 1900* 46. 4 (2006): 849 – 861.

Nemesvari, Richard. *Thomas Hardy, Sensationalism, and the Melodramatic Mode*. New York: Palgrave Macmillan, 2011.

Nishimura, Satoshi. "Language, Violence, and Irrevocability: Speech Acts in *Tess of the d'Urbervilles*." *Studies in the Novel* 37. 2 (2005): 208 – 222.

Norman, Andrew. *Thomas Hardy: Behind the Mask*. The Mill, Brimscombe

Port Stroud, Gloucestershire: The History Press, 2011.

O'connor, Alan. *Raymond Williams: Writing, Culture, Politics*. Oxford: Basil Blackwell, 1989.

O'malley, Patrick R. "Oxford's Ghosts: *Jude the Obscure* and the End of the Gothic." *Modern Fiction Studies* 46. 3 (2000): 646 – 671.

Page, Norman. *Thomas Hardy: The Novels*. Houndmills, Basingstoke, Hampshire: Palgrave, 2001.

Pandey, Amrit Lal. *The Novels of Thomas Hardy (A Study in Existential Perspectives)*. Varanasi: Mishra Trading Corporation, 2001.

Pinion, F. B. *A Hardy Companion: A Guide to the Works of Thomas Hardy and their Background*. London: The Macmillan Press Ltd, 1968.

Qi, Shouhua, and William W. Morgan. *Voices in Tragic Harmony: Essays on Thomas Hardy's Fiction and Poetry*. Shanghai: Shanghai Foreign Language Education Press, 2001.

Radford, Andrew. *Thomas Hardy and the Survivals of Time*. Aldershot, Hampshire, England: Ashgate, 2003.

Ramel, Annie. *The Madder Stain: A Psychoanalytic Reading of Thomas Hardy*. Leiden: Brill Rodopi, 2015.

Reid, Fred. *Thomas Hardy and History*. Cham, Switzerland: Palgrave Macmillan-Springer Nature, 2017.

Ruskin, John. *The Complete Works of John Ruskin Volumes Three and Four: Modern Painters Volumes Two and Three*. New York: The Kelmscott Society Publishers, 1900.

Russell, Bertrand. *A History of Western Philosophy and Its Connection with Political and Social Circumstances from the Earliest Times to the Present Day*. New York: Simon and Schuster, 1945.

Salmons, Kim. *Food in the Novels of Thomas Hardy: Production and Consumption*. Cham, Switzerland: Palgrave Macmillan-Springer International Publishing AG, 2017.

Schoenfeld, Lois Bethe. *Dysfunctional Families in the Wessex Novels of*

Thomas Hardy . Lanham: University Press of America, 2005.

Schopenhauer, Arthur. *The Cambridge Edition of the Works of Schopenhauer The World as Will and Representation Volume 1.* translated by Judith Norman, Alistair Welchman and Christopher Jana. Cambridge: Cambridge University Press, 2010.

Seimiya, Michiko. "Darwinism in the Art of Thomas Hardy." Diss. Japan Women's University, 2005.

Shaw, Bailey Justine. "Gender, Form, and Interiority in the Novels of Thomas Hardy." Diss. Southern Illinois University at Carbondale, 2017.

Stave, Shirley. *The Decline of the Goddess: Nature, Culture, and Women in Thomas Hardy's Fiction* . Westport, Connecticut: Greenwood Press, 1995.

Sumner, Rosemary. *Thomas Hardy: Psychological Novelist* . New York: St. Martin's Press, 1981.

Sumpter, Caroline. "On Suffering and Sympathy: *Jude the Obscure*, Evolution, and Ethics." *Victorian Studies* 53. 4 (2011): 665 – 687.

Suzanne, Keen. *Thomas Hardy's Brains: Psychology, Neurology, and Hardy's Imagination* . Columbus: The Ohio State University Press, 2014.

Tandon, Bharat. " '… Among the Ruins' : Narrative Archaeology in *The Mayor of Casterbridge* ." *Studies in the Novel* 35. 4 (2003): 471 – 489.

Taylor, Kevin. *Hans Urs von Balthasar and the Question of Tragedy in the Novels of Thomas Hardy* . London: Bloomsbury T & T Clark-Bloomsbury, 2013.

Thomas, Jane. *Thomas Hardy and Desire: Conceptions of the Self*. Houndmills, Basingstoke, Hampshire: Palgrave Macmillan, 2013.

Tomalin, Claire. *Thomas Hardy: The Time-Torn Man.* London: Penguin Books, 2012.

Trilling, Lionel. *Matthew Arnold: With an Additional Essay, "Matthew Arnold, Poet"* . New York: Harcourt Brace Jovanovich, 1954.

Turner, Paul. *The Life of Thomas Hardy* . Oxford: Blackwell Publishers, 2001.

Vidas, Louise Walczak. "The Single Green Light and the Splendid and Terrible

Spectrum: A Study of the Secular Romance Quest in the Novels of Thomas Hardy and D. H. Lawrence." Diss. University of Illinois at Urbana-Champaign, 1973.

Vigar, Penelope. *The Novels of Thomas Hardy: Illusion and Reality*. London: Bloomsbury Publishing plc, 2013.

Weber, Carl J. *Hardy of Wessex: His Life and Literary Career*. New York: Columbia University Press, 1940.

Wilkie, Mary Dale. "Functions of the Descriptions of Nature in the Novels of Thomas Hardy." Diss. The University of Wisconsin, 1972.

Williams, Raymond. *Culture and Materialism*. London: Verso, 2005.

Williams, Raymond. *Culture & Society 1780 - 1950*. New York: Columbia University Press, 1983.

Williams, Raymond. *Marxism and Literature*. Oxford: Oxford University Press, 1977.

Williams, Raymond. *The Country and the City*. Nottingham, England: Spokesman, 2011B.

Williams, Raymond. *The Long Revolution*. Cardigan: Parthian, 2011A.

Williams, Raymond. *The Sociology of Culture*. Chicago: The University of Chicago Press, 1995.

Wolfreys, Julian. *Critical Issues: Thomas Hardy*. Houndmills, Basingstoke, Hampshire: Palgrave Macmillan, 2009.

Wotton, George. *Thomas Hardy: Towards a Materialist Criticism*. Goldenbridge, Ireland: Gill and Macmillan Ltd, 1985.

Youngkin, Molly C. "Men Writing Women: Male Authorship, Narrative Strategies, and Woman's Agency in the Late-Victorian Novel." Diss. The Ohio State University, 2002.

Zhang, Chengping. "Moral Luck in Thomas Hardy's Fiction." *Philosophy and Literature* 34. 1 (2010): 82 - 94.

邓晓芒,赵林:《西方哲学史》。北京:高等教育出版社,2005 年。

丁世忠:《哈代小说伦理思想研究》。成都:巴蜀书社,2008 年。

范一亭:《阿诺德的文化观与〈无名的裘德〉的资本主义批判》,《外国文学评论》,2014 年第 4 期,第 97—113 页。

高万隆:《婚恋·女权·小说:哈代与劳伦斯小说的主题研究》。北京:中国社会科学出版社,2009 年。

郝涂根:《仁爱与纯洁:哈代小说中新宗教的二维研究》(博士论文)。上海外国语大学,2012 年。

何宁:《哈代研究史》。南京:译林出版社,2011 年。

姬生雷,冯梅,乔建珍:《从〈德伯家的苔丝〉看哈代的贞操观》,《河北师范大学学报(哲学社会科学版)》,2011 年第 4 期,第 101—104 页。

李增,王丁:《论哈代"性格与环境小说"中的"性格"和"环境"的关系》,《外国文学研究》,2004 年第 5 期,第 62—67、171 页。

刘放桐:《西方哲学通史:西方近现代过渡时期哲学——哲学上的革命变更与现代转型》。北京:人民出版社,2009 年。

刘磊,迟欣:《双重的哈姆雷特——一位人文主义者的自我建构与自我解构》,《安徽农业大学学报(社会科学版)》,2013 年第 1 期,第 94—98、140 页。

刘磊,胡婷婷:《从文化帝国主义到文化博弈理念——人本理念的空间嬗变暨其在中国文化背景中的扬弃》,《渤海大学学报(哲学社会科学版)》,2012 年 B 第 2 期,第 128—131 页。

刘磊,胡婷婷:《西方人本理念与中国文化传统的共通、龃龉及其扬弃》,《重庆交通大学学报(社会科学版)》,2012 年 A 第 4 期,第 1—4 页。

刘磊:《从整体主义的伦理观看莎翁喜剧〈皆大欢喜〉》,《乐山师范学院学报》,2013 年第 4 期,第 30—35 页。

刘磊:《覆灭前的挣扎——从〈印度之行〉中的两个人物看穷途末路的殖民主义道德体系》,《哈尔滨学院学报》,2011 年第 2 期,第 79—83 页。

刘磊:《利益生活空间与道德生活空间的联动博弈——哈姆雷特的宿命之源》,《淮南师范学院学报》,2012 年第 5 期,第 21—25 页。

刘磊:《人文主义理想情结之寄托——论莎士比亚第 18 首十四行诗》,《重庆交通大学学报(社会科学版)》,2016 年第 2 期,第 97—101 页。

刘磊:《英美文学中人文情结的嬗变》。北京:中国社会科学出版社,2019 年。

鲁春芳:《哈代乡土情结的演变》,《外语教学》,2006 年第 3 期,第 90—92 页。

陆扬,王毅:《文化研究导论》。上海:复旦大学出版社,2006 年。

罗影:《哈代〈还乡〉与〈远离尘嚣〉中的教育主题叙事与时代特征》,《文艺争鸣》,2020 年第 7 期,第 189—193 页。

马弦:《论托马斯·哈代的宗教思想》,《外国文学评论》,2003 年第 4 期,第 115—122 页。

马弦:《哈代小说的原型叙事和创作观念研究》。杭州:浙江大学出版社,2019 年。

马弦:《论哈代小说中的新女性形象》,《外国文学研究》,2004 年第 1 期,第 76—80,172 页。

聂珍钊,刘富丽等:《哈代学术史研究》。南京:译林出版社,2014 年。

聂珍钊,马弦编选:《哈代研究文集》。南京:译林出版社,2014 年。

聂珍钊:《托玛斯·哈代小说研究:悲戚而刚毅的艺术家》。武汉:华中师范大学出版社,1992 年。

钱乘旦,许洁明:《英国通史》。上海:上海社会科学院出版社,2012 年。

舒开智:《雷蒙德·威廉斯文化唯物主义理论研究》。北京:学苑出版社,2011 年。

宋希仁主编:《西方伦理思想史》(第 2 版)。北京:中国人民大学出版社,2010 年。

梯利,伍德:《西方哲学史》增补修订版。葛力,译。北京:商务印书馆,2013 年。

王泽应:《伦理学》。北京:北京师范大学出版社,2012 年。

王智敏,吴亭静:《〈德伯家的苔丝〉与哈代的"共同体形塑"》,《晋阳学刊》,2018 年第 2 期,第 134—137 页。

吴笛:《哈代新论》。杭州:浙江大学出版社,2009 年。

肖滨:《马修·阿诺德的古典主义》,《外语学刊》,2010 年第 3 期,第 164—168 页。

谢地坤:《西方哲学史(学术版)第七卷 现代欧洲大陆哲学(下)》。南京:江苏人民出版社,2005 年。

徐德林:《重返伯明翰:英国文化研究的系谱学考察》。北京:北京大学出版社，2014 年。

晏辉：《现代性语境下的价值与价值观》。北京：北京师范大学出版社，
　　2009 年。

叶胜年：《西方文化史鉴》。上海：上海外语教育出版社，2002 年。

于文杰：《英国文明与世界历史》。北京：生活・读书・新知三联书店，
　　2013 年。

张成萍：《哈代：文学与伦理解读》。北京：科学出版社，2016 年。

张旭东，刘益民，欧何生：《心理学概论》第 2 版。北京：科学出版社，2009 年。

朱立元，陆扬，张德兴：《西方美学思想史（上、中、下）》。上海：上海人民出版
　　社，2009 年。

图书在版编目(CIP)数据

个体性文化体系的失度：哈代小说主人公悲剧根源
研究：英文 / 刘磊著. —南京：南京大学出版社，
2022.7

ISBN 978 - 7 - 305 - 25897 - 8

Ⅰ. ①个… Ⅱ. ①刘… Ⅲ. ①哈代(Hardy, Thomas
1840—1928)-小说研究-英文 Ⅳ. ①I561.074

中国版本图书馆 CIP 数据核字(2022)第 114561 号

出版发行 南京大学出版社
社　　址　南京市汉口路 22 号　　邮编 210093
出 版 人　金鑫荣

书　　名　个体性文化体系的失度——哈代小说主人公悲剧根源研究
著　　者　刘　磊
责任编辑　刘慧宁

照　　排　南京紫藤制版印务中心
印　　刷　江苏凤凰通达印刷有限公司
开　　本　718×1000　1/16　印张 13.75　字数 249 千
版　　次　2022 年 7 月第 1 版　2022 年 7 月第 1 次印刷
ISBN 978 - 7 - 305 - 25897 - 8
定　　价　56.00 元

网　　址　http://www.njupco.com
官方微博　http://weibo.com/njupco
官方微信　njupress
销售热线　(025)83594756